INSPECTOR WEST
ALONE

John Creasey

Charles Scribner's Sons
New York

1 3 5 7 9 11 13 15 17 19 C/C 20 18 16 14 12 10 8 6 4 2

Printed in the United States of America
Library of Congress Catalog Card Number 75-7519
ISBN 0-684-14354-2

CONTENTS

INSPECTOR WEST ALONE

1

EVEN now, it didn't occur to Roger West that there had been anything faked about the message. He was just afraid in case Janet had run into trouble.

You could spend your life walking into trouble with your eyes wide open and feel hardly a tremor. When you began to wonder whether your wife was in danger, you had a sick feeling of dread; assuming that you were in love with your wife, of course.

Roger stood outside the back door.

It was locked, like the front door and like all the windows. It was a small, lonely house, and he had never been here before. He hadn't heard of the place until two hours ago. There was a rotting hurdle fence round the large garden, and the light was just good enough to show the distorted shapes of trees that hadn't been pruned for years. Grass grew knee high on what had once been lawns. The gravel drive was covered with weeds, dark blotches on the dirty yellow.

There wasn't a light anywhere.

A chilly wind blew on to his back, coming across the open moorland and hilly country of Surrey. Low clouds threatened rain.

Except for the wind rustling the grass and the leafless branches of the trees, there was no sound.

The message had been clear enough, but he hadn't taken it himself. Janet had telephoned Scotland Yard. Roger hadn't been in his office, so Eddie Day had spoken to her. Eddie wasn't a shining light, but a man who had been thirty years in the force and become a Chief Inspector; he didn't get messages wrong.

" Bit of trouble for you, Handsome—Janet 'phoned. All right, all right, you needn't get worried, there's nothing the matter with the kids! Janet's gone to see

7

a cousin of hers, Phyllis—the one that lives in Surrey. She says can you go straight there to-night? Copse Cottage, Helsham—not far from Guildford. Difficult place to find, she says. I've written the directions down."

The note was in Roger's pocket.

He'd followed the directions with ease; this was Copse Cottage. The big white stone at the corner, near the signpost, had been unmistakable. There'd been one odd thing about the old, rotting signpost; the pointing finger and the words Copse Cottage had been freshly painted. He'd smelt and touched the paint, which wasn't quite dry. The name board on the narrow wooden gate, also broken and dilapidated, hadn't been painted for years.

The house was as dark as the night.

He'd been startled on discovering that there was no light back or front; worried when there had been no response to his knocking. That seemed to echo about the garden now—heavy and sharp from the iron knocker and plate on the front door, dull when he had thumped the back door with his fist.

Janet *had* a cousin named Phyllis; an older woman, who lived somewhere in Surrey. He'd never met her, and didn't think Janet had heard from her more than twice in the past five years.

A gust of wind blew cold, making him shiver.

Be reasonable. Cousin Phyllis had probably been taken ill, Janet had hurried out here, taken things into her capable hands, decided to move Phyllis to a hospital, possibly even taken her to Chelsea. There was no reason to feel scared. He forced a grin and turned towards the front of the house. From here he could see the sidelights of his car, facing the main road and parked in the narrow, unmade lane. He would try once more at the front door, then go into the village—two miles away—and telephone home. This was all rational enough, and——

The lights of his car disappeared.

He stopped moving, and stared. Only one thing could blot those lights out—someone standing in front of them. They were still on; he could see a faint glow, and the vague silhouette of a—man? Or Janet?

No, it was a man. The lights appeared again. Yet he'd heard no footsteps, and any ordinary sound would have been clear. The vague figure was lost against the black outline of the car.

Then he heard a sound; of the car door, opening.

He shouted: " *Here!* " and broke into a run. The car door slammed and the engine hummed. He was ten yards from the open gate when the car began to move, and it was twenty yards along the road when he reached the gate.

" *Here!* "

The only answer was the snorting of the car.

Alarm sawed at his nerves. He ran, in desperate hope; the road was rough, the car couldn't make much speed, and would have to slow down at the sharp corner. But the pot-holes and loose stones made running difficult. He turned his ankle, grabbed at a tree to save himself and lost precious seconds and still more precious yards. The red light glowed, then turned out of sight as the driver swung the wheels towards Helsham. When Roger reached the corner, the car was out of sight down the winding hill road.

His forehead was wet with sweat, and the wind chilled it.

What was all this? How could it be explained rationally? There was a touch of fantasy about it, as well— let's face it—as a touch of the sinister. *Had* Janet come here?

The sound of the engine faded into silence, and the wind was hushed, but his forehead felt icy cold. It was pitch dark now. He turned and stared towards the house, and could only just make out the outline against the lowering sky. Suddenly, gusty wind swept down upon him.

He could walk to the village and back to reason; or return and force his way into the house. He didn't like to contemplate the possibilities of what he might find. He couldn't give a name to his fears. The sensible thing was to go for assistance; he could get a car from the village and come here with the local policeman. It wasn't easy to be sensible when fears for Janet crowded upon him.

Then a light went on in the house.

.   .   .   .   .

It wasn't bright; just the dim yellow glow one would expect from an oil-lamp, probably the only lighting in these wilds. It was on the first floor, above the front door; *and it moved*. Suddenly a shadow, large and shapeless, was thrown against a window. Someone was carrying the lamp from one room to another. It passed the window, and only a faint yellow glow remained; then it shone more brightly from another window, and became steady.

Janet?

She would have heard him call out, would have shouted after him by now. Whoever carried that light wasn't Janet.

Roger walked quickly towards the house, staring at the lighted window, but he could no longer see a shadow. As he turned into the open gate, another gust of wind swept down on him—and as the howling died, he heard the scream. Wild, shrill, eerie, it played on his taut nerves like a saw on an iron bar; and he knew that it was a woman's scream.

.   .   .   .   .

He smashed a stone against the glass of the window, and the crash was like an explosion. A splinter of glass cut the back of his hand, but he hardly noticed it. He bent his elbow and broke off the jagged splinters which stuck out from the side, then groped for the window catch. It sprang back sharply, and he pushed the window up.

It was pitch dark inside the room.

He used his torch for the first time. The beam shone upon oddments of furniture, the mirror of a huge sideboard, and a door. He climbed through, breathless, tense, but heard no more screaming. Whoever had carried that lamp must have heard the window crash, but there was only silence. He reached the door, pulled it open and stepped into the passage. A faint glow of light came from upstairs, enough to show him the narrow stairs themselves, the gloomy hall, the glass in the picture-frames hanging on the walls. He put out his torch and stood quite still.

There was no sound, no movement.

Had he heard that scream?

His teeth were set so hard that his cheeks hurt. He felt something warm and wet running down his hand and realized vaguely that it was blood. He wiped it off on his coat, and went slowly towards the foot of the stairs. Now that he was more accustomed to the light he could pick out the banisters, the shiny handrail, the dark, blotchy wall-paper; and he could smell the fustiness which told him this house had not been lived in for a long time.

He must go upstairs; he wasn't a victim of nerves.

He started up the stairs, keeping close to the wall to avoid creaking boards, and the only sound was his own breathing. The light still glowed, dimly yellow. He reached a small landing and stood quite still, recovering from the first attack of nerves, warning himself to be careful. There were three doors, one of them wide open, and the light came from this room. He stepped softly towards it, and peered inside. It was an empty bedroom; empty, that was, as far as he could see. A huge double bed, with big brass knobs on the posts, stood against one wall. Backing on to the window was a huge Victorian dressing-table with a big centre and narrow wing mirrors. The oil-lamp, without a shade, stood on this, and the light was brighter here because it was reflected from the mirrors.

He went to the foot of the bed and peered to the other side—and saw nothing.

Had that scream been a freakish trick of the wind?

He knew it hadn't; he also knew that it might have been uttered to bring him here. His heart pounded as he turned towards the door, fearful of being watched. On the landing he saw no one and heard no sound. Whoever had lit that lamp must still be here——

Hold it!

While he had been rushing towards the window and breaking in there had been time for man or woman to run down the stairs and leave the house by the back door. He couldn't take anything for granted. He went into the room, picked up the lamp, which gave off a grey smoke and an oily smell, and placed it on a chest on the landing so that it gave more general light. Then he approached the first of the two closed doors. He took out his handkerchief and wrapped it round the handle before turning it. The door opened without difficulty.

Another, smaller bedroom, as empty as the first, was all he found.

And silence——

It was broken suddenly, eerily, by a sound he placed at once, but didn't want to hear; by moaning. It jarred his nerves as he turned to look at the other closed door.

The moaning wasn't loud, but sounded clearly because of the general quiet. Undoubtedly it came from behind that closed door. It wasn't easy to tell the difference between a man moaning and a woman; but he thought this was a woman, and saw a picture of Janet in his mind's eye.

He moved slowly to the door, repeated the trick with the handkerchief, and pushed—but the door was locked. The moaning was continual now, low, frightening, working on his nerves. He ought to have no nerves, but he stood there with his teeth clenched. It was a stout door, and there was no key in the lock. He put his shoulder against it and pushed, a practised trick which would open a flimsy door in a modern house, but it had no effect on this one. He drew back and flung himself at the unyielding wood; all he did was to hurt himself.

The moaning went on and on.

He turned and hurried down the stairs, using his torch. He found the kitchen at the first attempt, and opened the door cautiously; there was no one there. Another door led to a scullery; there was always a scullery and wash-house in an old cottage of this kind. The scullery was drab, and cobwebs hung across the window. He opened a cupboard door and found what he wanted: an axe, lying rusted and dull on the cement floor, near a few logs and a heap of kindling wood, thick with dust. He wrapped his handkerchief round the grimy axe handle and went back upstairs. He felt more like a policeman, now; more in control of himself. Whether the moaning woman was Janet or not, he had a job to do. He paused at the head of the stairs, looking round again; no one appeared, and yet he had a feeling that the house wasn't empty.

He approached the door determinedly.

He could waste ten minutes battering at it; or open it in two minutes if he used his wits. He swung the blade of the axe powerfully against the panel just above the lock; the wood caught the blade and held it, he had to wrench it out. That eerie sound didn't stop. He smashed again, and splintered the wood; smashed on with fierce urgency until a strip of the panelling lay on the floor. He didn't fuss with a handkerchief now, but thrust his hand through the gap, hoping for the unlikely—a key on the inside.

There wasn't one.

He smashed again and again, until the lock gave way and the door sagged open. By then, he was dripping with sweat; and the moaning sounded louder. He shouldered the door wide open, flashed on his torch, and stepped inside the room.

A man stood by his side, pressed tightly against the wall, and Roger didn't see him until he leapt forward.

Sharp nails clawed at his face, a knee came up and caught him agonizingly in the groin. As he reeled back against the swinging door, hands clutched at his throat and squeezed; powerful, claw-like hands. He tried to use the axe as a weapon, but couldn't get it into position. He felt the air locked in his lungs, his chest heaved as he tried to breathe, as blackness descended upon him. He struggled, kicked, but he couldn't free himself. He didn't see the assailant clearly, but heard the harsh breathing—harsh, harsher, then suddenly less clear, as if it were fading into the distance. *He* was fading; consciousness was slipping away from him, the bands round his chest had the strength of steel.

He slumped to the floor.

2

THE DARK ROOM

IT was dark.

That was all he realized at first—darkness, and pain that was little more than discomfort at his chest, and a smarting soreness at his face. He didn't know what had happened until he heard a sound—a moan. Then everything flashed back.

He was lying on the floor.

He couldn't see where, but the moan was so near that he knew he was in the room.

There was a dull pain in his groin, and when he tried to get up, the pain became sharp and he collapsed, grunting. The moaning went on—a steady trickle of sound, as of a human being in agony. He stretched out his legs and arms, and made himself relax; minutes passed. He turned gently on to his right side, and began to get up. His head swam, but he managed to stand. He put out his right hand and touched the wall, swayed towards it and then leaned against it, drawing in deep breaths; his lungs still felt tight and locked.

Outside, the wind was howling.

He heard a different sound, neither the wind nor the woman—rather that of a car on the road. It faded. He bent down, and the blood rushed to his ears as he groped for his torch, found it, and switched it on. The light was so bright that it hurt his eyes. He didn't switch off, but swivelled the light round slowly until at last it fell upon the woman.

She lay on a single bed, two yards away from him, one arm hanging over the side—a slim white hand. Her body was flat, and she lay on her back. Her clothes were dishevelled, her long legs, sheathed in nylon, were nice legs. As the light travelled up, he saw enough to judge that she was young and comely; not her face, the light didn't touch her face yet—just her body. Her white blouse was wide open at the neck. Torn? The light fell upon the point of her chin, and it might be Janet's chin. Then it travelled to her face and her head——

He dropped the torch.

It crashed on to the floor and went out, plunging the room into darkness. But in spite of that he could see— he could screw up his eyes to shut out darkness and still see. He staggered and leaned heavily against the wall. His heart thumped, and his stomach heaved.

When the worst of the shock was over and his mind began to work, one thought came absurdly into it: how could she be alive? How could anyone so mangled be alive, moaning from the shapeless thing that had once been her mouth?

Then he heard the car again—much nearer. He didn't at first realize what it was, but when the engine stopped and a door slammed, he knew that someone had arrived outside. It took him a long time to realize it. He didn't move, but stared towards the bed, where the white blouse was now a pale blur. He heard footsteps, and then a heavy banging on the front door.

Someone shouted; he didn't catch the words.

He said aloud: " I'm a policeman. I'm used to seeing dead bodies."

He wasn't used to such a sight as that—or to the thing which brought the real horror—the possibility that the woman was his wife. Dark skirt, white blouse, long, slim legs, long, slim, slender arm and hand—he had seen the right hand, which had been ringless; Janet wore no rings on her right hand, but she often wore a dark skirt and a white blouse. Roughly, fearfully, he rejected the possibility that it could be Janet; for who would want to kill her?

No one would want to bring him here and do this thing to him ; but someone had.

" Get on top of yourself." His voice was hoarse, cracked.

There were other sounds, now, of men walking in the house, then along the passage. He heard them talking, but still couldn't catch the words, because they were whispered. There were two or three men downstairs. They started to come up. He put out a foot, feeling for his torch. He didn't touch it. Faint light appeared ; the men were coming cautiously and carrying a torch.

He licked his lips and called : " Who's there ? "

The footsteps stopped on the instant, and the light went out.

He called : " It's all right. Who's there ? "

He heard a shuffling sound, and then the creaking of boards—and suddenly a beam of light stabbed into the room and into his face. He shut his eyes against it, before he saw the two husky men and the third, behind them. Next moment, he felt powerful hands on his arm, and he was held tightly. When he opened his eyes, the torch light was shining towards the bed.

They were huskies—but the chill of horror which went through them passed itself on to him. For a long time— minutes—no one spoke, and there was just the sound of heavy breathing. Then one of the men said in a thick voice :

" You *swine*."

Roger said : " Don't be a fool. I——"

" Shut up ! "

He didn't want to talk, explanations could come later. And these were policemen ; before the night was out, they would be turning somersaults in order to please him. Two of them were police-constables, anyhow, the third was in plain clothes. Roger didn't recognize his lean face, and that wasn't because of the poor light. He couldn't be expected to know every plain-clothes man in the Surrey C.I.D. What he was expected to know didn't matter. Fear had been driven away for a spell, but came back in waves of terror.

Was that *Janet*?

The man in plain clothes said: " Better have some more light. Light the lamp outside, Harris."

" Yes, sir." Harris, the policeman nearer the door, seemed reluctant to release Roger's arm. When he did, the other man held on more tightly, and hurt; but that wasn't important, all that mattered was finding out whether the woman was Janet.

There was something different in the room; what?

The woman had stopped moaning.

The plain-clothes man approached the bed. Another car came along the road towards the cottage.

Roger said: " Look at her right shoulder."

The man, his back turned on Roger, did nothing of the kind, but appeared to be shining his torch into her face.

" Look——" began Roger.

" You keep quiet," said the big policeman, and dug his fingers more deeply into Roger's arm.

" This will be the doctor," said the plain-clothes man.

Harris came in with the lamp, alight but turned up too high and smoking badly. He stood it on the dressing-table, and the plain-clothes man told him to be careful not to touch anything. He trimmed the lamp clumsily. After the darkness and the beam of torchlight, it seemed a soft, gentle but all-revealing glow. It made the husky policeman seem sinister.

Roger said in a taut voice: " All I've asked you to do is look at her right shoulder."

The plain-clothes man was tall, with thin features; and the light made him look yellow.

" Why ? "

" See if there's a mole at the back of her right shoulder —egg-shaped."

" Want to make sure you got the right woman ? "

" You can be funny afterwards."

" With you, no one will ever be funny again," said the plain-clothes man. He made no attempt to look at the woman's shoulder. She lay absolutely still, and hadn't moaned again; she was dead, of course. It was better that she should be dead than alive, for her face would be hideously disfigured for ever, but—the question hammered itself against his mind, filling him with a wild terror which showed in his eyes and in his tension. *Was she Janet?*

He forced himself to speak calmly.

"Will you please look at her right shoulder and tell me if there's a mole on it."

The plain-clothes man said: "Take him downstairs, you two, and ask Dr. Gillik to come upstairs at once. If the squad has come with him, tell them to be very careful what they touch and to start on that downstairs window. I'll send for them when I want them. Oh, I'd better have the photographer up at once."

"Yes, sir." Harris and his companion pulled at Roger's arms.

He tried to wrench himself free, to go towards the woman on the bed. The top of her shoulder glowed, pale and creamy-coloured, in the light; move the blouse two inches, and he would see what he wanted.

A mole—and it was Janet. No mole—not Janet.

He got one arm free, and then sensed what was coming. He turned his head. A ham-like fist smashed into his nose, blinding him with pain and tears. The woman and the plain-clothes man became shapeless blurs. He felt himself dragged out of the room. Then one man took his arm and bent it behind him in a simple hammerlock, and pushed him downwards. The other followed. There were men in the hall, including a middle-aged man with greying hair and carrying a black bag; "doctor" was written all over him.

"Inspector Hansell would like you to go straight up, doctor, please."

"What's this all about?"

"*Very* nasty business, sir. Woman with her head smashed to pulp."

Cold grey eyes scanned Roger's face. The doctor didn't speak, but couldn't have said more clearly: "And you've got the man, good." Roger was thrust into a small front room, where a lamp burned, then pushed into a chair.

"That's too comfortable for him," said Harris. "Get up—sit on that chair." "That chair" was an upright one.

Roger didn't move.

"I told you to get up!"

It wasn't worth arguing. He stood up, then sat on the other chair, which was near a big heavy, old-fashioned standard lamp. He didn't realize what Harris was at until cold steel pressed into his wrist, and a lock snapped. He was handcuffed to the standard lamp.

So this was what it was like on the other side of the law; how they dealt with a suspect. No, be just; if he couldn't quiet the surging fear in him, be just, be rational and normal, being abnormal wouldn't help. They'd caught him, as they thought, red-handed; they felt vicious towards him, as he would have felt vicious towards a man caught in the same damning circumstances. They hadn't really manhandled him; Harris had been justified in striking him when he had tried to get away, and couldn't really be blamed for the power he'd put into his punch. The handcuffs were justified, because he'd made one attempt to escape.

His arm, stretched out, began to ache.

Men were going up the stairs, and there were others working at the window.

What had brought them so quickly and in such force?

Harris, red-faced and bucolic, kept staring at him from narrowed blue eyes.

Roger said slowly and deliberately: "I want to send a message to Inspector Hansell, from Chief Inspector West of New Scotland Yard." Harris started. "I want to know whether that woman has a mole at the back of her right shoulder, and I want to know quickly."

Harris shrugged.

"When the Inspector wants to hear from you, he'll tell you. Keep your mouth shut."

"Damn you, find out about that mole! Tell him that I'm West. Get a move on!"

Harris was startled. The other constable grunted, and they exchanged glances. Then Harris said : " I'm Queen of the May." But he went out of the room and made his way up the stairs ; they creaked at every step. The other man, husky enough but smaller than Harris, moved to the door, as if he didn't want to become inveigled into conversation. Roger leaned back. Discomfort didn't matter, whether from the hard back of the chair or the soreness at his face.

Fear that the dead woman was Janet hammered ceaselessly against his mind—but even before Harris returned he didn't really believe that the woman was Janet. It was fear, as of a nightmare from which he knew that he would wake up. But when he heard Harris's ponderous tread on the stairs again, the nightmare became reality. He sat upright, straining his eyes and his body.

A man spoke to Harris, whose rumbling voice came clearly ; his words had nothing to do with Janet. Roger half-rose from his chair, and the constable at the door growled :

" Don't try anything."

The rumbling went on, then stopped ; Harris appeared. A word burst out of Roger.

" *Well?* "

" No mole," said Harris.

3

WHY ?

FOOTSTEPS sounded above and on the ground floor, there was a ceaseless murmur of voices, odd, unexpectedly sharp sounds, creaking, and now and again the wild howl of the wind and a spattering which Roger didn't place at first. None of them mattered ; the dead woman wasn't Janet. Janet was alive, free, Janet was——

Janet *wasn't* here.

And what about Cousin Phyllis ?

What was behind all this?   Had he strayed by accident into trouble, or was it carefully plotted, making him the victim of a conspiracy.   The thought shocked and sobered him—sobered, because now that he actually contemplated it, he knew he should have thought of that before.

As a frame-up, it was nearly perfect.

Once accept the possibility that someone had wanted to lure him here and have him accused of murder, and the rest followed easily enough.   But swallowing that wasn't easy.   There was no rational reason why he should be framed for the murder of a woman he didn't know; or for any murder.   But the hall-marks of a cunningly contrived frame-up were here.   Just one thing made it ludicrous; that anyone would suspect a highly placed officer of the Yard of murder.   And Eddie Day knew where he was coming, it was no secret.

The sobering process continued.

Everything had been laid-on, even the call to the police with the convincing warning that it was a case of murder. Nothing else would have brought Hansell and his squad along so fast.

He'd learn the details when Hansell knew who he was.

He must get one thing clear.   Hansell had been summoned so that he, Roger West, youngest C.I. at the Yard, could be caught in the house with that dead girl.   Was he right in thinking he had only to convince Hansell that he *was* West, and the situation would switch in his favour?

No, he wasn't.

He'd been found on enclosed premises, with a girl battered out of recognition and with an axe by his hand. From what he remembered of the girl's face, it would take a better pathologist than most to prove that that particular instrument hadn't been used, *if* there were any blood on it.

As the man who had assaulted him had wanted him framed, presumably he hadn't overlooked a detail of that nature.

Roger murmured to himself: " I'm in a spot."

" About time you realized it," Harris growled.

Never mind Harris. Why should anyone frame him? Why should anyone telephone the Yard, leave a fake message—of course Janet herself hadn't telephoned—lure him here and then work this? Remember, too, that it had to be someone who knew he'd jump to any form of SOS from Janet, and who also knew that Janet had a recluse cousin named Phyllis, who lived in Surrey. That meant, someone who had taken a lot of trouble to unearth little-known facts about his relatives; and meant someone who wanted him framed at all costs.

Why?

There was only one possible answer; to get him out of the way. But the answer only led to a second *why?* He wasn't in the proper mood to go on answering that kind of question. If he accepted one thing, that the murderer desperately wanted him framed, there was another question he could think about—would it be a wise thing to *let* himself be framed? Or at least, let the world, and that really meant the murderer, think that Scotland Yard believed he had killed the unknown woman upstairs?

He smiled faintly at the thought.

Harris growled: "You'll grin on the other side of your face before this is over."

Roger shrugged and stood up. He could do that without pulling the standard lamp over. He hadn't a chance to get away, but both policemen moved towards him. He turned away from them and looked into an oval mirror above the mantelpiece. This was the first time he had seen his reflection since he had come round, and it gave him another shock, a nasty one which turned his stomach.

He **didn't** recognize himself.

His face was a dark blotch, looking sinister and brutal, reminding him horribly of the girl upstairs.

·   ·   ·   ·   ·

Hansell came in. Roger didn't notice, because he was still staring at his reflection. The panic was subsiding into reason. His face was badly scratched, the scratches had bled a lot, and the blood had dried on it, in a brown

mess which looked black in the mirror. He put his right
hand to his cheek and felt a sharp pain in the back of the
hand, looked down and saw the long cut in it—the cut
which he had received from the window-glass.

Then he was aware of Hansell standing behind him
and staring into the mirror. He turned. The two
policemen had gone out, and the door was closed.

" Admiring yourself? " asked Hansell.

" I'm something to look at! What kind of detective do
you think you are? "

Hansell smiled faintly.

" Pretty good."

" I don't like your methods. There's an old saying in
England that a man is presumed innocent until he's
proved guilty. It's usual to make a charge before you
use handcuffs, and it isn't usual for burly constables to
try to break a suspect's nose."

Hansell's smile grew wider.

" Who are you? "

" I'm——" Roger paused, as the vital question reared
up in his mind again; would he be wise to allow this
frame-up to succeed, for the time being? Was that a way
of finding out what was at the back of it.

" Aren't you sure? " Hansell sneered. " Perhaps
you've a split mind, schizophrenia is a favourite ailment
of murderers. Or perhaps you're just suffering from loss
of memory. Why were you so interested in that mole? "

" My wife has a mole just where I asked you to look."

" So that makes you not a wife murderer."

" That's right."

" Stop fencing. Who are you? "

He liked Hansell; he had a feeling that the man was
a good officer, one in whom there was a full sense of
responsibility. And going part of the way with the
murderer might get him into a worse jam than he was.
Once Hansell was convinced of the truth, he would hold
his tongue.

" Roger West, Chief Inspector, Scotland Yard."

" So you remember you've told Harris that. Mind if
I see your wallet? "

Roger moved his left hand to get it, and the handcuff
stopped him. "Help yourself."

Hansell took out his wallet. In the poor light, this
was an eerie experience, but he faced it out. He didn't
look at the wallet, but at Hansell's lean, narrow face and
the drooping lips—this man had the face of a cynic.
Several letters were in the wallet, and Hansell took them
and turned towards the light. Only then did Roger see
that it wasn't his wallet; it was brown, his was black;
this was much thicker, too; and he saw a wad of one-
pound notes, many more than he ever carried.

"That's not——" he began.

"Three letters, addressed to Mr. Arthur King—at
least you got the number of syllables right," Hansell said
sardonically. He probed into the wallet. "Registration
card—Arthur King. Driving licence—Arthur King.
What gave you the idea of pretending to be a policeman?"

Roger sat down heavily.

"You're Arthur King, of 18 Sedgley Road, Kingston-
on-Thames," Hansell said, "and I charge you with the
murder of a woman, as yet unknown, and warn you that
anything you say may be used in evidence. Any legal
quibbles about that?"

Roger said slowly: "It'll do, for now."

"I still want to know why you pretended to be West."

"Work it out later, and don't try any rough stuff,
Hansell." Roger spoke sharply, seeing the other's hands
clench. "What's your evidence? Wholly circumstan-
tial? I was in the room with her, you saw me and jumped
to the conclusion and charged me. That story ought to
please your superintendent and give the magistrate
apoplexy."

"I like giving beaks apoplexy," said Hansell. "You
were next door to the axe with which she was killed.
Your prints are on the axe, on the torch you were using,
and they're all over the place—including the window,
where you forced entry. That girl put up a fight and
clawed your face, and skin and blood off your face are
under her finger-nails. Give it up, King, and admit that
you did it."

Roger looked at the door—it was now ajar; if he made any kind of admission, it would be thrust open, so that Hansell could later present a witness to the statement.

He said : " I didn't kill her. I was outside, heard a scream, broke in, and then heard moaning. I broke the door down with an axe and when I went inside, a man attacked me and knocked me out. I hadn't been conscious again for five minutes before you arrived."

" How long did it take you to work that one out? "

Roger shrugged.

" How did you get here? "

" By car."

" What car do you use? "

" A Morris 12, supercharged engine, registration number *SY 31*."

Hansell laughed. " That's why a Chrysler with registration number *XBU 31291* is parked in the road outside, I suppose."

That made the frame-up as near perfect as one could ever be, by breaking down the story of how he had approached the house. His assailant had scratched his face to make it look as if he had struggled with the girl. There was even a chance that he'd transferred blood and skin from Roger's cheeks to the girl's fingers; he would be as thorough as that, and yet it didn't make sense. How could the man prove that a senior officer of the Yard was someone else? How could he hope to make that stand up?

He couldn't.

He stood a chance of proving that Roger had been *pretending* to be someone else.

Roger laughed; there wasn't much amusement in it, but the spasm caught him, and he couldn't stop for a few moments. Hansell stared down at him, and when Roger had checked himself, said :

" I still don't think it's funny. Why not give up trying, King? We've caught you with everything."

" Then you ought to be happy."

" I'll be more satisfied when I know why you killed that kid upstairs."

" I'll be more cheerful when you start looking for the murderer. Give me a cigarette, will you? " He always kept his cigarettes in his hip pocket and couldn't reach it with his free hand.

" No, I don't smoke them. I wouldn't give you a cigarette if I did. Harris! " Hansell raised his voice, and the door opened at once. " Go through his pockets and put everything from them on that table," Hansell ordered. " You stay here with them, Lister." So the other big constable was named Lister.

Hansell went out, and Harris began to go through Roger's pockets. Out of the right-hand jacket pocket he took a slim gold cigarette-case; not Roger's. From the waistcoat, a lighter, watch, and diary—none of them Roger's. He was used to the idea now—that his assailant had taken everything out of his pockets and put someone else's stuff in its place.

P.C. Lister made a note of everything, calling it out aloud as Harris placed it on the table. When that was done, Roger sat down and eyed the cigarettes longingly.

Hansell came in.

" Finished? "

" Yes, sir," said Harris.

" Anything marked with ' *R.W.*'? "

" No, but several things have '*A.K.*' on them, sir."

" Good enough," said Hansell. " Sergeant Drayton is outside, and he'll take you and the prisoner down to the station. He can be tidied up, but before that I want you to scrape some of that dried blood off his face, and keep it. You can give him something to eat, and let him have a packet of cigarettes but no matches—when he wants a light, he will have to ask for it. Don't let the Press get at him. Take him in the back way, and see that he doesn't see anyone except our people."

" Yes, sir."

" Ever heard of the accused being allowed to see his solicitor? " asked Roger heavily.

" I'll talk to you about that later. You don't have to say anything without a lawyer, but just now I've more important work to do. All right, Harris."

Harris unlocked the handcuffs.   Roger rubbed his wrist gently.   Both policemen kept close to him, and once they were in the hall, Lister held his arm tightly, just above the elbow.   Outside, there was a blaze of light with silver streaks stabbing through it; rain was coming down heavily.   The lights came from several cars parked in the lane, most of them facing towards the road and Helsham, but one, a glistening American model, was facing the other direction; this was " Arthur King's " Chrysler.   Yes, the job was masterly, but it didn't make any sense at all.   It was one thing to frame a policeman, another to fasten a false identity on to him—oh, it wasn't worth thinking about yet.   His thoughts became muddled, he hadn't yet absorbed all the facts.

He came back to early questions : where was Janet, and where was Cousin Phyllis?   He didn't feel as anxious as he might have done.   Janet was probably safe at home, and the two boys would be asleep by now.   Janet would be expecting to hear his car at any moment.   The message had been faked, only her name and not Janet herself had been involved.   But as soon as he was at the local police-station he would make sure that someone telephoned her, to find out whether she was there.   Once he knew that she was safe, he might play ball for a little while with the perpetrator of this vicious hoax.   If she were in danger, he'd make them send for someone from the Yard.   If he exerted himself he could do that, he'd soft-pedalled so far.

He got into the back of the car.   Harris sat next to him, Lister took the wheel, and a bulky plain-clothes man, presumably Sergeant Drayton, sat next to the driver.   It was a roomy car.   Roger watched the other cars as they passed slowly, and then saw the big white boulder and the newly painted signpost which had told him that he was going to the right cottage.

Why had this happened?

He sat back and closed his eyes, feeling Harris's arm against him.   If he made a move, Harris would use that ham of a fist again.   There was no point in trying to escape, anyhow, Harris could rest easy.   His thoughts flashed from one thing to another.   But for that girl's face and head, this would be laughable; farcical. This was how it felt to be sitting next to a policeman, under arrest on a charge of murder! He snorted, and Harris glared at him. They were going cautiously down the steep hill, which Roger had come up, in third. There were several dangerous corners, and none of them was marked, because the road was little used. The headlights shone on the spears of rain and the leafless hedges bent beneath the fierce March wind. Road and banks glistened. Trees stood out like grey spectres, and dropped behind, only to be replaced by others. He saw lights, some distance ahead—the little cluster of lights of Helsham Village, but they wouldn't take him to Helsham, they would go on to Guildford. Whom did he know at Guildford? There was Inspector Masterson——

The driver turned a corner and then jammed on his brakes. All of them were jolted forward, Roger before he caught a glimpse of the road block or of the men who darted forward the moment the car stopped.

4

HOLD-UP

THE glow of the headlights shimmered on the rain, on huge branches of trees which had been flung across the road, and on a man who stood huddled up in a raincoat, with a hat pulled low over his forehead and a gun pointing towards the car. Roger caught a glimpse of all this as he straightened up. He saw other men, one of whom wrenched open the driver's door and poked a gun inside.

Harris grunted and grabbed Roger's wrist. Cold steel brushed his hand, and then the handcuffs clicked—he was manacled to Harris.

"Take it easy." The man who poked the gun into the car had a smooth voice. A scarf, tied round the lower half of his face, served as a mask. "Do as you're told, and you won't get hurt."

" You're crazy." That was Sergeant Drayton, in a shrill voice.

" Not so crazy as you'll be if you try to pull a fast one. We want West."

" You're crazy." Drayton either had a one-track mind or was stupefied by the hold-up.

" No one named West——" began the driver.

" Okay, forget who it is, we want your prisoner—he's a pal of ours." Bright eyes showed in the pale light inside the car. " Get out, pal." He looked at Roger.

They were remarkable eyes; fierce, glittering; like silvery fire.

" We're the police! " howled Drayton.

" And you're telling me why the police are so bad, sergeant. We'd still want our boy friend, even if you were the Army, Navy and Air Force rolled into one." The gun swivelled towards Roger. " Get out."

The door by Roger's side opened; another man with a gun stood there. The rain hissed down until wind caught it and sent it in a wild flurry about the car, spattering inside.

" I can't——" Roger began.

" You can, pal. And hurry, we haven't got all night."

" That's enough of *this*," said Harris heavily. He breathed like a grampus, and had been fighting to retain his self-control. Harris was good—ten times better than Drayton. " You clear off, the lot of you." He might have been talking to a crowd of gapers gathered about a street accident. " This man's our prisoner. Clear off."

" What do they train policemen on? " marvelled the man by the driver. " Get out! " He waved the gun at Roger.

" Take me, take my friend," said Roger. " I'm hand-cuffed to him." It wasn't easy to make the words sound casual, or to try to sum this up; except to see that it was the next stage in the framing.

Why?

Harris sat back in his seat, as if determined to stay there for ever. It would be no fun trying to get him out of the car by force, he must weigh sixteen stone.

"He's got a key, hasn't he?" The man with the strange eyes said harshly.

"I told you to clear out," Harris growled. "Another car will be along in a minute, and then——"

"We'd make fools of more policemen," said the spokesman. The rain hissed and spattered, and the wind howled; it was bitterly cold. "If you know what's good for you, you'll unlock those handcuffs."

"Oh, will I," said Harris. He moved his left arm. Something bright glistened in the light, flew across the car and out of the door—the key. Thrown with that force, it doubtless went into the hedge, it would take hours to find it. Harris licked his lips, and pressed back in his seat again, satisfied that he'd foiled the assailants.

Then the door at his side opened.

As Harris turned, a man struck at him with the butt of a gun. The heavy blow caught him on the chin. Quickly, the man with the gun tipped Harris's helmet over his eyes and struck again—not savagely but with cold calculation.

Harris slumped down, and didn't move.

"Look here, you're crazy!" gasped Drayton.

"That's right. You just do what you're told. Sit still —you'll get more than the ox if you're awkward."

By then, men were dragging Harris out of the car, shoulders first. Roger slid towards the door, unable to help himself, utterly at these men's mercy. The tug at his wrist was painful, but the man eased Harris out gently, and helped him. It seemed an age, but was actually no more than five minutes, before Roger crouched over Harris's huddled figure, still fastened to him by the single handcuff.

The rain pelted down.

"Take it easy," said the man who had knocked out Harris. Another came forward and held Roger's arm, so that the steel connecting bar of the handcuffs was visible, and Harris's hand hung limp from it. The newcomer started to work with a small file, and the rasping sound added to the wild bluster of the night. Water trickled down Roger's neck, was bitterly cold on his sore face; it hurt. His clothes began to get soggy. The two policemen in the front of the car did nothing, for they were still covered by the gun. The man with the file seemed prepared to work all night; but he didn't, the job took only five or six minutes.

No other car appeared.

Harris's hand dropped limply by his side.

" Come on, West." That was the spokesman, now standing by Roger. He took Roger's arm in a grip as tight as Harris's, and another man was close behind, pressing a gun into his back. There was room to pass between the hedge and the branches. Suddenly, the headlights of the police-car went out. Doors slammed. A little group of men, five in all, followed Roger and the spokesman. Farther along the road, pointing towards Helsham, were two cars—dark, looming shapes, with only their sidelights on. Roger was bundled into one, the spokesman got in beside him.

Soon they were moving down the hill.

·   ·   ·   ·   ·   ·

Roger simply let impressions rest on top of his mind.

Take one detective. Lure him to a lonely cottage with a faked message. Kill a helpless girl. Make it obvious that he'd killed her. Give him a false name. Capture him from the police, and use his real name so clearly that the police couldn't mistake it. *Then* take him away.

" Cigarette? " asked the man by his side. Those fantastic, silver-fire eyes glowed.

" Thanks."

The man lit cigarettes for them both, handed one to Roger and sat back. It was too dark to see his face clearly, but he had pulled down the scarf, and the cigarette glowed red and showed the pointed tip of his nose. They turned off this narrow road to the main road which ran through Helsham and then towards London through Guildford. The car was powerful, and well sprung; the engine made scarcely any noise.

" Enjoying yourself? " asked the man next to Roger. His voice and manner didn't go with his eyes.

" So-so."

" I must say you take it well, policeman."

" King Canute ordered the waves to recede, but he didn't keep his feet dry," said Roger.

The man laughed.

" I think we'll be able to work with you."

" Sooner or later you'll be asking yourself whether I'll work with you," said Roger, " and that'll be the question that matters."

The man laughed again. It wasn't an unpleasant sound; it denoted a man who knew exactly what he was doing and had no thought of failure.

" Another question, just to set my mind at rest," said Roger mildly.

" Let's hear it."

" My wife? "

" Expecting you home, probably. Unless she's telephoned Scotland Yard, to report you missing."

" Thanks."   .

There was no reason why he should believe the man, but he did. He felt much easier in his mind, almost content; that didn't make sense. It wasn't any use worrying about Harris, or the ruthlessness of the hold-up, or the future. Janet had been used as a decoy, and it wasn't much good blaming Eddie Day for failing to make sure that it had been she who had actually telephoned.

His clothes were soggy from the rain, but it was warm in the car.

They sped on, carving an avenue of light through the blustery darkness. They soon reached the Guildford by-pass and drove along the wide road between rows and rows of small houses, many with lighted windows. There was little traffic. The car in front, as large and powerful as this, was never more than twenty yards ahead of them, and so made sure that no one cut in. A car with a blue " Police " sign coasted along in the opposite direction, and the man by Roger's side laid a hand gently on his knee.

The police-car passed.

" Nervous? " asked Roger.

" I shouldn't have liked anything to happen to you,

and it would have done if you'd tried to attract their attention." They sped along the by-pass then suddenly swung left, off the main road. "I always heard it said that if there was such a thing as a good policeman, it was Roger West."

"Thanks. But I'm just a beginner."

"If you behave yourself, you'll have a lot more time and promotion ahead of you. Care for a drink?"

"No thanks."

"You'll have one, just to please me," said the man by his side. "It'll taste all right—Scotch. You won't notice anything wrong with it, and you'll have a nice rest for a few hours. After that, we'll talk business."

"And what if I spit it out?"

"Then you'll get the same treatment that the ox had back on the road. Why risk a bad head?"

As he spoke, the man took a flask from his hip pocket. He unscrewed the cap and then switched on the roof light. He had a narrow, pale face, and those flashing eyes had long, dark lashes. His hand was as steady as the car would allow. Roger took the flask; it certainly smelt like whisky. Roger sipped: it wasn't any use fighting against this. He sipped again, and the whisky warmed and encouraged him.

"That'll do." The man took the flask away and screwed the cap on. "If you stay as sensible as this, we'll get along. Any idea what it's all about?"

Roger laughed.

"Have you?" The man's voice sharpened.

Roger laughed again.

"You can be too clever," the man said. "But I'll talk to you when you wake up." It was like a threat.

He didn't like the possibility that Roger had some idea of what was behind all this; so it would be a good thing to make him think a lot was known. Roger leaned back, comfortably, not yet drowsy. He didn't know what road they were on now. Both cars sped through the night, and the rain came down in silvery streaks.

Gradually drowsiness came upon him. The man by his side hadn't spoken since the threat. He wasn't sulky,

but worried.   He stared straight ahead of him, with that
molten silver for eyes.

Roger's eyes began to feel heavy, he couldn't keep them
open.   He yawned.   There should be something frightening about going under to knock-out drops.   It was
possible that he would never come round, but the thought
didn't really alarm him.   They wouldn't go to all this
trouble, simply to poison him.   They wanted his help.
A ruthless, powerful, well-organized gang of crooks, the
existence of which he hadn't even suspected, wanted the
help of a man from the Yard.

That was as far as he got in his thoughts before un-
consciousness captured him.

.   .   .   .   .

He'd slept a long time, because it was daylight when he
woke.   He lay in a comfortable bed, drowsy, unaware of
any aches or pains, but his face felt stiff, and so did the
back of his left hand.   Thoughts and recollections came
to him as through a haze.   He felt no sense of alarm, even
when he remembered what had happened in the car;
he felt as if he were awake in a dream.   He closed his
eyes for a few minutes, opened them again and looked
round the room.   It was small but delightfully furnished;
more a woman's room than a man's.   On the dressing-
table was a bowl of daffodils, yellow heads drooping.
Chintz curtains at the narrow window matched the
flowered chintz on the bedspread, the eiderdown, and the
two easy-chairs.   The colours were gay, the quality
good.   The furniture, of light oak, was reproduction;
he didn't know the period.   There was a corner wash-
hand basin.

All he could see out of the window from the bed, was the
grey sky.

He knew that he ought to get up, but didn't feel inclined
to move.   His mouth was dry—parched; the thing he
would like most was tea.   Weak, hot, sugarless tea, pints
of it, and after that, something stronger.   He grinned to
himself—and then had a mental picture, of a battered
head.   That was his first bad moment since waking, he

was really beginning to *feel* again. He no longer wanted to lie in bed. He pushed back the bed-clothes and sat up. His legs were stiff; he swung them over the side of the bed. His head began to ache, and he felt more in need of that tea than ever. When he was steadier, he walked slowly to the window. He looked out on to a trim lawn, daffodil beds and, beyond, a beech-hedge with massed brown leaves, trees. There seemed no end to the trees. There were some dark firs and pines; but mostly they were leafless trees, spiky-looking beech and birch; silver birch, he could tell from the trunks, which looked like silvered alligator hide. He heard nothing—absolutely nothing— but the tops of the trees were bent by the wind. So sound didn't come into this room through the window. The window was a single pane of glass, and when he examined the frame, he saw that it was really a false one— this window wasn't made to open. He pressed nearer and looked upwards, studying the glass. It had a yellow tint, a characteristic of toughened glass. Whatever these people used would be good, so that glass was nearly unbreakable, almost as good as iron bars.

He went to the door.

It had a handle, but no lock—no keyhole. He tapped on it gently, and it didn't sound like wood, it was more like steel. If he tapped louder, to make sure, he might attract attention. Well, why not? He turned from the door, and searched the room. He was wearing a pair of pyjamas with a broad blue-and-white stripe, and at the foot of the bed was a dressing-gown and a pair of slippers, but no day clothes were in sight. He looked inside the wardrobe; there was nothing but clothes hangers. He let any idea of getting away quickly slide out of his mind —in any case, he didn't want to get away yet, he wanted to find out what it was all about.

He caught a glimpse of his face, and it surprised him because it was so normal. He went closer to the mirror, his face reflected above the daffodils. He could see the pink scratches and the shiny, greasy salve which had been rubbed into them after the blood had been cleaned off. His hand had been treated with the salve, too—that was why he felt little discomfort. He studied his face. By habit, he laughed when they called him "Handsome" at the Yard, but it wasn't really a surprising soubriquet. His curly fair hair was ruffled, but undoubtedly it had been combed the night before, while he had been unconscious; they'd made sure that he would be presentable when he came round.

He went to the wash-basin, washed his hands and face carefully in tepid water, and dabbed them dry. As a result the pink streaks turned red. They tingled, too. He went to the door and banged on it with his clenched fist, and then stood back and waited for someone to come.

Before long, he heard footsteps.

5

MARION

He knew, before the door opened, that a woman was outside. The footsteps were quick and light, and he heard them distinctly, which argued against the door being steel. He heard a key scrape in the lock, so it had a lock on the outside. He sat down on the bed, looking towards the door with a faint smile on his face.

The girl came in, started back when she saw him, and then smiled also, and closed the door behind her. He caught a glimpse of a man who remained in the passage outside.

" Good morning," the girl said brightly.

Roger's smile widened. " Hallo. Seeing you makes a good morning."

She laughed—an easy, unaffected, friendly laugh.

" Is there anything you want? "

" Tea. In urns, if possible, if not in pint mugs."

" Some will be sent up in a few minutes."

" Cigarettes and a lighter."

" I can give you a cigarette," she said, " but I'm not

allowed to leave matches with you, or to let you smoke when you're alone."

"That's a good argument for staying with me for a long time," said Roger.

She laughed again, took a small plastex case from a pocket in her pale-grey frock, and a lighter. She had to come near, to light his cigarette. Few men would complain at being near her. She wasn't beautiful, she just looked—good. It was in the clear grey of her fine eyes, the soft colour of her cheeks, the curve of her lips. She wasn't used to a lighter, and concentrated on flicking it; the moment of concentration brought her lips together in a rose-bud shape. She had a heart-shaped face, and light-brown hair—he supposed she would call it auburn. It was cut short, in the fashion, but not too short, and if the waves and curls in it were machine-made, he would be surprised. Her hands were not small, but well-shaped, and her nails were varnished a pale pink—pale enough to look natural.

He drew at the cigarette.

"All right?"

"Yes, thanks. Who are you?"

"You may call me Marion."

He leaned back, nursed his knees with his hands, and looked at her without frowning.

"That's thoughtful of you. What are you going to call me?"

"Mr. King."

"Oh, I'm a king again, am I?"

"If you really think about it," said the girl he could call Marion, "every man is a king to someone, isn't he?"

She wasn't joking; she was earnest, sober, almost sombre—and she looked just a little scared and a little wary. She backed away until she reached one of the arm-chairs, and sat on an arm. She crossed her legs. She wore a long dress, but it didn't hide the shapeliness of her ankles or the lower part of her legs. She was slim, but not too thin, tall for a woman, and grace was made for her.

" I wonder who I'm a king to," he said.

" Please don't worry about that now," said Marion.
" You will feel much better when you've had breakfast."

" Ah, yes. Even kings and princes have to eat. Did
you patch my face up last night? "

She looked relieved at the change of subject.

" Yes, how does it feel? "

" As if it needs patching up again."

" Now? "

" Yes, please."

She went to the wash-basin and opened the tiny cupboard above it, took out a small pot of white salve, and
came towards him. " Sit up straight," she said, and
when he obeyed, she took some of the salve on her fingers
and began, gently, to rub it along the scratches ; immediately, they felt easier. When she had finished, she
stood back and said :

" What about your hand? "

He held it out obediently.

" Thanks very much," he said when she had finished.
" You're as good as a trained nurse."

" You have to learn a little of everything." She
seemed anxious to make sure that he didn't think she was
a trained nurse. She remained wary, watching him as if
it were possible that he would attack her. She glanced
out of the window, and for the first time he caught a
glimpse of her profile; it was lovely. She had a short
nose, slightly tip-tilted, and tiny pale-pink ears. In every
way, she was a wholesome creature, and the word " goodness " came to his mind. Then he imagined her as she
would be with her face smashed in ; the word faded.

The door opened.

This time, he'd heard no footsteps.

A man came in, a little fellow wearing a white jacket,
with a grey, bullet-shaped head and mournful brown eyes.
His brown shoes were polished brightly enough to attract
attention. He carried a large tray with the experienced
poise of an accomplished waiter, and placed it on the
bedside table. Roger ran his eyes over the tray. The
oddest thing was the ivory knife; more like a very blunt

paper-knife than a table-knife. There was tea, toast, marmalade, butter—plenty of them all—and two plates under silver covers.

" I should sit in bed and have it," said Marion.

" I never like breakfast in bed."

" You don't want to overdo anything," she said, but humoured him by placing an upright chair in front of the table. He poured himself out a cup of tea; ah! He finished it before he lifted the covers. By then, the waiter had gone.

Porridge; and eggs and bacon.

The bacon was cut into small pieces; he could manage the egg with the ivory knife. All these things added up to one unavoidable conclusion. He didn't speak of it. The girl sat on the arm of the chair, her legs still crossed, watching him or looking out of the window. He finished every scrap. He had a feeling that it was wrong to enjoy the food as much as he did. Afterwards, the girl said:

" Wonderful! "

" What's wonderful? "

" Your appetite."

" You haven't seen anything yet," said Roger. " Now, I'd like to shave."

" I'll arrange it," she said. She leaned forward and pressed a bell by the side of the bed, and the little waiter came in. Without a word, he took the tray out. The girl followed him, saying at the door: " I won't be long."

When she had gone, he went to the little cupboard above the hand-basin. There were no scissors; no razor; nothing made of steel. He grinned crookedly to himself as the adding-up process went on apace. He waited for ten minutes, as far as he could judge—he had neither watch nor clock. Then the door opened again, and the girl and the waiter came in; the waiter carried a little black bag and reminded Roger of Dr. Gillik.

The waiter spoke for the first time in a voice that was unmistakably Cockney, from the very heart of the East End.

" Goin' to git in bed, or sit in front've the mirror? "

" I'll sit in front of the mirror," Roger said.

" S'right." The man went over to an upright chair,
then opened his little bag. Out of it he took a large pink
sheet. Roger sat down, the sheet was tucked round his
neck in a professional manner. Then he was lathered
and shaved with a safety razor. They weren't even going
to take a chance that he could snatch a cut-throat from
the " barber's " hand!

He was regarded as dangerous; the girl, presumably,
considered him a dangerous lunatic.

.   .   .   .   .

No knife, no razor, no weapon of any kind, no clothes,
no watch or clock, no newspapers, neither pen nor pencil;
at least, there were some books. These were on a little
shelf in the bedside table. He glanced at the titles.
They were mostly classics—the popular classics, Scott,
Dickens, Macaulay, Trollope—with a book of verse and
two modern novels. He didn't open any of them, but
went to the window again and looked out on to the trim
lawn and the nodding daffodils and the trees which
crowded upon the garden—an impenetrable mass of
them, many more than there had been at Copse Cottage.
How far was he from Copse Cottage? How many miles
had they travelled after he had lost consciousness? Why
was he here? When would he see his silvery-eyed companion of the night before?

.   .   .   .   .

The waiter brought his lunch, and stood by while he
used the ivory knife again. Five minutes after he had
finished, Marion came in with coffee on a tray, and two
cups and saucers. He was sitting in an easy-chair by the
window.

" Do you mind if I have coffee with you? "

" I was hoping you would."

" How are you feeling? " she asked.

" Mystified, but quite content."

" I'm so glad." She passed over the " mystified "
and poured out the coffee. He was fascinated by her
hands. They were so like Janet's; not quite so roughened

at the tips with work, but still the hands of a capable person who knew exactly what she wanted to do. Except for that wariness, so easy to understand now, she was at ease—a comforting companion. Handmaiden to a murderer too—did she know it?

" Another cup? "

He passed his empty one. " Thanks. When are you going to tell me all about it? "

" There's nothing I *can* say." She was earnest.

" Do you think I'm mad? "

" No, of course not! " Coffee spilled out of the jug into the saucer. " That's ridiculous. You haven't been well, but you're getting better, and soon you'll be perfectly fit again. I want to help you. I wish you'd talk freely to me."

" What about? "

" Anything that comes into your mind."

" Applied psychology? Or psychiatry? Or what? "

" Just talk. It always does one good to talk."

" Supposing I talk about my wife? And the boys." She had the wary look again, and he decided that Mr. Arthur King had neither wife nor children. She poured the spilt coffee from his saucer into her cup. " Janet isn't like you, except her hands. Hands reveal a lot—did you know? "

" Yes," she said.

He made himself sound dreamy. " The only known infallible ways of telling one person from another are by comparing the tips of the fingers and the lines on the soles of their feet; its easier to take finger-prints than footprints. But I was going to talk about my family. Janet we'll take for granted. The boys—there are two of them. The elder is Martin, but we call him Scoopy. Odd name, isn't it? "

" I rather like it." She was pretending to believe him.

" It's grown up with him. Derived from the family expression, windy-pops. You know, wind-up. Scoopy's a big chap. Rising six. Tough as they come and a plodder—he takes life pretty seriously. Richard is a year younger and a very different kettle of fish—he takes life as it comes, a gay young man who will go places if he

can only develop half of his brother's power of concentration.   You don't believe a word of it, do you?"

" Please go on."

" Why don't you believe it?"

" Please go on."

" Why do you work for a killer?"

" I just have my job to do."

" Being handmaiden to a murderer shouldn't appeal to
you."

She smiled.

" Do I strike you as being insane?" he demanded.

" I can't talk to you about that," she said.   " I know
you have dreams—nightmares.   The dreams are good,
the nightmares—I'll help you to forget them, help you to
sleep without them.   It's only temporary, as a result of
the strain.   Don't worry about them.   Just *tell* me about
them.   That's all I want you to do.   You won't shock me.
I've heard so many strange stories and helped so many
people.   Just tell me about the worst of them.   Please."

It wasn't going to be easy to convince her that she was
wrong.   At this stage, it was hardly worth trying.   She
was convinced he was here as a patient and that he was
dangerous.

Why?   Why had they used these methods?

He felt himself grow cold;   and shivered.

" Do the nightmares frighten you like that?" she asked
softly.   " Speak about them, talk freely, and they'll recede.   I promise you they'll recede."   She came closer,
took his hand in hers and smiled into his eyes.   " I want
to help you."

He shivered again.

What did they want to do?   Make *him* think that he was
crazy?

6

NIGHTMARE

HE could hear the moaning. . . .

And he could see the girl with the battered face and the white blouse and her hand lying over the side of the bed. The moaning had a note of horror which made him writhe, the sight made him want to close his eyes against it—but the tighter he closed them, the more vividly he could see. The nightmare gripped him with a feverish intensity, and went on and on, but was always exactly the same—the girl, the moaning, the blood—clearer, louder, clearer, louder. He wanted to shout, and opened his lips and screamed; but no sound came. He tensed his nerves and muscles to yell, but couldn't make a sound, invisible hands were holding him tight—tighter.

At last words burst from his lips.

" *No, no, no !* "

Then, he was awake.

The nightmare was no longer real, just vivid memory. He lay in the darkness. He felt the hot sweat bathing him, and his arms, legs, and face twitching. He peered up at the darkness of the ceiling, and felt afraid. He didn't try to move. He had only to stretch out his hand and switch on the light, but he didn't want to. He had to overcome this new terror—a terror of the dark.

This was the third night of these nightmares.

It was always dark when he woke; and he knew that if he submitted to the terror and gave himself light, then he would have lost a battle.

He lay panting, horribly hot, with his eyes closed.

He heard no movement, but suddenly it was no longer pitch dark. He opened his eyes. A small light burned by the door, which Marion was closing gently behind her. She wore a dressing-gown, her hair was in a net, and she was smiling reassurance. She came straight to him, and her hand was cool and gentle when she pressed it against

his forehead.   She went to the basin and damped a sponge,
came back and sponged his face and hands; he wanted
her to go on doing it.

" You'll be all right, when you've told me about them,"
she said.   " If you'll only tell me, there's nothing more to
worry about."

She'd said that a dozen times in the past three days, but
always in daylight.   She hadn't come in just after he had
recovered from a dream before.   He lay looking at her
fresh, wholesome attractiveness, and felt that he hated her.
She was the only human being he had spoken to, except
the waiter, since he had first come round.   She was
always the same, and nothing he could say would make
her change her attitude—he was ill, she was there to help
him.   He'd tormented himself, trying to fight against it;
just as submission to the fear of darkness would mean a
lost battle, so would the narration of his dream to her.

They could *make* him dream; they had.

" You'll feel better soon," she said softly.

He sat up.

" Water, please."

She went and got him a glass of water.   He sipped it,
looking at her all the time.   It didn't matter how he glared
or looked or talked, she was always exactly the same—in
complete control of herself, reality where there was only
unreality.   They had lifted him out of his daily life and
surrounded him with fantasy, and the question which had
started when he had seen the dead girl at Copse Cottage
became a shriek which filled his whole mind: *Why?*

She was like Janet.

It wasn't just her hands; she was like Janet.   If
Janet were here, he would feel better.   Being away from
her for so long—three days!—was agony in itself.   Knowing that she was worried, frightened because he was
missing, was perhaps the worst thing of all, except that
insistent, screaming question—why?

He hadn't seen a newspaper or heard the radio, he had
no idea what was happening outside in the world.   Whenever Marion came in, there was always a male guard at
the door, and he had no doubt that the man was armed.

If there'd been no guard he might have overpowered her and tried to get away, but—would that be wise?

"Tell me what it was about?" she whispered, and leaned over him. A wisp of her hair brushed his cheeks—the scratches had practically healed now. "Then you'll be all right."

He mustn't lose the battle.

"I'm too hot."

"I'll take off the eiderdown." She stood up, slim in spite of the dressing-gown, which was of wool, and folded the eiderdown back, took off one blanket, folded it and laid it across an easy-chair. "Lie down," she said, and when he obeyed, she lay on the bed beside him. She was cool and impersonal; it wasn't as if a girl were lying there, but someone unreal and unhuman; unhuman, not inhuman. She put a hand on his arm, then adjusted the pillow so that her head was more comfortable. "Just tell me about it."

That quiet, insistent demand was always the same.

"You'll feel much better."

So was the promise.

They wanted to make him lose the fight, wanted him to talk to her, and he'd be damned if he would let them win. They could try as much as they liked, but——

He became rigid.

"It's all right, I'm with you," she said.

He wasn't thinking about her, now, but the idea which had come suddenly. It made him want to laugh, and he hadn't felt like laughing since the first morning he had seen her. The next stage wouldn't be reached until he *had* talked, until "they" thought he had succumbed.

"Just tell me——"

He shook off her hand, sat up sharply and pushed her away.

"Mr. King——"

"Get out! Get away. I hate the sight of you!"

"If you'll only——"

"Get out!" He pushed her again, and then suddenly raised his hands and clutched her neck. He didn't hold tightly, but enough to scare her. She called sharply:

"*Come in!*" He was still clutching her neck when the door opened and two men sped silently across the room. One held his wrists and forced his hands from her neck, the other helped her from the bed. She looked pale and shaken. The man didn't hurt him, just held him down in bed until she had left the room. Then they went out, and left him alone.

What time was it?

He felt cool, now—cool and more in command of himself because the cloying helplessness had eased a little. He had a plan of campaign. Three days had sapped his energy and dulled his mind, making it soggy, filling it with one obsession—and he hadn't seen the obvious, that nothing further would happen until he had done what she wanted him to do—talked freely.

He got up and went to the window.

There were stars, but it was very dark. There was no moon, nothing to help him to judge the time; he never knew the time, except that it was day or night. He went back to bed and closed his eyes, and felt rested, but that didn't mean that he had slept for long before the nightmare. He waited, and waiting was an agony in itself. Judging time was almost impossible, but before he tried again, he must wait for a quarter of an hour, or a little more. It wouldn't work unless he waited.

He wasn't sleepy.

Now and again he smiled.

He wanted a cigarette, but the only time he was allowed to smoke was when the girl or the barber–waiter were with him—which meant that, ostensibly, they were afraid he would set fire to the room. Everything they did was done to convince him that he was a dangerous lunatic.

He got up again, put on his dressing-gown and went and stared into the dark garden, shifting his position from time to time, until at last he decided that he had waited long enough. He went back to bed—and began to shout.

"*No, no, no!*"

Nothing happened.

He screamed again. "*No, no, no!*"

Was he losing his reason? Could a sane man lie here and shout like that, in an otherwise empty room, with no one to hear him? Idiot—he could laugh at himself, couldn't he? He did, weakly, and then shouted again: "*No, no, no!*"

The light came on.

Marion stood in the doorway, smiling, calm. The light was just above her head, and her face was framed in that wispy auburn. She closed the door gently, and this time he didn't see the guards, although he was sure that they were there. She approached him, and said:

" Did it come again? "

" I—I can't stand it." He licked his lips, and wondered whether he appeared frantic enough to be convincing. Apparently he did, because she went to damp the sponge again, came back and bathed his forehead, face, and hands. She smiled gently all the time, as if she were completely unafraid. Did she really think that he had attacked her, and that if help had not come, he would have strangled her?

She lay down beside him.

" Tell me," she said.

" It's—so foul. *Foul.*" He made his voice break.

" Yes, it must be, but don't worry—I'm used to hearing all kinds of strange stories. The nightmares will stop when you've talked about it. What happens? "

He told her the simple truth of what he had seen in Copse Cottage. His voice kept breaking, twice he stopped and turned his head away from her, his body becoming rigid; and each time she rested a hand on his arm and waited, until he went on again hoarsely. He left nothing out, but he stopped at the moment when the police had arrived. He told the story over and over again.

Strangely, he felt easier in his mind.

She put an arm round his shoulders, and her face was very close to his, but it was still impersonal and unreal.

At last, he stopped.

" Don't worry," she said. " Just go to sleep."

" What—what time is it? "

" It's the middle of the night.   Don't worry, just go to
sleep.   You won't dream."

.   .   .   .   .

He didn't dream.

.   .   .   .   .

It was full daylight when he woke, and the sun was
shining.   He felt more rested and calmer than he had for
three days—now nearly four.   He lay for a while, looking
at the sun shining into a corner of the room, then got up
and went to look into the garden.   The grass smiled, and
the daffodils' heads were raised; the scene was beautiful
and as quiet as his mind.   He didn't ask himself whether
he had succeeded in doing what he had set out to do.   He
knew that he had; and that although he might have to
pretend again, this part of the ordeal would soon be over.
He leaned against the window and pondered over everything that had happened, calmly and dispassionately, and
he didn't think he had said anything wrong, or that he
had exaggerated any incident.

She brought him his breakfast.

The man with the white jacket and the mournful face
shaved him.

Afterwards, Marion brought in a suit of clothes.

.   .   .   .   .

Except for a handkerchief, there was nothing at all in
the pockets, but he felt more himself, fully dressed.   The
clothes fitted well.   He wasn't allowed a tie, the shirt
had a collar attached.   He was brought a pair of leather
slippers, but not shoes—and therefore no laces.

Marion allowed him twenty minutes to dress, and then
came in.   She left the door wide open.   No one was in
the narrow passage behind her.   She looked fresh and
delightful, with nothing to show that she had lost so much
sleep during the night.   Her eyes were gay and sparkling,
and he thought that she was pleased with what had happened, it was a kind of professional triumph.

" Would you like to walk round the garden ? "

" Er—may I ? "

" Yes, it's a glorious morning," she said. " And afterwards you can sit downstairs for a while, a change will do you good. Did you sleep well after I left you? "

" Er—yes."

" No dreams? "

" No."

" I told you so," she said; and she had.

He laughed inwardly, but was haunted by an uneasy feeling; she had prophesied it, and it had happened—her " cure " had worked. He was getting confused in his own mind, in spite of his dispassionate mood of the night before. What would she say if she knew that he had told her that story deliberately, not just to ease his fears, but to bring about the change?

The passage was narrow, with cream walls. There were four doors in it. It led to a landing and a narrow staircase, and he didn't think that it was the front of the house. Downstairs, in a small hall, she took an overcoat from a peg and helped him on with it, slipped a coat over her shoulders like a cloak, and then opened the door. The sun shone brightly on them, warm and spring-like. It was good to breathe fresh air. He walked slowly; he didn't think he could have walked briskly had he tried.

The daffodils nodded gently in a soft breeze, and the lawn had hardly a weed. A bent old man approached a herbaceous border, but quickly disappeared again. The beech-hedge was higher than it had seemed from the window—seven or eight feet high, and it looked thick; it wouldn't be easy to get through or over that hedge. As they walked, Marion talked idly about trivial things.

At the end of the garden he stood and looked at the house.

There was nothing remarkable about it. The walls were grey, most of the windows small—only those on the ground floor appeared to open. Radio music came from one of the rooms. He guessed she didn't want him to study the house closely, and she pressed his arm gently. He turned—and as he did so, a man appeared at a ground-floor window.

He knew it was the man who had talked to him after the hold-up. Even at this distance, those silvery-steely eyes were unmistakable.

7

NEWSPAPERS

THE man withdrew, as if anxious not to be seen.

Roger kept his face blank, let his gaze roam past the window towards the daffodils near it. He knew that Marion was looking at him intently, but he wouldn't meet her eyes. She held his arm lightly and exerted a gentle pressure as they moved on.

" What is the matter? " she asked.

" I'm all right."

" You must learn to tell me exactly what passes through your mind when you're frightened."

" I'm not frightened."

" You are," she said, and he couldn't look away from her any longer, had to meet her eyes. They were so clear and grey—restful eyes. The wholesome goodness in her was so apparent that he wondered if she were completely fooling him, whether anyone could be as good as she both looked and appeared to be. " I felt your arm go taut. Did you recall the nightmare? "

" It's nothing."

" Unless you talk freely, you won't get better," she said. She hadn't talked so openly before about his being ill. " Why don't you trust me? "

" You've been very good."

" I want to help, that's all, and I think I can."

" How many other patients have you had here? "

" Quite a lot. And——"

" You've helped them all." There was a sneer in his voice, but it didn't seem to affect her.

"I 've been able to help some of them, and I'm very

anxious to help you." The gentle pressure of her fingers increased. She slipped her arm through his.

" So I'm a favourite patient. Why don't you tell me what's the matter with me, instead of hinting? "

" Don't you know what's the matter? "

" No." He tightened his lips. " I'm as sane as you are. You seem to think I'm crazy."

" You've been ill, and its affected you differently from many people," said Marion, " but as soon as you've learned how to forget yourself and your fears, and to trust me, you'll be better."

" I want to leave here."

" You may, as soon as you're well."

He pulled his arm free and stalked ahead of her, and she made no attempt to catch him up. The gardener went on working and showed no interest in him, behaving as if this were an everyday affair. He walked across the lawn glancing towards the window where he had seen the man with the fierce silvery eyes, but without staring. He caught a glimpse of the man, standing by the side of the window with a hand at the curtains. So he was under surveillance; no need to be surprised about that. What was his best move? What did they expect of him?

He turned, and saw that Marion was walking slowly across the lawn. The sun shone on her hair, filling it with golden lights, giving her beauty. She smiled pensively, as if she were humouring him and his mood didn't matter, whatever it was she would always be the same. He waited for her, feeling—and looking—like a sulky school-boy. She made no reference to what they had been saying.

" I expect you're tired, you'd better come indoors."

" I'm all right out here."

" It's the first time you've been out for several days, you shouldn't overdo it," she said. She took his arm again and drew him towards the side entrance to the house. This time there was no doubt; she pressed gently against him, liking the physical contact. He went into the house, which seemed gloomy after the bright sunlight, and she led the way to a door on the right—overlooking the back garden. Was it the room where the man had been?

It was large, pleasant, sunlit—a drawing-room, furnished with the same taste as his bedroom, quite delightful. In one corner, near the window, was a grand piano, and on it a huge bowl of daffodils and early tulips. Freshness seemed to come from them. There were several sofas and easy-chairs, the carpet was pale green and yellow, on the cream-papered walls were water-colours—good ones. She led him to a chair and waited for him to sit down, pulled up a small table on which was a box of cigarettes and a table lighter. She offered him a cigarette.

" Thanks."

" Just sit here for a while, I'll see you again soon."

She left him with the lighter—the beginning of trust. The door closed softly behind her. He fought back a temptation to jump up and follow her. He smoked, sitting tensely, straining his ears for any sound of conversation; she had probably gone to report. He heard the murmur of voices in the next room, stood up and went to the wall; he could distinguish no words, just heard the hum of voices.

He went back to his chair, and as he began to sit down, saw the newspapers.

The sight had a curious physical effect. He became rigid and stared at them—at this first contact with the real world in four days. The papers were in a rack, near the piano, with several magazines. He turned and looked at the door; it was still closed. He glanced out of the window, and no one appeared to be looking at him. Then he warned himself that nothing would be left about by accident, shutting him up in here with newspapers meant that he was intended to see them. He went across and picked them up. Before he did so, he thought wearily : " It's a trick." They would be old newspapers, of no real interest.

They weren't; there were four, each a *Daily Cry*, the first dated March 14, the day he had left the Yard. He looked at the others; *March 15, 16, and 17*. He looked at the second, and the headline leapt up at him :

GIRL MURDERED IN LONELY COTTAGE

The body of an unknown girl, her face savagely mutilated, was found by the police in Copse Cottage, Helsham, one of the loneliest parts of Surrey. The killer had smashed a window in order to force entry, and broken down the door of the girl's room with an axe.

There was a great deal more, but nothing about Roger or the hold-up. A girl had been brutally murdered, and the police were investigating—just that. He dropped the paper and picked up the next.

GANG RESCUES KILLER—

POLICEMAN SAVAGELY ATTACKED

There was the whole story; much more than there had been in the first paper. He scanned it swiftly, for names. The man who had been charged was " believed to be Arthur King, with an address at Kingston-on-Thames "; there was nothing about Roger West. He glanced through the rest of the paper quickly, seeking only headlines, and found what he wanted on an inside page—a short paragraph with a small heading: *Yard Man Missing.*

Chief Inspector Roger " Handsome " West, youngest C.I. at Scotland Yard, left his office late on Monday afternoon, and has not been seen or heard of since. The Yard authorities believe that West, who has been working at high pressure for several months, may be suffering from loss of memory or some other illness.

There was much more behind that; he could see the wary hand of the Yard, requesting the newspapers to play down the fact that he was missing. There was no photograph, nothing to suggest a hue and cry, nothing to hint that his disappearance might be in any way connected with the murder. He felt his forehead damp with sweat as he dropped that paper and picked up the fourth—that morning's.

POLICE HUNT MURDER GANG

Everywhere in Great Britain the police are seeking the gang which rescued a killer from a police guard near Helsham, Surrey, late on Monday night. It is believed that an arrest will shortly be made. The rescue, described fully in yesterday's *Cry*, was the most daring in police annals.

The dead girl has not yet been identified. There was nothing at the house where she was found to suggest that she lived there, and the house has been empty for several months, the owner, Mrs. Ethel Malloy, being abroad. The police theory is that the murderer made an appointment with the unknown girl, who discovered his evil intentions too late and locked herself in. Her face was so badly mutilated that photographs cannot help with identification.

Sir Harry Gregg, chief pathologist at Scotland Yard, says that the girl was probably in the early twenties, but there were no distinguishing marks on the body. The police are anxious to have details of any young woman who has been missing from her home since Monday last, and who answers the following general description: Height: 5 ft. 6 in.; medium to dark hair; blue eyes; well-developed; Weight: 10 stone 4 lb. At the time of her death, the victim was wearing a pleated black-serge skirt, white-silk blouse with four mother-of-pearl buttons, the size of two-shilling pieces, a three-quarter-length coat to match the skirt, nylon stockings size $9\frac{1}{2}$ (French make), black suede shoes, rayon underwear (peach colour). The names of the suppliers and manufacturers of all these articles of clothing had been removed.

Roger groped for another cigarette and lit it without thinking of that token of trust—he was left with a lighter. There was plenty to go on; absence of name tags shouldn't prevent the police from tracing the clothes. The " French make " introduced a difficulty; was it possible that the girl had come from France? No more than an outside possibility, a lot of French nylons found their way into

England, any woman travelling home from France was allowed, unofficially, to bring in two or three pairs. Many gave them away as presents, it wasn't reliable even to say that the girl had been in France. How many tourists went there each year? Hundreds of thousands— forget the French angle.

He was thinking almost as if he were at his office.

He turned the pages, and again found what he wanted— another reference to himself, this time with a small photograph; and a poor one.

YARD MAN STILL MISSING

Chief Inspector West (*photo side*) is still missing from the Yard and from his home in Bell Street, Chelsea. There has been no trace of his movements since he left the Yard late on Monday afternoon to keep an appointment with his wife. The police theory that he is suffering from loss of memory is supported by his wife, who says that the pressure of work for the past few years has affected his health.

Nonsense! Janet knew better. Janet had been visited by the pundits, had been told what to say to the Press— and the pundits were still influencing the Press. There was not a hint that he was even remotely connected with the Copse Cottage murder, nothing which gave any inkling of the truth.

Janet, by now, would be in agony of mind.

.   .   .   .   .

So mystery was piled upon mystery. The dead girl was unknown, which meant that the Yard wasn't getting far in its inquiries. That was trivial, compared with the greater mystery—what did these people think they were going to do with him? Why had they brought him here, why had they identified him with Arthur King, and then talked so plainly during the rescue that the police must realize that he was in fact West? Why had they treated him like this, as if trying to convince him that he was ill, in need of treatment—that his mind was unbalanced?

He couldn't see any point in it, no matter how he flogged his brain.

He gave it up. If he couldn't puzzle that out, at least he could decide what line to take next—when he saw the man with the fiery silver eyes. It was easy to imagine those eyes everywhere in the room, piercing and compelling. That man wanted his help—but how could he help, now? What good was he to anyone if the Yard had reason to believe him to be a killer?

He lit another cigarette.

He stood up and went to the window, looking into the garden, and then he saw that this window was exactly the same as the one upstairs—of toughened glass, and without a movable frame. They meant to make sure that he didn't escape. He hadn't thought of escaping! They were atrophying his mind, he was completely soggy, he—no, be fair to himself: it was much more important to find out what these people wanted than to escape from here. His job was to find out.

He turned from the window and picked up the newspapers again—and then he heard a sound behind him. It made him swing round. He stared blankly. A shutter was falling over the window from the outside, a shutter like a venetian blind, blotting out the sun from the top half of the window, then descending over the bottom half. When the shutter was nearly down he rushed to the window and touched the glass, but there was nothing he could do. All he could see was a little of the lawn and the heads of a few daffodils; they disappeared when the shutter fell right into position, and he was left in absolute darkness. Only the glowing tip of his cigarette relieved it, and that faded when he stopped drawing at it.

The hairs at the back of his neck seemed prickly.

He heard no sound, now—just stood with his back to the window, staring into darkness.

He heard a whirring noise, which came suddenly, and turned his head to the right. Then he saw light—a beam, as from a powerful torch, shining on the opposite wall. There, the wall was bare. The light hit the wall, much like that from a cine-camera and about the same shape;

it made an oblong of light, two yards across, a yard and a half down. Yes, it was from a small projector, and the whirring was explained, they were going to put on a film. He forced himself to walk slowly to a chair facing the wall; he could just pick it out, among the other furniture. He sat down and crossed his legs.

A picture appeared.

A girl was walking along a narrow street—that was all. He didn't recognize the street, but there were things in it which told him that it wasn't in England; more likely, France. The houses were tall, terraced, and the windows had shutters fastened back against the walls. There were several little balconies at the higher windows. The street was empty, except for the girl, who appeared to be walking towards him. She looked tall, although he had so little by which to compare her. She walked quickly. She was smartly dressed and seemed thoughtful. In a way, she wasn't unlike Marion; but he might also say that she wasn't unlike Janet. She kept on walking—was the street as long as that, or was it a trick of the camera? She *was* young; in spite of her thoughtful expression there was a hint of eagerness in her face.

There was something else; that quality of goodness which he had recognized in Marion.

A man appeared; was that significant?

No, he passed her. She turned into another street where there were more people, into yet a third. This was a wide busy thoroughfare. He caught a glimpse of a single-decker bus with a crowd of people standing on the platform at the back—peculiar to Paris. There was a newspaper and magazine kiosk, which as far as he knew one wouldn't find in the same form anywhere but in Paris.

The dead girl had worn French nylons.

He wasn't being shown this film just to entertain him.

He had forgotten that sharp nervous fear of the sudden darkness, was absorbed in the pictures.

The girl was lost among the crowds; no, not quite lost, she appeared occasionally, once stood and looked into a shop window—at handbags. Then she walked on—and there was a cut in the film, but he knew it wasn't finished, for the whirring of the projector continued.

Another picture came, this time of a small café, with a big striped awning over a dozen or so small tables, a waiter standing in white jacket by the open door, one couple drinking out of long glasses—*bock*. Then the girl appeared and sat down as far as she could get from the couple. The waiter approached her, eager, smiling; she shook her head, said something, indicated that she was waiting for a companion. The waiter took up his position in the doorway again. Now he smiled at the girl's back, benign, understanding; a middle-aged romantic. The girl lit a cigarette, adjusted her long skirt, looked up and down the street, which Roger couldn't see clearly. Twice she glanced at her wrist-watch. She began to frown. The waiter's smile widened, he nodded his head, as if he could share her anxiety.

She opened her handbag, and took something out—a letter? She studied it closely. Yet her eyes didn't move from side to side, as they would have done had she been reading. She put the thing down, and he saw that it was a photograph; he thought it was of a man, but couldn't be sure. The girl finished her cigarette, and now there was no doubt that she was frowning and worried. Another couple appeared, and the waiter went inside to get their order. The girl began to tap her foot on the ground, impatiently.

Then a shadow appeared over her.

She glanced up—and although the frown disappeared, she didn't smile, but looked anxious. She said something, and Roger wished this weren't a silent film, then scoffed at himself for the inanity of the thought.

The shadow grew into a man, who had his back to the camera. He pulled up a chair and sat down. The waiter reappeared and smiled broadly, nodding as he went to the other patrons. The man with the girl leaned forward and hid most of her from Roger. The man was hatless; he had fair wavy hair which needed cutting. There was something familiar about him; Roger couldn't place it. Then the man turned, as the waiter approached, and

Roger caught a glimpse of the profile—and sat up, a chill shiver running up and down his spine, a physical thing which he couldn't prevent.

It was *his* profile.

He had never seen that girl in his life before, but he was sitting there as if in the flesh and talking to her. He looked grim, sombre, and paid the waiter scant attention. Then man and girl leaned forward, talking earnestly.

The picture faded.

But the whirring continued, it hadn't finished yet. The light seemed bright. The sweat on Roger's forehead was cold; this was getting on his nerves, he could sense unnamed terrors hidden from him.

Another picture flashed on——

Of the girl—without a face, or with a face that was unrecognisable. She was just as he had seen her at Copse Cottage.

And then a man spoke from a corner of the room.

" Why did you do it, West? *Why?* "

8

CONVERSATION

ROGER hadn't heard him come in; hadn't dreamt that anyone was there. The voice affected him more than the words. He started violently, and peered towards the corner. He could see a vague shape, which faded as the light from the projector died away and that dreadful picture disappeared.

" Why did you do it, West? *Why?* "

There was nothing sinister about the voice; it was just a man's voice, earnest, rather grim. He'd heard it before, in the car driving down the hill near Helsham. He licked his lips, and his mouth was dry.

The man moved; Roger heard the sound, but it was too dark to see anything.

" Why don't you tell me? Why did you do it? "

Roger didn't answer.

"You wouldn't have done a thing like that without some reason," the man said. "Confess, West."

This was the half-way stage to madness; the man, who knew he had not done that foul thing, was charging him with it, adding to the unreality. But underlying all this there was a sinister purpose, he mustn't lose his grip. Everything "they" had done was intended to make him lose it.

"Well, West?"

Roger said: "Can't we have some light?" His voice was hoarse.

"So you don't deny killing her."

"Let's have some light." Roger stood up. The door was immediately in front of him, but for all he knew, the man might be standing in his way. He put his hand down and picked up the silver cigarette-box; fingered it, as if to throw it, and then put it down. It clattered, and he thought it fell on its side.

The man moved again.

Light came on, not bright, just a single wall-lamp near the door; everything in this affair seemed to be played out in semi-darkness. The man was little more than a shape, but his eyes were like silver fire; it was a relief to see that it was the man whom he remembered, that he hadn't been misled by that voice.

"Why did you do it?"

"I don't get this. I didn't do it." The denial sounded weak—he wasn't really on top of himself, could easily behave like a fool.

"Who do you think will believe you?"

"Anyone with sense."

"Anyone who sees that film, and knows the rest, will believe that you killed her, West. Why don't you think up a reason that would satisfy your friends the police? It ought to be easy for a man with an agile mind like yours."

Roger turned and sat down. The cigarette-box was on its side, and the cigarettes were spread over the table. He took one and lit it; it was a relief to smoke. The man stood staring at him, accusingly.

" What do you want? " Roger rasped.

" I want you to get some facts straight. Don't you remember going to Paris? Don't you remember going to the cottage? "

" I haven't been to Paris for over a year."

" You could have seen her then."

" I didn't see her. I've never seen her before." This was like trying to reason with a blank wall. Was the man still trying to make him believe that he was ill, trying to convince him that he had done things of which he had no recollection?

The man drew nearer.

" West, you don't seem to realize your position. You went to Paris and saw that girl—the camera doesn't lie, the film is here, a copy of it can be sent to Scotland Yard. You went to Copse Cottage, you were alone there when the girl was killed. You appeared to be someone other than yourself—to fool the police. You were rescued by friends, who nearly killed a police-constable. Your colleagues at the Yard have been very moderate, so far. They've made it apparent that you're not well, that you might be suffering from loss of memory, but you know why, don't you? They think you killed the girl. The evidence is so strong. That film, proving that you knew her before and had an *affaire* with her, gives you a motive. You met her by assignation in a lonely country cottage. You arranged that someone should telephone the Yard with a faked message, pretending to come from your wife, but you didn't realize that your wife would deny having sent such a message. You thought you'd get safely home and no one would suspect you, didn't you? But you didn't have the luck."

Roger said : " One of us is crazy."

" No one at Scotland Yard would believe that you're crazy. You're too well known, too clever. This has all the hall-marks of a crafty crime—the kind of crime that a man who knows the law might commit. You're a police-man." The voice maintained its monotonous level, there was no sneer, no hint of a gloating smile, it was just factual.

" You know how the police build up their cases, you've

often collected the evidence to send a man to the gallows. You've briefed the prosecuting counsel a hundred times. Imagine him being briefed with all this evidence! That you once went to Paris; that this girl is French; that you saw her there; that she came to England and threatened to break up your home life; that you planned to meet her and to kill her, to save your domestic life from collapse. Don't just tell me that you didn't do it, West, tell me what you think a prosecuting counsel would make of it."

Roger said: " In every trial, there's a defending counsel, too."

" I'll leave you to think it over," said the man abruptly. He put his hand to his pocket, pulled out an envelope and tossed it into Roger's lap. He turned towards the door, and as he went out of the room the shutter began to fold up, and sunlight came in through the window again, but it didn't bring reason.

Roger fingered the large envelope, which seemed to have several folded papers inside. He groped for another cigarette. His hand was unsteady. He'd been unsteady enough before seeing that film; he knew that everything that had happened to him from the moment he had smashed the window at Copse Cottage had been intended to make an impression on his mind, unnerve him, convince him that a case could be proved against him.

He saw the old gardener, working—and looking at him.

He took the contents from the envelope. There were three smaller envelopes, each of them stamped with a French stamp; each with a Paris postmark, each with a blue sticker reading *Par Avion*, each addressed to Arthur King, at 18 Sedgley Road, Kingston-on Thames. The writing was large and feminine, the ink bright blue. He took out the first letter, and the words which flew up at him were: " *My Darling Arthur——*"

The writing was the same as on the envelope. The address was simply: *Paris*, with the date. He scanned the first. It was a love letter, as from a woman pouring out her heart. It was a good letter, written in fair English with a few odd turns of phrases, and an occasional word or expression in French; the signature was " Lucille." There was a postscript : " *Soon, I must see you, when can you come ?* "

He opened the second letter, dated two weeks afterwards, and the first words were the same, and then it went on with a fierce directness which shook him badly. " *I am coming to see you. Yes! I am able to come to London, very soon, I am delirious with the delight of it. Chéri . . .*"

The third letter was very brief; she would be in England on Saturday, March 12, and he was to write to her at the Oxford Palace Hotel, London, to say when and where he could meet her.

. . . . . .

He could tear the letters up and be no better off. They would have anticipated that, would have photostat copies, and there would be other letters, too, not just these three. Letters addressed to Arthur King, and passionately written. Put these into the hands of the prosecuting counsel together with everything else, and no jury in the country would acquit him. If he wanted to be rational, he would have to accept that. He couldn't put up a defence—or only one which wasn't at hand and was never likely to be at hand. The only defence lay in proving that all this was a cunningly built-up plot to ensnare him. *Why?*

What did the man want?

Why had a girl been sacrificed for this?

All right, *be* rational; they'd wanted the girl dead for another reason, and found it useful to use her for this plot. Dead, she couldn't deny a thing. Where was the weakness in the case? The film was faked. It wasn't hard for experts to fake a film, and it might be possible to get other experts to testify that it had been faked, that one had been placed upon another—but by itself that wouldn't be a defence. He had been superimposed on the picture; that was all—a simple technical problem. Someone had photographed him, taken away the background—or it needn't be a faked film. Make-up could create features

like his for the purposes of a film. The camera didn't
lie! What a farce. Anyone with good photographs to
go by and with the gift for make-up could have made-
up a man of the same size and general appearance to
stooge for him; it was elementary in film work. Oh,
forget it and face the facts—there was a murder charge
against him, the only defence was the truth, and he
would never be free to find the truth because once away
from here he would be in custody.

He wiped his forehead.

The gardener was hoeing rhythmically, slowly, ignoring
him completely.

He lit another cigarette and squashed it out almost at
once, stood up and went to the door. There was a handle
but no keyhole, and when he turned the handle, nothing
happened.

Was he being watched? For the first time, he glanced
up at the wall from which the camera had projected.
He saw an oblong opening, stood on a chair and looked
through it—but all he saw inside was a wooden board—
wood or steel, what did it matter?—painted with the same
colour as the wall itself. No, he wasn't being watched
now, he was being left to " think it over ". He went back
to his chair and read the letters through again and felt
something of the passion in them and *knew* one thing;
Lucille had been in love with the man to whom she had
written. They weren't faked letters, they had a quality
which reflected sincerity. So Lucille had had a lover,
and had come to London to see him.

Who was the lover?

The man with the fiery eyes?

.　　　.　　　.　　　.

The man came in again.

.　　　.　　　.　　　.　　　.

Roger really saw him, this time. Apart from his eyes
there was nothing remarkable about him. He had a thin
face, not ugly, not handsome—a vague kind of face. His
lips were unusually well-shaped and red. He had brown
hair, brushed straight back from a high forehead, with

a wide centre parting. He was dressed well in dark
grey, but apart from those eyes—which were unfor-
gettable—there was just an ordinary man who might be
seen anywhere. He walked easily, and this time he
smiled and sat down.

" Have you read them? "

" Yes."

" Have you asked yourself what a prosecuting counsel
would say? "

" The defence would want proof that the letters were
addressed to me."

" Oh, they'd have proof. Admirable proof. From
two or three blameless people who would swear that you
often went to 18 Sedgley Road to collect these letters—
irreproachable witnesses, West. You might *know* that
they were lying, but you wouldn't convince your colleagues at the Yard. You've sent many men to the gallows,
now you know what it's like at the beginning of the
walk."

Was this—*revenge*?

Had Roger once garnered the evidence to send a friend
of this man's on the nine-o'clock walk? Would anyone
go to these fantastic lengths for such a reason?

" Do you like it? "

Roger said: " Not much. When are you going to
tell me what it's all about."

The man laughed—as lightly as if this were a normal
conversation, and Roger had made some casual quip.

" Now you're being sensible," he said. " You're half-
way towards doing a deal. Before you've finished you'll
have to come all the way, because it's the only thing that
will save your neck from being stretched. I'll tell you,
later, possibly to-morrow. I've one or two other items of
information for you. This house is a private asylum.
You're not the only borderline case they've had here.
The doctor, like those witnesses, is irreproachable. The
staff is thoroughly trained. Some time ago, a Mr. King
was brought here by his friends, because he was a psycho-
pathic case and given to moods of violence. He received
treatment for a few days and was released. He came back

once, before this week. He came when you were away from the Yard on special jobs, and you would have great difficulty in proving you had been somewhere else. He was a fair-haired man, who might be mistaken for you. The only two members of the staff who really saw him at close quarters and could be sure it wasn't you, were the male nurse who shaves you and the doctor. Your own nurse never saw him—nice girl, isn't she? She's very sorry for you. She thinks that you've committed some violent crime and are under the proper treatment. The doctor who is prescribing for you will swear that Arthur King and you are one and the same. The theory will be, of course, that as Roger West you knew something was going wrong with your mind, you called yourself King and submitted to treatment. Now the defending counsel might make something of that, but—think what the prosecutor would say."

He stopped.

Roger said harshly: " Do my thinking for me."

" Very well. The prosecutor would say that this was all carefully planned, so that if you were caught, you would be able to offer evidence that you were a mental case. The resident doctor here would swear to it, but others would say—truthfully—that if a man wants to pretend that he's over the border he can do so, and fool almost anyone. You've simply fooled this resident doctor."

The man laughed.

Roger eased his collar.

" The case rests," said the other easily. " Spend the rest of the day and to-night seeing if there's a way out of it. If I were in your shoes, I'd come to a conclusion pretty quickly. The only courses open to you are to play ball with me *or* kill yourself. And if you don't play ball with me, you will kill yourself. Your body will be found with those letters in your pockets, and a veil will hastily be drawn. Your wife will have a bad time for a while, but she'll get over it. It's surprising how quickly human beings recover from the worst of shocks, and she'll have plenty of helpers. Your friend Mark Lessing will help her to bear the burden stoically, won't he? And he'll probably become step-father instead of uncle to your two boys. Nice kids, I've seen them several times. What's the name of the elder one? Something unusual, Marion was telling me—she doesn't believe you've any children, of course, she just thinks you're a bad case. A violent case, who——"

There was just so much one could stand . . .

At the first mention of Janet, Roger had felt his muscles tensing; at mention of the boys, he'd felt a savage hatred which locked him in his chair. And that question— "what's the name of the elder one"—brought a vivid picture of Scoopy, big, eager, and trustful, looking at him. Red rage took possession of his mind, and he leapt up. He hardly saw the man, didn't know whether the other had sensed that the attack was coming. With one half of his mind he knew that he was being crazy, but he couldn't stop himself. He smashed at the blurred face, hit something—and felt agonizing pain in his stomach, from a kick.

Next moment he was surrounded by a surging group of people, fighting wildly, but feeling remorseless pressure on the back of his neck, then on his arms. His right arm was forced behind him in a hammerlock, he felt sick with the pain, and the rage cleared. He saw three men as well as his tormentor; two were holding him, one of them was holding something that looked like a coat harness. In the doorway stood Marion.

Marion said: "Oh, please——"

The men ignored her. Roger's arms were forced through holes in the "coat"; and he knew it wasn't a coat, but a strait jacket. It was wrapped round him and tied tightly. There were tears in Marion's eyes.

He was taken out of the room—upstairs; not into his own room, but to one much smaller—a padded cell.

.   .   .   .   .

He stayed there for the rest of the day and during the dread, dark night. There was a couch on which to lie. Before daylight had faded, two men had come in and fed him with a spoon; that was the only food he had. He couldn't rest; dozed fitfully, and dreamt as soon as he dropped off. They weren't nightmares, and he wasn't sure whether they were dreams of waking or sleeping. He saw Marion with tears in her eyes, and Janet, with the two boys, and sometimes he saw the girl walking along that Paris street, so vividly alive.

He remembered the battered face, but it didn't affect him now.

* * * * *

When daylight came, he was lying on his back on the couch, looking at the ceiling: at least that wasn't padded. There was a small window, set high in the wall, and no sunlight, although the morning was bright enough to tell him that the sun was shining; and outside there was a quiet, bright, and happy world. Happy! He tried doggedly to reason with himself, but always came back to the ultimatum: to do what the other man wanted, or to be killed—they'd make it seem like suicide. Suicide depended a lot on motive, and there was one strong enough. Any man who had gone to these fantastic lengths wouldn't bungle a "suicide". The criminal always made a fatal mistake, but this man hadn't made one yet. You might convince the man in the street that this type of criminal never got away with his crimes; a Yard man knew better. He could get away with them.

But it wasn't as simple as the man had made out. He could choose, now, between living and at least pretending to help—and no pretence would satisfy his mentor for long—and dying, and thus defeating the man's mysterious purpose. That was a simple fact. If he refused to "play", he would be killed; the other would simply have wasted a lot of time and painstaking effort.

He could make sure of bitter victory by refusing to play.

But that wouldn't avenge the dead girl.

It wouldn't help Janet.

It wouldn't give Scoopy and Richard back their father. If he lived, there must be *some* chance of doing all that, the scheme couldn't be foolproof.

He lay like that, unmoving, even when the door opened;

movement wasn't easy, once he was lying down. He expected to see the two male nurses, but instead it was Marion. She smiled at him, fresh as the dawn. She closed the door, determinedly, came across, and as he started to sit up, helped him. Then without a word, she began to unbuckle the strait jacket, at the back. She took it off.

His arms were numbed, pins and needles began to run up and down them; agony came. She rubbed his arms briskly, sitting very close to him and smiling.

" Do you feel better? More rested? "

He didn't answer.

" I'm so desperately anxious that you shouldn't have another relapse," she said. " Don't think I'm boasting, but I volunteered to come here alone. I felt sure that you wouldn't hurt me. You mustn't attack your friends, you know."

She spoke with great simplicity, as if to a child whom she was anxious to impress. He looked at her with his head on one side, and wondered what she would think if she suspected the truth. *Was* she sincere? Had the man told the truth about her? If so, she might become a useful ally, and——

No, leave her out of it, for the time being.

" You understand, don't you? " she asked.

" Yes."

" I am going to ask them to let you return to your room again. I think perhaps you were out too soon after the last attack. Dr. Ritter believes in giving patients every possible chance, and I know he is particularly anxious about you."

He would be. And at last he had a name: Dr. Ritter. It brought reality a little nearer.

" I'll soon be back," promised Marion.

She didn't close the door.

That was deliberate, either because she was putting him on trust, or because the man wanted to find out whether he was desperate enough to try to escape. What could he escape to? The certainty of arrest and the near certainty of conviction; it would be crazy to try.

He couldn't try anything. He was forced back to the choice; whether to "play" or whether to let himself be killed. He'd play, of course; he'd have to play.

Marion was soon back, and her face was radiant. No one was in the passage outside.

They were on the second floor; they walked down to the first, and she led him into the bedroom in which he had first come round. He went straight to the window, for he wanted to see that real world beyond the beech-hedge. He saw three men talking together: the gardener, a tall, thin man with a hooked nose, and the man whose eyes impressed themselves so deeply on his mind.

Roger gripped Marion's arm.

"You ought to rest," she said, and he thought she sounded scared.

He relaxed his grip. "Who are the men in the garden?"

"Don't pretend you don't know the doctor!"

"Ritter—the tall man." He didn't have to think that out very deeply. "Who is the other?"

"Don't be silly, Mr. King."

"I've seen him before somewhere, and can't place him." He put his hand in front of his eyes, as if to shut out a dread vision, and her voice became soft and soothing again as she led him towards the bed. He sat down, but didn't lie flat. She went towards the door, and said quietly: "That's your very good friend, Mr. Kennedy. He brought you here."

Here was another name to use as a handle.

Marion went out.

9

THE GAME

KENNEDY came in during the afternoon; the sun was low in the west, and Roger had finished lunch an hour—or was it two hours?—ago. Kennedy came in softly and closed the door behind him, and Roger looked up but didn't move. Kennedy was smiling a faint, sardonic smile, as if he were now beginning to enjoy the joke thoroughly. He came straight across and offered cigarettes. Roger would have liked to throw them in the man's face, but he felt desperately in need of a smoke.

" Aren't you scared of me? " he sneered.

" I shall never be frightened of you, West," said Kennedy easily. " I've only to call for help, and my friends here will come at once. They know they're dealing with a dangerous lunatic. Have you had time to realize the hopelessness of your position? "

" I'd like to change it."

" You can," said Kennedy softly. He walked to the window and looked out, beyond the trees. It was almost as if he were pointing, although he kept his hands in his pockets. " Out there, the world is going on much the same as usual. Your wife, your children, your friends—all of them are living, eating, sleeping, behaving normally. Each has worry, anxiety, fear of some kind to contend with, except the fools, and the fools don't really count. If you ever want to go back into that world you'll have to do what you're told."

" It would help to know what you want."

Kennedy turned the full force of those shimmering eyes on him; they did not look like the eyes of a sane man. But his smiling nonchalance was sane enough. He didn't move; he didn't speak. Waiting caused agony; he knew it and played on it.

Roger sat with clenched teeth, the cigarette jutting straight out, right eye screwed up against the smoke.

Kennedy spoke at last, smoothly, suavely:

" I want you, West. The man and the policeman. Your knowledge of crime and of police methods. I want the expert on criminal investigation. The man who knows Scotland Yard as a doctor knows his patient—and *better*. I want inside knowledge of the C.J.D. All the tricks of the policeman's trade. You can lay your finger on anything at Scotland Yard, and I want everything. I want you, not part of you. Mind, body, soul, if you're fool enough to think you've got a soul. The rest steps out and I take possession."

He meant every word.

His eyes were the true guide to his mind; he wasn't sane, or he wouldn't ask for the impossible.

He said: "No, I'm not mad, West. That's an idea you've got after being here. I haven't really started on you yet. If you're fool enough, you'll refuse. Then you'll know how patients can be treated when they're locked in a soundproof room in a lonely house. You can scream. Maybe Marion will cry tears of pity for you. No one else will."

Roger said: "What's in your mind? To send me back to the Yard, whitewashed?"

"Forget it. You're wanted for murder. I've made the evidence too strong. If you ever left here alive and alone, you'd swing. Thinking about escape won't help you. You can only escape to death."

Be *rational*; use reason.

"It sounds wonderful. I work for you and forget my past."

"You haven't got a past."

"Wife? Family?"

"They're alive. They're well. They're not in danger. Forget them."

"Every C.I.D. man in the country, every patrol man, every village copper, every journalist, and about thirty million people who'll know what I look like when the Yard really releases this story, will be on the look-out for me."

"They won't find you. You won't look yourself. You won't be yourself."

Roger swung round, to stare into the peaceful grounds, to convince himself that this was happening, to grope and gasp. Kennedy didn't speak or move. A thrush flew down and drove a dozen sparrows away from crumbs which lay white on the lawn.

"Make up your mind," Kennedy said.

"What do I get out of it? I'm to lose plenty."

"You'll be alive."

" I suppose I'm to live on air."

Kennedy threw back his head and laughed. It wasn't a pleasant sound, but high-pitched and grating; it matched his eyes. He clapped his hands together, crossed the room and slapped Roger on the back. One clenched fist driven into his stomach, another into his face, and he wouldn't have much to laugh about in future. Roger stood rigid, although the touch was loathsome.

" You're like the rest, Roger! High-minded while you've no temptation. What you mean is—what's in it for you? "

" Well, what is in it for me? "

" A fortune. An easy life. Plenty of the right kind of company. Do what you're told and put your best into it, and you can have the world."

" But nothing out of my past? "

" *Nothing*," said Kennedy.

Roger said: " You say you want the man as well as the policeman. Both have memories."

" It's easy to forget." Kennedy's voice was soft, now, almost a hiss. He turned away, as if to hide the glitter in those frightening eyes. " I know it's easy, because I've forgotten." He was haunted by memories at this moment, they crowded upon him and he fought them away savagely. " You won't remember anything for long, not in a way that hurts. You'll think of the others as dead, like the past. They'd better seem dead, or you won't live. Going to play, West? "

There was more in it than this: the whole plan wasn't unfolded, only a corner was turned up.

" I don't want to die."

" You don't have to."

" What do you want me to do? "

" Will you play? "

" It looks as if I'll have to."

Kennedy threw back his head and laughed again. The outburst lasted a long time, and he was nearer Roger, his chin up, perfectly placed for a blow that could break his neck. Roger bunched his hands inside his pockets.

Kennedy stopped.

" You'll be given paper and pencil. Write out a list of all the senior officers at Scotland Yard, and their special duties. Indicate the particular qualities of each man. Make a précis of the way the organization works. That'll fill in your spare time for the rest of the day. Make sure it's right in every detail."

He went out, abruptly.

.   .   .   .   .

There was no great betrayal in this; few secrets; none Roger need give away. He wrote until his fingers and wrist ached. The male nurse came in with his evening meal, and took away all he had written.

.   .   .   .   .

Night came slowly, but he wasn't tired. He had a watch, now, all the cigarettes and matches he needed, and whisky; the beginning of the " easy " life. His mind was alert, things were crystal clear. His first task was to convince Kennedy that he would really " play ". Kennedy wasn't convinced yet; there'd be trick-tests and crafty traps, and he would have to be on his guard every waking moment.

Until Kennedy was finally convinced of his goodwill, the real motive would be concealed.

He began to think, dispassionately, of how he could send word to Janet and the Yard, and if he found a way, whether he should do it. Janet, when vexed and sharp-voiced if he'd worked too late, had a trick of gibing: "You're a policeman first, man second." There was truth in it; never more truth than now. He could argue and reason with himself night and day and not shift an ounce of one mountainous fact; Kennedy had a fantastic conception of crime. No man who had planned as he had planned so far was without that. He had a scheme for turning a leading Yard man's knowledge and experience against the law. He thought no more of murder than of swatting a fly.

The battle was on—a strange, tenuous, bitter battle.

.   .   .   .   .

He was asleep when Marion came to him, and the warm touch of her hand and breath disturbed him. For a moment, he thought it was Janet. Then recollection came. He started up. Only the dim light was on, and she sat on the bed, looking fragile, ethereal. Her eyes glistened.

He hadn't been dreaming; hadn't called out.

" What is it? "

She said: " I'm terribly frightened."

" *You're* frightened! "

" Yes." She conveyed an impression of fear in her soft voice, in her manner.

" Why? What's happened? "

She asked: " Who *are* you? "

He nearly answered, telling the truth; he would have done so but for the dark shadow of warning that came into his mind: beware the traps.

" Don't you know? "

" I thought—you were Arthur King."

" Aren't I? "

" *He* called you by another name."

" Who? The doctor? "

" No. Kennedy." She spoke as if she were afraid of being heard, and looked over her shoulder towards the closed door.

" When? "

" I heard you talking in here to-night."

She might have; much more likely she was in the plot and came as an *agente provocatrice* from Kennedy.

" Forget it," he said roughly.

" Please! Don't raise your voice. I want to help you, if you're in trouble I saw a photograph— "

" I'm ill. You know that."

" But *are* you? " She gripped his hands tightly. She wore the woollen dressing-grown, and it parted at the neck; her nightdress was a filmy silken thing. " I've been unhappy about you, you seemed so rational at first, not like the others. I thought——" She paused, and her fingers pressed hard enough to hurt.

" Well? "

" I thought it was because I—liked you."

" That's happened to me before."

" Oh, *please*. Tell me the truth. If you're someone else I can get a message sent for you. It would be a hideous crime to keep a sane man here. Perhaps I could tell your friends, or the police. I have time off to-morrow, and can go into the village—to London—anywhere. I want to help you."

" Seriously ? "

" Oh, yes ! "

" Then let me get some sleep."

She drew back, as if he had struck her, and her eyes seemed filled with pain. Could any woman act like that? Behave too quietly and naturally? Was he wrong about her? Could a word be sent out so easily and safely?

She went slowly towards the door; for the first time, her shoulders drooped as if the vitality had been drained out of her. She opened the door; there was still time to call her back.

He let her go.

.   .   .   .   .

The safety razor felt unfamiliar in his hand, but he didn't cut himself. When he looked into the mirror afterwards, he saw that the last traces of the scratches had all but gone, anyone would have to peer closely to discern them. He'd slept well and felt fresh.

The male nurse brought him a *Daily Cry*. There was a little paragraph about the nation-wide hunt, and more about him, with a larger photograph, and the words:

Reliable reports say that Inspector West was last seen on Monday evening, in the Guildford area. Anyone who saw him after six-fifteen that night should communicate at once with Scotland Yard or the nearest police-station.

That was placed close to the murder story; so, slowly and reluctantly, the Yard was allowing him to be connected with that affair.

He put the paper down as the door opened. Kennedy came in with a little sparrow of a man. The newcomer had a beak of a nose and beady eyes, a fresh complexion and tiny, bloodless lips. He stood hardly higher than Kennedy's shoulder, but was immaculately dressed in black coat and striped grey trousers, pale spats, a diamond tie-pin in a silvery grey tie. His voice was high pitched, almost shrill.

" Good morning, good morning. So you're the patient."

" For what? " asked Roger.

" You'll see," said Kennedy.

" Yes, yes," said the little man. " Yes, I see. Mr.—ah—King, go over to the window, please, sit sideways to it, and look at the wall. Please."

Roger obeyed.

The little man came close, peered, breathed on him, and kept nodding. It went on for an age. Then the man pinched his cheeks, his forehead, and the flesh beneath his chin. Roger felt like a biological specimen.

" Yes, yes, that will do."

" A good subject? " asked Kennedy.

" Quite satisfactory."

" Mind it is, damn you! "

" There is no need to be abusive," said the sparrow perkily. " When? "

" This morning."

" Very well, I will get ready." The sparrow went out, bustling and confident.

Roger felt the glittering eyes on him; felt hot and frightened, but schooled his voice to calmness.

" What's on? "

" The second stage in the transformation of Roger West. You don't need to worry, you won't feel anything." Kennedy laughed, and then Marion came in with a tray on which were two cups of coffee; a departure from daily practice and therefore suspicious. She spoke, as if to lull his suspicions.

" As you were here, Mr. Kennedy, I thought I would bring two cups."

" That'll do."

" Thank you."

" Drink coffee, West ? "

" I prefer tea."

" You'll like this for a change."

He drank it.

.   .   .   .   .

It was drugged. He knew that from Kennedy's grin,
and had proof in his own drowsiness, ten minutes after he'd
had the drink. Kennedy left him and the male nurse
came in, said: " Follow me " and went out again, expecting unquestioning obedience. Roger followed him
along the narrow, plain-walled passages. The nurse
opened a door. A powerful smell of antiseptics stung
Roger's nostrils ; the bleak white austerity of an operation
theatre met him. Panic rose inside him like a tempest, he
stopped and gripped the door. No one took any notice
of that.

His mind was numbed with the drug, or he might have
drawn back then, and fought to escape.

Beneath a single bright light was a chair ; a barber's
chair. It stood beyond the operating-table. The nurse
led him to it, and said : " Coat off." He took off his coat
and the nurse pushed him into the chair. As he sat down,
the sparrow came hopping in. He went straight to a
steaming metal pan, where surgical instruments gleamed
through steam. Roger closed his eyes and leaned back
against the chair ; the neck rest was of hard rubber, quite
comfortable. The mist rising from the pan seemed to
become thicker, a billowing cloud, hiding the window,
turning the light to an iridescent haze The sparrow
loomed out of it, or else was enveloped and almost invisible. He kept clicking his tongue ; or was it his false
teeth ? He put on a long white coat. The mist looked
like ectoplasm, and the sparrow a wraith. Roger's head
whirred as if the cine-projector were inside it. The speed
increased, the harsh sound grated in his ears, eyes, the
whole of his head. The mist became a billowing cloud
stirred by up a strong wind. Men became shapes. On a

tray in front of him instruments gleamed—glittered—it was as if Kennedy were staring at him from the tray.

He lost consciousness.

. . . . .

He groaned. Someone spoke, softly, soothingly. He groaned again, but not from pain. There was no pain, only fear of something he could not comprehend.

A hand was at his shoulder, and the voice came again, but in spite of its gentleness, it was not soothing; the voice reflected fear. He remembered much, recalled his last vision of knives which had become eyes. He tried to open his eyes.

He could not.

Panic, a hundred times worse than when he had been in the chair, took hold of him and shook him violently, his whole body seemed to be in physical turmoil. He felt pressure on his hands and—worse—on his eyes; that was why he couldn't open them, something pressed firmly against the lids. That wasn't all; there was pressure against his cheeks, chin, lips, and throat, a constricting pressure, as if his face were in a special " strait jacket "

" Mr. West ! "

He knew that voice.

" Please don't struggle, please don't."

Was he struggling? He felt as if he were convulsed by forces stronger than himself. But he became calmer and more conscious of the gentle pressure of Marion's hands.

" You'll be all right," she promised, " you'll be all right."

He was still; and he was hot; prickly heat affected his whole body, and there was a warm glow over his face. He tried to speak, and couldn't move his lips.

" Don't try to speak yet. You'll be all right. You've had an operation on your face."

How could that soft voice create such cold and frightening terror?

" You'll be all right in a few days."

Would he? He felt as if he were on fire.

" Just rest. I'll get you something to drink. Just rest and don't struggle any more. If you do, they'll——"

She broke off, but he knew what she had been going to say; they would put him in a strait jacket. Had his struggles been so violent? He lay quite still, aware of the ˥tiff warmth of his face, clearly understanding what had happened. The sparrow was a plastic surgeon; Kennedy had talked of the second stage in the transformation of Roger West—a transformation in his looks, of course. No wonder the man had been so sure he would be safe from the police.

He moved his right hand.

He felt the same warm stiffness at the tips of his fingers —so they'd taken the skin off them, and grafted new, to prevent identification through his finger-prints.

He heard a rustle of movement.

" I'm going to help you to sit up," said Marion.   " Then I'll feed you."

Her arms were young and strong, and soon he reclined comfortably against the pillow. She put something to his lips and it seemed hard, cold, and round; like a cigarette.   It was a rubber tube.   Warm sweetness filled his mouth, and he gurgled as it ran down his gullet. He didn't want much, and eased his face away. She stopped at once.

" Are you fairly comfortable?   Just nod."

He nodded.

" Does it hurt badly? "

He shook his head.

" Is there anything you want? "

He wanted freedom; Janet; the boys; all the things which were impossible to have.   He shook his head.

" I'll come and see you again, soon."

He wanted to ask how long this would go on, but he couldn't move his lips, and so he had to let her go.   The rustling movement faded and he was alone.

·   ·   ·   ·   ·

An hour or an age passed before she was back.

·   ·   ·   ·   ·

" Mr. West, I want you to listen carefully to all I have to say."

He nodded.

"You can talk now, if you try. Your lips are free of the bandages, but your chin and nose aren't. If you try to talk without moving your lips much, you'll manage."

Old lags knew that trick; he'd often demonstrated for fun, and sent the boys off into peals of laughter. He tried now.

"Okay. I can hear." The voice didn't sound like his own.

Had they changed *that*?

"You'll be here just for a day or two, and after that more of the bandages will be taken away and you'll feel easier."

"Okay."

"There's a cord above your head. Pull it if you want someone to come."

"Thanks."

"Would you like the radio?"

"No!"

"If you would, just pull the cord. And please remember this. I want to do everything I can to help. I know who you are now, I've seen the newspapers, and——"

She broke off in a choking voice, and he heard her rush out of the room.

. . . . .

Routine.

Special feeding, liquids only; visits once a day from the sparrow. Radio music in half-hour doses. After the third day, some of the bandages were removed. The burning sensation went completely, but his face and fingers felt numb.

Routine: practise speaking; practise moving his fingers. Radio music; dull radio comedians, bright radio comediennes—no news. Never any news.

Routine: look forward to Marion's visits. Wait for them. Hear a faint sound and hope she had entered. Feel sick with disappointment if she hadn't, exhilarated if she had. Routine: stop thinking about Janet. Stop it, stop it! Stop an avalanche, stop the waves, stop thinking about Janet and about the boys.

Wait for Marion.

Feel desperately lonely.

Wait—hope—forget.

Policeman first, man second; whose joke was that?

Routine——

Lie back and listen to Marion reading. She chose Trollope, soft, soothing, benign, unreal, wholly artificial and yet warm and friendly—of Barchester, bishops, beauty and beatitude.

She read to him at intervals, and he always wanted her to go on. He had five minutes exercise in talking at the beginning of each session. His voice *was* his voice, there'd been no miracle about that.

Each day for seven days a little more of the bandage was removed.

On the eighth day, the awful darkness lifted, for the bandages and pads were removed from his eyes. He opened them to a subdued light, and the hazy face of the sparrow in front of him—a perky, peering sparrow, who seemed fully satisfied with the results.

" Two or three days now, and you'll be all right, quite all right; perfectly satisfactory case. No complications. You'll be weak, but you'll get strong quickly. Having any solid foods? "

" A little."

" I'll increase it."

He did.

Roger hadn't argued about being confined to bed, had taken that to be inevitable.

On that eighth day he got up. Marion helped him. His legs were ridiculously weak, and he would have fallen but for her arm. She led him to a chair, and while he sat there and she read to him, he saw himself in the mirror. He was a mask of bandages but for his lips, nose, and eyes; they weren't his eyes, and it wasn't his nose; the shape of his lips was all wrong, they were turned down at the corners and they looked thinner.

Routine: *wait*.

10

NEW MAN

Rain hissed and spattered against the windows, heavy grey clouds hung low, and the garden was a sorry drenched mass. Many of the daffodils were dead or dying, and there was little colour in the borders, except green.

Roger stood there, looking out.

The door opened. Marion? His heart leapt, because hers was the only friendly voice and friendly face. But this was the sparrow, and Kennedy was with him. Kennedy nodded and smiled, as if in an affable mood; even the dullness of the morning could not hide the glitter in his eyes.

"Good morning!" The sparrow rubbed his hands together briskly. "Feeling better?"

"Yes."

"Good, good. Come and sit down."

Roger sat in a chair in front of the mirror. The pale white bandages covered most of his face, and he had become familiar with the "new" eyes, nose, and mouth since seeing them three days ago.

Kennedy stood behind him, looking at his reflection in the mirror.

"Now!" chirruped the sparrow.

Bright scissors snipped the bandages at the back of Roger's head, nimble but gentle fingers plucked the gauzy stuff away, and it peeled off, almost like a skin. There were several layers. Roger gripped the arms of his chair and deliberately closed his eyes. The sparrow said: "There!" After that there was silence, until Kennedy spoke in a marvelling voice.

"Wonderful!"

"Yes, yes, it's good. I knew you'd be satisfied."

Kennedy sneered: "Aren't you going to look at yourself, West?"

Roger clenched his teeth, and his fingers seemed stuck

to the arms of his chair. He could imagine the delight
in the sparrow's eyes and the gloating satisfaction in
Kennedy's. Very slowly, he opened his eyes. The vague
shape of his head and shoulders appeared first, and he
stared as through a mist. That cleared.

He looked into the face of a stranger.

It wasn't a bad face; not evil. His good looks had
turned into ruggedness. His nose was broader at the
bridge, his eyes were narrower—he knew that skin had
been taken out of the corners. His chin jutted, and
seemed less pointed. His lips were thinner, but not
turned down at the corners. As a face there wasn't much
the matter with it, but it wasn't his. His usually long and
wavy fair hair was cut very short, showing the shape of
his head.

The sparrow took the gauze from his fingers. New
skin, new whorls, and loops and ridges had been grafted
on, taken from another set of human fingers.

No one who knew him would believe the thing had
happened, would believe he was his real self.

.   .   .   .   .

After the others had gone, Marion came in. She
saw him sitting by the window, gazing out on to the rain-
swept garden and a prospect as desolate as his own future.
She came slowly and softly, as if afraid of what she was
going to see. He wouldn't turn his head, made her come
round in front of him. She put her hands to her breast
and opened her mouth as if to cry out, but no sound came.

Roger growled : " Satisfied ? "

" It's—a miracle ! "

" Nice, tough-looking guy, aren't I ? "

" I've never seen anything like it ! "

" Battling Beauty, pride of the ring."

" It's not—so bad. You look normal, but different,
that's all.   No one would think——"

" That's the whole idea. Satisfied with your share in
it ? "   It was hard to say why he felt that he had to be
harsh with her.

" I've tried to help."   She was near tears.

" And this is the result."

" If only you'd let me send for others——"

" *Let* you! Did I stop you? "

" Yes," she said. " I didn't tell the police because I thought you were afraid of them. I wanted to help *you*. I'd give my life to help you."

From the beginning, she had been strange, possessed by that simplicity as rare as it was refreshing—and so rare that he had distrusted it. She had seemed the epitome of goodness and truth, but that hadn't squared with anything here, so he'd rejected it. Now, her heart seemed to be in her eyes and in her voice. He was reminded of the love letters of Lucille.

She whispered : " I didn't care—I don't care—whether you killed her or not."

" I didn't."

" Then why didn't you let me——"

" Oh, forget it." He stood up abruptly, for he was fit enough bodily now.

" All right, Marion. Tell me how it is you've been nursing me since you stopped thinking I was mad. You know that your precious Dr. Ritter and my dear friend Mr. Kennedy are crooks, don't you? "

" I—yes."

" You knew all the time—didn't you? "

" No," she said dully. " I'd no idea there was anything wrong when you first came. After I'd looked after you, Dr. Ritter told me that you'd killed that girl and had to be—changed. He gave me the chance of helping you. I took it. I had to take it. I think he knew why."

" Why? "

" I love you," she said.

.   .   .   .   .   .

Was she lying?

Or was she trying this way to win his confidence? Was she a tool of Kennedy's, or simply a victim?

.   .   .   .   .

Kennedy was in the lounge downstairs when Roger went in. He put down a newspaper and raised a hand.

" Hallo, West.   Are you as well as you look? "

" I'm all right."

" Good.   After a spell like you've had, you want to get
back into civilization slowly.   I'm going to let you take
Marion around a bit.   You'll both be closely watched,
but I don't think you'll try any funny stuff."

" I'm tired of doing nothing."

" I've plenty of work for you—when I'm ready.   For a
start, here are the newspapers for the past ten days.   Get
yourself up to date with the news.   Then you can take
Marion to the flicks.   Dance around a bit, afterwards,
start living.   You know that no one in this world would
ever recognize you, don't you? "

" Yes."

" Remember it," said Kennedy.   " Also remember
you're in my service now, and I expect absolute obedience
and loyalty.   You'll have to do a lot of things you won't
much like, but you'll get used to that in time.   I'll see
that the pill is sugared, too."

He went out.

Roger read newspapers until he could take in nothing
more.

The Copse Cottage murder had gradually faded from
the *Daily Cry*, and the story of his disappearance replaced
it.   The disappearance of Roger West was—or had been,
it was deep in the past already—a nine-days wonder.
But there had been no official connection between that
and the murder, all the statements were guarded.   Only
one thing hurt: a photograph of Janet.   He stared at
that for a long time, teeth clenched, emotion getting the
better of him.   This was only the beginning.   How long
would it be before he knew the whole truth about Kennedy, and could declare it?   Never mind the misty
future—but an obsession began to take hold of him:
he must get word to Janet.   If she received even a hint
that he was alive, then he could rely on her faith to support
her, to help her over the agony she was suffering now.

Marion?   *Could* he trust her?

Would he have a chance to send word when he was back
in circulation?

There was one obvious conclusion: he must go cautiously at first, whatever the cost to Janet.

.   .   .   .   .

It was no longer raining. A weak sun pierced the clouds, birds chattered, the air was fresh, crisp, exhilarating. Roger, dressed in well-made new clothes, stood beside Marion, by a small car, outside the front of the house. Beyond were dripping trees and hedges, and great fields, where a few cattle grazed. He could see no other sign of habitation.

" Get in," he said.

Marion climbed in.

She wore a red plastic raincoat over a blue dress. Her eyes sparkled, her freshness seemed to match the day, fears were gone, and she was set fair for enjoyment: being with him. They settled down, and their chauffeur, the male nurse, let in the clutch. This winding road led for miles between trees, and then they came upon a main road. There were telegraph poles, wires, cars, lorries, the half-forgotten things. They passed through a village where a constable stood leaning on his bicycle, talking to two old men; they showed a countryman's interest in the passing car, no more.

They came to a town.

It was bustling and pleasant, had a friendly atmosphere. The streets and wide market-place were thronged with people, cars, single-decker buses, a few horses and traps. The nurse took them to a car park, near a huge Odeon Cinema.

" Do you want to see a film at once? " he asked Marion.

" We're to go to tea at the *Royal*, first."

" Film later, perhaps," He didn't really care.

They walked on. He was mingling with ordinary people again, and felt numbed with the strangeness. There were several policemen here; none showed any interest in him, yet each would have scored a rousing triumph had he but guessed. They passed a police-station; Roger caught sight of a photograph on a " wanted " sheet and started, then stopped. " Steady," he said, and Marion looked at the photograph—a good likeness of the man he had been.

Had been, *had been*; he was no longer Roger West, because Roger West would be hanged for murder. Remember that—and remember also: policeman first, man second; there was a great deal for the policeman to do.

They walked past a sergeant of police who had seen them study the photograph, and who didn't even trouble to watch them walk towards the end of the street. Roger felt a burning inward excitement, his stomach heaved and his nerves began to quiver. This was like being born anew into a familiar, precious world.

Marion held tightly on to his arm.

No one appeared to follow them, but he was sure that they were being watched wherever they went; that sixth sense which came from years of experience, hadn't died. They came upon a large hotel, where a sign outside read: *Tea Dance, Daily*, 3s. 6d.

" Where are we ? " Roger asked.

" Worcester."

He recalled it, now. The old town cheek by jowl with the new. They went in. The atmosphere was friendly, a good band was playing, but only three couples were dancing, half a dozen others sitting round a large room. The waiter came up promptly.

They danced; Marion was as light as a feather, and her eyes were brimming over with a kind of happiness which he could not believe was spurious.

" If we could go on like this," she said.

He nodded, but made no comment. Her presence hurt because she reminded him of Janet in her complete contentment at being with him. He danced mechanically a quick-step with a gay lilt and quickening rhythm.

Then he saw a couple enter and froze.

Marion said: " Don't look like that ! " He turned away, but looked at the new-comers out of the corner of his eye. It wasn't fancy. His blood ran hot, he missed a step again. Marion asked urgently:

" What is it ? "

He didn't answer, but led her towards their table, feeling physically sick and racked with pain. The newcomers looked around—man and woman.

Man—and *Janet*.

.   .   .   .   .

The man was Mark Lessing, his one close friend.

.   .   .   .   .

"What is it?" demanded Marion. "Please tell me."
"Never mind."
"Have you seen someone you know?"
"Yes. Please don't talk."

She fell into a reluctant silence. Janet took off her coat, the now shabby black sealskin which he had bought her years ago. Mark put it over the back of her chair, Janet was sideways towards Roger, not five yards away. She began to look round her, and he hated what he saw in her grey-green eyes. She was older—careworn and tense. Her hands were clenched in her lap. Her eyes sought out every man here, and Roger knew she was looking for him. She'd come here, hoping to see him, but the hope was already dying. She looked at him, but her gaze didn't linger for a moment; she showed no interest in Marion.

Her eyes were so tired, her hair, dark yet usually so full of light, had lost its lustre. Mark Lessing gave her a cigarette, and she began to smoke nervously, agitatedly.

Mark sat back, looking about him with less obvious tension than Janet, but eagerly, searchingly. He was good-looking—in his way, handsome. His expression was austere, and those who did not know him well took him for a snob. His skin was rather sallow, his dark hair was wavy, and worn too long; it looked affected. He was almost as familiar as Janet, the sight of him hurt nearly as much.

No two people knew him, Roger, so well.

"Please tell me," Marion whispered.

"A friend—of mine."

"Oh. Kennedy——"

" Sent us here.　This is a test of my nerves and goodwill.
I'd rather not talk."

" All right,"　Her reluctance remained.

The music stopped, and the bandsmen put down their
instruments and sauntered out of the room.　The hush
was broken by murmured conversation, and Roger
strained his ears to catch what Janet and Mark said.
Janet began.

" He's not here."

" I was afraid it was a hoax."

" It's—damnable."

" We had to come and see."

" Mark, I can't stand it any longer."

" You'll be all right."

" I just can't stand it!"　She spoke in passionate
undertones.

" He'll come back."

" To—*what*?"

" He didn't do it, Jan."

" Of course he didn't, but why——"

" Jan, don't keep tormenting yourself.　Believe in him."

" He's dead, Mark."

" Nonsense!"

" I can feel it," said Janet.　She looked about her again,
listlessly;　saw Roger and glanced away.　Roger half-
rose from his chair, and Marion put a cold hand on his.
In the corner sat a man on his own—Kennedy.　He
looked boldly at Janet, who stiffened when another couple
came in, but her interest died away as quickly as it had
been born.

" It's your wife," Marion said in a flat voice.

Roger nodded.

" She's——"

" Don't."

" She's very sweet."

" Let's get out of here!"

" No!　Kennedy's watching."　Marion feared Kennedy so much.

Kennedy was grinning, as if to himself.

" Come on," said Roger.

He led the way, and Kennedy still grinned. Mark glanced at him; was there a puzzled gleam in his eyes? Roger paid at the cash desk, and when he looked round, neither of the others was looking at him. He was sticky hot. He went into the lobby and saw a man sitting in an easy-chair, from which he could see into the ballroom. It was all Roger could do to look away from the watcher who was Detective Inspector Sloan of New Scotland Yard —and no man at the Yard knew Roger more intimately.

Sloan stared at him blankly.

. . . . . .

The film didn't matter; all he saw was Janet. It was dark when they left. The male nurse was outside with the car. The journey to the nursing-home took an hour. He wanted to get to his room and be on his own, but Kennedy called him into the lounge. Marion made to follow.

" Not you," Kennedy said. " Close the door and leave us alone."

Marion obeyed.

Kennedy grinned. " Good, isn't it, West? "

" Is it? "

" I'd call it good. In future, you're to be known as Rayner—Charles Rayner. I've a passport, registration card, business, home, past history, and everything else you might need. Don't forget, Mr. Rayner."

" You forget my bad memory."

" Your memory is all right, so far, but it won't hurt for long. Marion's a nice girl, and she's yours for the asking. Oh—*Rayner*."

" Well."

" You might have the bright notion of sending word to your wife. Don't. I sent her a message, saying she might see you in Worcester to-day. So she hasn't given up hope. I knew she was on the way, when you left. Know how I knew? "

Roger didn't answer.

Kennedy laughed.

" Your wife has a new maid. She's spent so much time

away on wild-goose chases after you that she had to have a *reliable* nurse for the boys. She's got one. That nurse will be loyal to her for exactly as long as you're loyal to me. Not a day longer. You're no fool, West. If your wife got a message which convinced her you're alive, she'd tell the nurse—or at least, give it away. Remember all this. The nurse is a nice girl, and fond of children. But she'll do what I tell her. I don't want to have to hurt the kids."

.   .   .   .   .

Roger now accepted the fact that he was unrecognizable. He also accepted the fact that he must live only for the present. There was strength in that, as well as weakness. If the time came, he could escape. He would work with and for Kennedy until he knew exactly what Kennedy planned; then he could wreck those plans. For the time being, he must live the life of a new man.

The past *was* the past.

.   .   .   .   .

He left the house again a week after he had seen Janet. London!

Fresh under an April sun, but with her great buildings dark with smoke and grime. London, a seething, toiling mass of people, crowded streets, giant red buses, box-like taxis, shops, shops, shops—and factories, docks, the broad, smooth Thames. The London he knew and loved, revealed to him again as he was driven along the straight, wide tawdriness of Oxford Street, into Regent Street with its curving stateliness. Piccadilly bustle, Leicester Square a quiet, friendly green patch with gargantuan cinemas around it, Trafalgar Square, Whitehall, massive Government buildings and—Scotland Yard. The driver turned towards Scotland Yard, but didn't go past the gates. He stopped the car so that Roger could see the reddish brick of the old building, housing the civil police. Constables on duty looked at them disinterestedly, as at all sightseers. They drove past Cannon Row Police-station, dark, low-roofed, and dingy, with its barred

windows. He knew every inch of it—and of the Yard.
It had been his life.

The Embankment; the white new building, housing
the C.I.D. Then they drove off the cluttered road near
the pale-grey austerity of the new Waterloo Bridge, and
into the Strand.

Roger, by the driver's side, hadn't said a word since
they had reached London. Now:

" Where are we going? "

" You'll see."

They turned out of the Strand, near Covent Garden,
empty and desolate and waiting for the next day's business.
They stopped in a narrow street. Here the buildings
were old—a mixture of flats and offices.

" This is you," said the driver. " Number 15."

Roger got out. Number 15 was opposite—with an
open door, a dark hallway, and narrow stairs. He went
in, completely mystified. The driver sat in the car and
grinned at his back. He glanced at the notice-board:
there were six names, and one newly painted sign read:

> *Charles Rayner.*
> *Commission Agent.*
> *Wholesale—Retail.*
> *4th Floor.*

There was no lift. He walked upstairs slowly. He was
Charles Rayner, and this was where he would work, what
" business " he would do. It was dark on each landing;
darkest on the fourth where a broken window was boarded
up. He stood undecidedly outside a door marked with
his new name; took the plunge and opened it.

A man leapt at him from the corner behind the door.

11

GINGER

WILD eyes burned in a pale face. An iron rod clenched in a claw-like hand brushed Roger's shoulders as he swung to one side. The rod hit the door with a metallic clang, and clattered on the floor. Roger thrust out a hand to fend the man off—and had a vision of the attack at Copse Cottage, launched with this same savagery. The man kicked and missed; sucked in his breath noisily, and swung powerful blows that didn't land. Roger ducked and dodged, then went into the attack, striking out savagely.

Right to the stomach; left to the chin. The first blow brought forth a soughing groan, the second, a screech. The man backed away helplessly, banged against a chair and sprawled into it. He didn't try to get up, but stared with those burning, hate-filled eyes. His mouth was open, he breathed harshly and noisily

The hate faded; he looked dazed, then stupefied.

Roger closed the door, and listened intently. He could hear a typewriter, going at speed; that was distant, the only audible sound. The man in the chair sat up, licked his lips and put out a hand as if afraid of further violence.

" Can you give me one reason why I shouldn't break your neck? " Roger growled. His voice was hard and grating, the voice he'd trained himself to acquire, and he spoke with little movement of his lips.

" I—— "

" Or use the iron bar on you." Roger picked the rod up. It weighed heavy and wasn't an easy weapon to use. He struck at the air.

" No ! "

" You would have cracked my skull if I'd let you."

" No, no ! "

" So you were just practising." Roger felt savage; he wanted to hurt, wanted to be cruel. He wasn't used to

the feeling, it was alien to him.   In the fury of his punches
there had been the hatred which he felt for Kennedy.

The man cowered back; hardly a hero.   He wasn't
difficult to read.   He had screwed himself up to make that
assault, and when it had failed, courage went out of him
like air from a punctured balloon.   Now he was desperately frightened.

He was thin, his pallor sickly.   He needed a shave, and
his gingery hair wanted cutting.   His clothes were poor;
navy-blue suit frayed at the cuffs, and a choker-scarf,
not a collar and tie.   You could pick up his like, almost
a facsimile, in a dozen poorer parts of London.

This was a waiting-room; the high, cream-washed
walls were bare, and there were two leather arm-chairs
and four good uprights, reproduction Hepplewhite.
On a plain walnut table, a dozen new magazines were
neatly placed; alongside it was a similar arrangement
of trade periodicals.   There was a faint smell, dry and
not unpleasant, of distemper.   Two doors led from here.
One was marked: *Inquiries: Please Ring*, with a sign
beneath a bell-push; the other, *Charles Rayner, Private*.
There were frosted-glass panels in each.

With a practised eye, Roger took it all in quickly;
professionally, he would have judged this a prosperous
place, with the mental reservation that it might be a smart
front to hide failure or fraud.

He swung the bar again.

" No! "

" Why did you attack me? "

" I—thought—— '   The man hesitated, thrusting out
his hands appealingly.   " You're not the man I expected."

" It would still have been murder."

" I came to kill him."

You couldn't mistake the touch of dignity which came
unexpectedly with the words; the man was proud of what
he had come to do, and had simply attacked the wrong
man.

" That's—*true*."

Roger said: " Stay there."   He turned, pushed open
the inquiries door and saw a large office, with six or seven

desks, three typewriters, several telephones, cabinets—a well-equipped place, where everything was new. There was a large cupboard, with hooks for hats and coats. He went back, gripped the ginger-haired man and took him into the room and locked him in the cupboard.

Another door led from this room—to the " Private " one. Roger opened it ; the office beyond was sumptuous ; more study than office, with a thick carpet, panelled walls, a library of books, and several easy-chairs. No one was here. He studied the ceiling and the panelled walls ; a policeman again, knowing exactly what he wanted and knowing pretty well where to find it. He saw a small panel, one of several in the wall behind the desk, and prised it open with his fingers.

He grinned broadly ; that was his first natural smile since he had left Scotland Yard.

Inside a foot-deep cavity was a tiny dictaphone recording outfit. He switched it off, using a pencil, and closed the panel. Then he scanned the ceiling and panelling again until he was sure there was no peephole through which he could be watched or heard. He went to the outer room. The ginger-haired man stepped meekly out of the cupboard.

" In here," Roger said.

He locked the outer door with the key on the inside ; there was no way of getting in except by the windows. These overlooked a blank wall, and the drop to the area below was sheer. He stood first at one side, then the other, to make sure that the office could not be overlooked. Finally, with the ginger-haired man gaping and nervous, he stood on a corner of the desk and examined the ceiling ; no, there was no break to mar the white paper ; no peep-hole through which he could be watched here, either.

He jumped down.

" Who did you expect to find ? "

" Not—not you."

" I've believed you, so far. Who did you want to kill ? "

" Rayner," said the ginger-haired man.

So he had inherited an enemy as well as a name.

" Why? What had he done to you? "

" He killed my wife."

" Murderers get hanged."

" It wasn't known as murder," the ginger-haired man said wearily. " It just wasn't discovered, but *I* knew. I was inside when it happened. He always told me he'd kill her if she wouldn't do what he wanted. She didn't, and he killed her."

The man thought that another man, named Rayner, had killed his wife: if you could believe his word. But could you? Was it natural for a man to lose his spirit so quickly and completely? Or had that been pretended rage? Was this another of Kennedy's little tricks?

" I'm—Kyle."

" Why did they put you inside? " Kyle, Kyle? The name was familiar, and rang a distant bell in his memory; few cases in which he'd played any part were completely forgotten. He'd never seen Kyle before, so it wasn't one of his cases.

" Forgery," Kyle said simply. " I'm an engraver. I'm a good engraver." That incongruous hint of dignity came again. " My products were practically undetectable, the police had to devise a completely new process to find them out. The Treasury use a new process to manufacture notes since my forgeries were discovered. I——"

That was true: yes, *Kyle*. He'd been caught and tried in Manchester. It was one of those cases in which a provincial force had stolen a march on the Yard. Eddie Day, purveyor of faked messages, had gone to Manchester to hold a watching brief for the Yard, and had come back shaken by the cleverness of the forgeries. Roger had only to stretch out his hand to the telephone and check what Kyle was like in appearance. They'd get it for him in five minutes at the Yard; or they *would* have done, once.

" When did you come out? "

" A month ago."

" What have you been doing since? "

" Looking for Rayner."

" Are you still on your ticket? "

" Yes, I report twice a week.   I go to Bow Street while I'm in London."

" What does this man who calls himself Rayner, look like ? "

The watery pale-blue eyes, with their pink lids and thin fair lashes, looked puzzled.

" Don't you know ? "

" I *am* Rayner."

" No, no ! You can't be ! You——"

" The other man used my name. What's he like? What's his most noticeable feature ? "

Kyle said softly and in a voice which seemed to be filled with hatred :

" You would never forget Rayner. His eyes—how I hated his eyes. Denise did, too, although they fascinated her, she—she was attracted to him, but he frightened her. He wanted her to go with him and leave me. She was very, very beautiful. You may not believe that I had a beautiful wife, but I did. *Beautiful*. The loveliest woman you would meet in a lifetime, that's why he wanted her. He used to say he would take her or kill her. Oh, not when I was about, I was too valuable to him. I learned afterwards. From friends, inside. You would be surprised how much news is passed on in jail. I complained, had an interview with the Governor—but at Parkley, he's a *swine*. An absolute swine. He said I couldn't expect any wife to do without me for seven years and not look at another man. That's what the swine said."

The Governor of Parkley Jail had the worst name in modern prison history; it was a byword among the police as well as among crooks.

Kyle put his hand to his pocket. Roger watched cautiously, in case the man had another weapon, but all he brought out was an old, worn, brown wallet. He smoothed the leather between his fingers.

" My friends told me that Rayner told her he would kill her if she didn't go to him. She didn't go. She was killed in—in an accident. Accident ! " Shrillness put an edge to his voice, and his eyes blazed. " She was run down by a car, all her beauty spoiled. *All* her beauty."

He took out a photograph slowly, and his fingers trembled. He stared down at it, and tears glistened in his eyes. He whispered: " Look! "

She was gay and smiling, a queen to this man's slave. It was easy to believe that Kyle had worshipped her.

Roger said: " I can understand why you don't like Rayner. Let me have a look at your wallet.'

" I—no! "

" Come on."

Kyle handed it over, reluctantly. Roger shook the contents of the wallet on to the brown-leather surface of the desk. He saw the expected oddments: a ticket of leave, prison-discharge form, registration card—an old, tattered, dog-eared letter dated eight years ago, a ten-shilling note, and another photograph. He turned the photograph over. He knew that Kyle was watching him, jealously intent, and kept his face set.

It wasn't easy, for this was the girl from Paris—Lucille. The smiling face seemed to fade into a reddy brown mess. He stared down at it, then at the picture of Kyle's dead wife.

These were alike, with unmistakable family likeness.

.   .   .   .   .

" You pick good lookers," Roger growled, after a long pause.

" Please! " Kyle's dignity rose again. " That is my daughter."

" Sure? "

" I am quite sure," said Kyle. " That is Lucille." He gave a gentle smile. " Years ago, I sent her to France, to my wife's family. I met Denise during the first great war. Lucille was so good and clever, and I did not want her smeared with *my* reputation. My wife and I agreed it was best. We had anxious days during the last war, my wife suffered most, because I wasn't there to help her bear her loneliness, but all was well, Lucille was in a country district, no harm befell her." The pedantic phrases had a touch of dreaminess.

" Lucky Lucille," Roger's voice seemed to stick in his throat. " Where does she live now? "

" In Paris."

" What's her address? "

" That I shall *not* tell you."

" You want to revenge yourself on Rayner, don't you? "

" I shall not die happily until I do."

He would die in anguish if he knew the whole truth.

" All right, then. Tell me where to find Lucille. I
know your Rayner. I can keep a check on him. If I
don't know where to find Lucille I shan't be able to find
out if he's interested in her, shall I? "

" I thought you didn't know him."

" I know those eyes. Let me have that address, Kyle.
You'll regret it if you don't. Afterwards, you can clear
out of here. I'll stake you for a few weeks." Roger took
out his wallet, and counted ten one-pound notes; Kennedy had given him fifty.

Eagerness but not avarice gleamed in Kyle's eyes.

" I'll stake you for ten a month. I'll send them to your
address."

" No! No, that wouldn't be safe, I'm at Joe's." Joe's
was a verminous den, a doss-house that remained a blot on
London, as it had been in the dark, squalid London back
streets of Victorian days. " Send it to—but *why* are you
going to stake me? "

" I don't like men who use my name. You'll keep quiet.
If anyone asks, you came here to beg, and I kicked you
out."

" Yes, yes! "

" Where's Lucille? " In a lonely pauper's grave, somewhere in Surrey, a nameless corpse.

" She is at 23 Rue de Croix, Paris 8." The information came out slowly and reluctantly; but it came.
" You won't harm her? "

" No. I'll post ten bars a month to you in the name of
John Pearson at the Strand Post Office—Trafalgar Square
end. Now clear out. If anyone worries you, telephone
me here." Using block capitals, he wrote the number,
taken from the telephone, on a strip of paper, printed the
name of John Pearson, c/o the Strand G.P.O., as a re-
minder, and pushed it across the desk. " Don't write,

don't come again unless I send for you.   Is that understood?"

" Yes, but—I don't under*stand*."

" You don't have to."   Roger stood up.   " Pull your
hat over your eyes when you go out, don't let anyone get
a good look at you.   You might be in trouble if your friend
knows you've been after him."

Kyle nodded.   For years, in prison, he had done exactly
what he was told, the habit of obedience was strong in
him.   He was almost friendless, and here was a man who
offered help.   So he nodded agreement.

Roger went into the outer office with him, watched him
pick up his cap and go out, small, spindly, nervous.
Roger followed him down the creaky narrow stairs, a few
steps behind him.   No doors opened at the other floors.
The car wasn't outside.

Ginger Kyle slipped away towards the market.

Another man came along the street, walking briskly—
like impending doom.

Detective Inspector Sloan of the Yard, tall, blond, with
an alert, eager face, good blue eyes and powerful body
and shoulders, watched Kyle keenly.

Roger, his heart hammering, went upstairs.   At the
second-floor landing, he paused.

Sloan was coming in from the street.

12

TEST

ROGER opened the dictaphone panel, switched the machine
on, then sat at his desk.   He opened a drawer, took out
some papers—the first that came to hand—and spread
them out.   Sloan's footsteps sounded on the landing.
Roger heard the outer door open.   If he locked this door
he could pretend that no one was in; there was hardly
time now—wrong tactics, anyhow.

Kennedy was a fool not to have primed him.   But was

he? This had all the signs of a trap; the empty office, and Sloan's visit. Would Kennedy have let him stay here alone without a purpose?

No.

Something may have gone wrong with his plans, but those usually worked out perfectly. There must be a good reason why he had brought his victim here and left him alone. But Kyle might have been the unexpected accident, of the kind which made mockery of plans.

Had Kyle been a stooge? Had he, Roger, swallowed a tasty bait? Wasn't it too much of a coincidence that Ginger Kyle should have been here just then?

What of Sloan?

Sloan was one of the few men at the Yard who had never called Roger crazy for taking chances such as he had with Kyle; for trusting his sixth sense as to whether a man was lying or not.

Sloan's footsteps were firm, not heavy: they had worked on a hundred cases together, and were Roger and Bill.

Sloan tapped.

Roger wiped his forehead, and called: " Come in."

Sloan thrust the door open firmly and took a good look round the office before coming inside and closing the door. He looked hard at Roger, in full appraisment, as at a man he was seeing for the first time. There would be no recognition *if* Roger could maintain his new voice.

Roger said: " Well? "

" Mr. Rayner? Charles Rayner? "

" Yes."

" Sorry to worry you, Mr. Rayner." That was perfunctory, Sloan was already enjoying himself. A friend had become a deadly enemy—and seemed almost to realize it. You couldn't mistake Sloan's hostility as he pulled up a chair and sat down. He took out his cigarettes, in a familiar yellow packet.

" Smoke? "

" Not with strangers. Who are you? "

Sloan lit up and took out a card and held it forward. Roger glanced at it.

"You may be a policeman, but you don't own the world."

"I just help to keep it clean," said Sloan. "You had a visitor just now."

"You say so."

"I know. A certain Mr. Kyle, who spent a lot of time behind bars."

"So he told me." The dictaphone had that, so Kennedy would learn about Kyle's visit.

"Didn't you know before?" Sloan challenged.

"No."

"What did he want?"

"Work."

"Did you give him any?"

"No."

"Why did you see him off."

"To make sure he left the premises."

"So you've got all the answers, Mr. Rayner."

"That's right."

Bill Sloan was a sly dog. This wasn't really an official call, he was reconnoitring. The build-up was obvious, and there was reason to feel easier in his mind. Kyle was watched, being known to have had accomplices who had never been caught. Sloan had been told where he'd come, and was here to try to shake information out of Rayner by direct approach. The tactics had a high risk, because they gave warning of the deep interest of the police.

Why *had* Kennedy let Roger come here without a briefing? Was it because the Kyle interview had been a plant, or because something had prevented Kennedy from getting here?

"I hope you've some more answers up your sleeve, Mr. Rayner." Sloan was heavily sarcastic. "This is an informal call. Can I take it that you'd swear in court that you'd never seen Kyle before?"

"Yes."

"What business do you transact, Mr. Rayner?"

"I'm a commission agent."

"That covers a multitude of—things." The pause

made the words an accusation. " How long have you been in business here? "

" I haven't."

That startled Sloan.   " This is your office."

" I open here next week." The place obviously hadn't been much used.

" Did you have another office, before this, or have you just started in business, Mr. Rayner? "

" You've a lot of men to help you find out things like that."

" Meaning you won't answer."

" That's right."

" A peculiar attitude to adopt, Mr. Rayner."

" If there's anything peculiar here, it's your manner."

" I see." Sloan read the obvious into that—the obvious that wasn't true, and which made Kennedy's failure to give a briefing almost a tragedy. " So you don't intend to help the police, Mr. Rayner."

" When I know how I can help, I will."

" Is this a new business? "

" How will the answer help you? "

Sloan said: " People who are awkward with the police often regret it.   Don't forget that."

" Policemen who come on their own aren't entitled to all the answers."

" So you're clever, too.   Where do you live? "

" This is my address."

" Morning, noon, and night? "

Roger said slowly, heavily: " Inspector, I don't like your manner.   I don't know the man who came here just now.   Don't blame me if he's a crook.   I'm not. Next time you want information, come and ask nicely. Don't get off to a bad start by accusing me of being a liar and helping a crook.   Now I've work to do."

" Who for? " asked Sloan.   " Kennedy? "

.   .   .   .   .

It was like looking at the world from the moon; he knew what lay behind every word, was familiar with every inflection of Sloan's voice.   He'd had a split second of

warning that a bombshell was coming. He hadn't
known what, and the " Kennedy " came out with shatter-
ing effect, but he kept a poker face.

" Who's Kennedy? " he asked.

" So you don't know? "

" Out in the office there are telephone directories.
Have a look at the hundreds of Kennedys in it, and then
tell me which one I'm supposed to know."

Sloan had been happy, until then; or at least satisfied
that he was getting somewhere. Now his manner changed,
because he didn't like what had happened—which meant
that Roger's reaction to the bombshell had defeated him.
Sloan might bluff others with his cold stare and set face,
but Roger knew how he looked when he was baffled—
owlish, too wise, too hard eyed.

" You're making a mistake, Mr. Rayner."

" Try making one yourself," Roger said.

" You insist that you don't know Kennedy."

" Tell me which Kennedy and why you want to know,
and I'll tell you—if I like your reasons."

It was fascinating to sit and watch, to guess—to *know*—
the thoughts passing through Sloan's mind. He was
deciding whether to make a final effort or to call it a day.
They stared each other out, and then Sloan's eyes went
blank, which meant he was going all the way.

" You are Kennedy," he said.   " Let's have the truth."

.   .   .   .   .

He was Roger West, *alias* Charles Rayner.

Kyle knew Kennedy as Rayner.

Sloan had guessed that Kennedy and Rayner were one
and the same person; and Sloan wouldn't make a wild
guess, he had reason for thinking that.

.   .   .   .   .

" You can't keep facts from the police for long," Sloan
said, but he knew that his challenge had failed.

" I can't stop the police making fools of themselves.
I'm Charles Rayner. I'm in honest business, and I've a
lot of work to do." Roger stood up, but Sloan stayed
in his chair, looking puzzled. Why? Was the voice

striking a chord in his memory? That voice was the Achilles heel in Kennedy's plans.

What would happen to that eager but now wary face if he leaned forward and said in his natural voice: "Crazy business, isn't it, Bill?" With the thought came temptation and a flood of emotionalism. No one at the Yard could seriously believe that he had killed Lucille. If he told the truth now, Sloan and everyone at the Yard would rush to help.

Sloan narrowed his eyes, as if conscious of some mental turmoil in the other man.

"Changed your mind?" he demanded. "Going to talk?"

"I've said all I intend to." Reason brought a cold douche to emotionalism. A detective was a policeman first, man afterwards; he had to be, and Sloan was no exception. Anyhow, there was a microphone close at hand, recording every word that was spoken.

Sloan said: "You'll regret it, Mr. Rayner."

He got up and went out, baffled, highly suspicious. Roger waited until the outer door closed; waited, and heard a faint sound in the outer office. He smiled tautly, and saw the handle of the door turn; but Sloan didn't come in, just left the door ajar and stood outside, listening—an old trick, almost all tricks were old. Tension faded. Roger picked up the telephone and banged the cradle up and down, making the bell ring faintly. Sloan would feel himself to be on the verge of a triumph, expecting him to telephone an accomplice, ears strained for every word. Another temptation came; call the Yard, ask whether they had a Chief Inspector Sloan. This time, he succumbed. He dialled, and could imagine Sloan's eyes bulging. A calm, familiar voice answered him, and the flood-gates of temptation opened wide again.

He had been a fool to do this.

"Scotland Yard, can I help you? . . . *can* I help you?" As he didn't answer at once, the man at the exchange spoke more sharply.

"Er—yes. Can you tell me whether you have an officer named Sloan—Chief Inspector Sloan."

" We have Detective Inspector Sloan, sir."

" Is he a tall, fresh-faced——"

" Who is that speaking, please? "

" My name is—oh, never mind." He put back the receiver, but derived no comfort from the puckish impulse. He saw the door close, heard the faintest of clicks, and knew that Sloan would now be doubly suspicious. Only a man on the look-out for a trick would have done that; Sloan had ample proof that " Rayner " was no innocent.

Here he was, at the end of a telephone which could connect him with the past which was to be drummed out of his mind. Lift the instrument and dial a familiar number, and *Janet* would answer. Janet—what would *she* do if she heard his voice?

Forget that! He could call Mark Lessing; a dozen, a hundred friends. Forget it!

He pushed the telephone away and lit a cigarette. His hand was unsteady, he had never felt more in need of a drink. He opened a cupboard in the big desk, and felt no surprise at sight of a whisky bottle, a set of glasses, and a soda syphon. He poured himself out a drink.

This was a pretty good start; whisky in the middle of the afternoon. And it wasn't the only good start; plunged into an unfamiliar office, with no information, no knowledge even about himself as he was supposed to be; murderously attacked in mistake for Kennedy; accused of being Kennedy. Where *was* Kennedy? How much of Kyle's story had been genuine? He pictured Kyle's wife being crushed beneath a car; and Lucille, lying dead. He finished his drink, and opened a drawer sharply, barked his knuckles and muttered to himself as he licked them.

Then he began to go through the papers in the desk; routine, everything was routine. He had done something like this a hundred times; gone through papers which belonged to someone else, with the sole purpose of finding out everything he could about the owner. Business documents betrayed a great deal to knowing searchers.

There were account books, order books, files of letters from customers, details of the business he handled; it could hardly be more varied. He lost himself in the task of studying it all. Charles Rayner had a flourishing business, and dealt in practically anything from tobacco and cigarettes to wines and spirits, tubular-steel chairs to plastic goods, bric-a-brac manufactured in Birmingham for sale in the bazaars of India and China—he had an export business as well as that at home, but apparently imported nothing. The business had been conducted from offices in Leadenhall Street; there were " change of address " cards which had been sent out to all customers; he was plunged into an established business, and much was explained by a stencilled circular letter:

> Mr. Samuel Wiseman begs to inform you that he has disposed of his business to Mr. Charles Rayner, and will remain with the firm for a short while in an advisory capacity. He takes pleasure in assuring you that Mr. Rayner will have personal charge of the business, and you may be assured of his close attention to your special requirements at all times.

This letter was dated 1st March: two weeks before Lucille's death. Had Kennedy been so sure of himself that he had planned that far ahead, or had he had another man in mind for " Charles Rayner " and thrust Roger into the position at the last moment?

What were his real plans?

There was nothing illegal about anything Roger had discovered here; but commission agents could be undercover agents for almost any kind of black market, any kind of smuggling, knavery, fraud. Outwardly, this was a respectable business with a large circle of customers.

In a drawer of the desk, he found " his " passport; he leaned back as he glanced through it, smiling with reluctant admiration. As a Yard man, he knew that it was comparatively easy to obtain false passports, but this was a prime example; it had been used, had visa and customs stamps for the United States, several European countries, even Germany; and his photograph was unmistakable. He hadn't even realized that he'd had one taken in his new personality, but here it was—a good likeness as passport photographs went. He hadn't discovered any foreign correspondence; there must be some in one of the cabinets; if he worked hard he would find out where he had been. He laughed—and the telephone bell rang.

Kennedy?

He hesitated; the harsh ringing sound jarred his ears. He took the instrument off its cradle, hesitated, then put it to his ear. He schooled his voice, spoke with little movement of his lips.

" Hallo."

" Roger! " His heart leapt at the name, for this was a woman—and in distress. " Roger, please help me, I——"

This was *Marion*—Marion, in trouble.

" What's the matter? "

" I can't tell you here, I must see you. I'll be at Piccadilly, by Swan and Edgars in an hour. *Please* help me."

" Marion, listen I——"

But she'd gone.

.   .   .   .   .

Roger stood outside Swan and Edgars, hub of London, watched the traffic and jingled the office keys in his pocket. He hardly noticed people, but every policeman in sight seemed to be twice life size. There were dozens of them, and from habit, they peered covertly at everyone standing outside the shop window and watching the swirling traffic; this was a rendezvous for the oddest people, the most noticeable spot in London. A dozen other idlers stood waiting, some standing, some walking impatiently up and down, some looking at their watches. Now and again, couples met; most linked arms or kissed and went off together, happily. The flower-sellers on the steps of Eros were doing little business; newsvendors called out tirelessly in their raucous voices. It was nearly four-fifteen, approaching rush hour.

Marion was a quarter of an hour late.

Half an hour——

It was no use waiting, she hadn't been able to come.

He had grown fond of Marion, as one could grow fond of the only really friendly soul in one's life. He had once had the opportunity to use her to help himself, and had missed it because he hadn't trusted her.

Had it been a mistake to come here? And a mistake to talk to Kyle, a mistake to——

The male nurse appeared, short, flashily dressed in a loud-blue suit and bright-brown shoes and a spotted red-and-white bow tie. He strutted. The vagueness which his white coat had given him had gone, he became a personality, aggressive and unpleasant. He approached briskly, and grinned; he was still ugly, but looked less faded.

" Getting tired? " he asked.

" What do you want? "

" You, *Mister* Rayner. You're wanted at the office. If I was you, I wouldn't come away so easy in future." He held up his arm, and a passing taxi stopped. " Inside." Roger obeyed; if he argued he would only attract attention, and too many people were watching. The male nurse gave the office address and followed him into the cab.

" What's all this? " Roger demanded.

" You'll find out."

There were three traffic blocks; a ten-minute journey took them twenty minutes, and not another word was exchanged. The male nurse waited for him to start up the stairs. He went towards the office door, and the man said :

" Other side—that's where you live." He tossed Roger a key. Roger opened the door opposite the office, and stepped into a well-furnished, bright, and colourful sitting-room.

A radio was on, and Kennedy sat with his legs stretched out and his eyes closed, a dreamy expression on his face, listening to Brahms. The male nurse closed the door and then went out of this room into another; that door slammed. Kennedy kept his eyes closed, but as the music stopped, he said :

" So you had a visit from Ginger Kyle, did you? "

His manner was overbearing, even threatening.   Revolt
had to start some time.

Roger chose now.

13

REVOLT

THE announcer was telling the world about Brahms and
the artiste who had just been interpreting his music.
As he stared at Roger from beneath his lashes, Kennedy
kept his eyes closed, or nearly closed.   Roger strode across
the room and switched off the radio, took out his cigarette-
case, and lit up.

" I spoke to you," said Kennedy, and opened his eyes
wide; they burned as if at white heat.

" I heard you."

" Then answer me."

Roger said: " One of these days I'll break your silly
neck. Are you congenitally crazy? You let me come here
without a briefing, easy meat for anyone who happened
along.   Kyle doesn't matter, but Sloan does."

" What did you say to Kyle? "

" Just now I'm asking the questions.   Why didn't you
brief me properly?   Or did you think I had a sixth sense?
If I'd been able to tell Sloan all about the business, who
I'd bought it from, what it was, he'd have gone away
satisfied.   Now he's rushing around London with the light
of battle in his eyes. I know Sloan. He's a bull-dog
type.   He'll keep at me until he's satisfied that I'm all
right, and that probably won't be for a long time.   You've
weakened the whole set-up.   I thought you were supposed to be good."

Throughout all this, Kennedy gradually sat up in his
chair and drew in his legs.   He didn't blink, didn't look
away from Roger, who glared at him.   The cigarette
tasted unpleasant.   Had he misjudged the moment for
revolt?   He stood his ground, and Kennedy said softly:

" I was detained."

" Being detained means that I'm now watched by the
police. I've a dozen little mannerisms which friends of
mine know well, and I do subconsciously. You might as
well tell them who I am, and be done with it."

" It was unavoidable," Kennedy said defensively. He
stood up. He had submitted to the first squall of revolt,
which was a minor triumph, but there would be many
more storms to come. " I also had a visit from the
police at my office, and I couldn't be here to meet you."

" So they're after us both."

" They've asked a few questions. You've got to find a
way to stall them. That's your job—understand, Rayner? That's what you're here for—countering the work
of the police. You'd better do it well."

" You bungled this. I should have been briefed before
I got here. Your funny-funny business will get you to the
gallows if you're not careful."

" You'll come with me."

" That's why I'm worried about it."

Kennedy smiled slowly; when he smiled, he had a
predatory look, and there was something of the vulture in
his face.

" That's a good frame of mind to be in," he said. " I
think I chose the right man. But watch your step,
Rayner. I'm the boss."

" What I do, I'll do my own way." Roger relaxed,
went to a chair and sat down heavily—and flung out the
next question: " What happened to Marion? "

" Why should you worry? "

" She called me, asked me to——"

" Sure, I know. But you don't answer appeals for
help from pretty women, you go where I tell you to go,
and forget all the rest."

" Where is she? "

Kennedy leaned back and thrust his legs out again.

" She isn't," he said softly.

The significance of it was a long time dawning on
Roger. It might not have dawned when it did but for
that slow, cruel smile. " *She isn't*." Marion wasn't alive,

they'd killed her. He sat rigid, and couldn't bring himself to utter a word; and Kennedy gloated.

"She met with an accident," he said.

"Accident?" On the tip of his tongue were the words:
"Like Kyle's wife," but he bit on them. "So you——"

"That's right. Haven't you realized who you're
working for? A man who wipes out anything and anyone
who gets in his way. Marion was useful. She made it
easier to handle you. But she wasn't reliable. She fell
in love with you. She listened at keyholes and learned
this address and enough of the truth to be dangerous. She
was silly enough to threaten to tell the police all she knew,
and you wouldn't have wanted that, would you, Rayner?
She knew it was a mistake, managed to get to a telephone,
and asked you to meet her. She didn't get that far. She's
in a morgue now, but she isn't cold yet."

Roger said: "Every detective at Scotland Yard
could tell you what I'm going to tell you now. You've
had it. You can get away with one murder, maybe two—
but in your frame of mind, you go on until you get caught.
Once they catch you, you haven't a chance in hell.
You're as good as hanged, Kennedy. Don't forget it."

"Very nice. I've been telling you, your job is to keep
me free from the police."

"I can't, if you kill as a habit."

"I only kill when it's necessary." Kennedy stood up
and went to the window. This one overlooked the narrow
street. "I don't want to turn you into a yes man, you
won't be any good to me that way, but don't forget who's
the boss, and don't forget that if I get caught, you'll be
caught with me. I've laid it on that way. And just
to make sure you've a proper incentive to work, don't
forget that girl who's living with your wife. If anyone
else calls you up with an SOS, forget it. So far, you've
done fairly well. You had a stiff job with Sloan, and it
couldn't be helped—but you got out of it as well as any
man could. You can handle Sloan all right. I asked
you what you said to Kyle."

"How did you know about Sloan?"

"I'll talk about a lot of things that mystify you, and you

won't say much I don't get to hear. The question is—Kyle."

" He was waiting when I got here. He expected to see someone else, although he didn't say so. He pitched a hard-luck story, and I flung him out on his ear."

" What kind of hard luck? "

" He wanted money. If I'd had time, I'd have listened to his story, but there wasn't any time, because I wanted to be alone. I didn't want anyone to find me with an old lag."

" Who told you that Kyle was an old lag? "

Roger stared—and laughed. He managed to sound amused. He lit another cigarette and waved his hand, as if at something which was ridiculous.

" I've been dealing with them most of my life. I've only to set eyes on them to know where they've been living. Kyle's been inside for at least four years, you don't get that way until you've had a stretch or longer. I wanted to get into the main office and look as if I belonged to the place. I succeeded."

That ought to answer the question Kennedy was really asking: how was it that the conversation with Kyle hadn't been recorded? He nodded and seemed satisfied.

Roger didn't give him much time to think about it.

" Why build up this front for me, Kennedy? Is the business genuine or phoney? "

" It's genuine, and its good. I use it for a lot of things, and some of them you'll know about—in time. You just settle down and get to know all about the business. There's a secretary you'll meet in the morning. She's good, and she knows everything, from A to Z. She also knows you're green at the game. She thinks you've put a lot of money into the business. You were to have taken it over a month ago, but you've been ill. She's been managing it for you."

" Why leave the old office? "

" It wasn't big enough. This business is going to expand! You can leave all the details of staff and the daily running of the business to the secretary—Rose Morgan. You'll get your instructions for the rest from me. You'll travel a lot—didn't I promise you an easy life?" He sneered. "This is your home address in England. There are two rooms and a kitchen besides this. You'll have a man to look after you—named Harry. He'll be along later in the day. Just settle into your new life, Rayner."

"When are you going to tell me what it's all about?"

"You'll learn. I've told you enough for a start. When the police poke their noses in, you'll handle them. Set a cop to fool a cop! Don't waste a lot of time guessing. Just remember what happens to people who won't play the game my way. The girl at Copse Cottage was one. Marion was another."

Kennedy got up and went out. He hadn't given much away; the truth would be let out gradually drop by drop.

Roger sat quite still, looking at the ceiling. Images on his mind were far too many and too vivid; Marion was added to them, now—good, wholesome, attractive Marion, who had wanted to help him; had *begged* to help him. If he'd trusted her, he might have avoided all this, or much of it. The ruthless devilry of it swept over him like a stinking cloak of corruption.

He had to find out how corrupt; what it was all about; who Kennedy was, in actual fact; who else worked with him—or whether he was working for others, unknown. There was a touch of the bizarre in the conception; of boldness, too. The one thing that could not be in doubt was the size and scope of it. This business had its tentacles all over the place; in England, on the Continent, perhaps as far afield as the United States. This was crime organized with painstaking care; big stuff—and remember it was boldly conceived and as boldly carried out. It wasn't *new*. That had been obvious from the beginning, but he hadn't faced it as a fact. It wasn't *new*. It had been going on for a long time, and the police hadn't discovered it, knew very little about it. That was only a half-truth; Sloan and the Yard were interested in the original Charles Rayner and in Kennedy. So something had leaked out.

How?

Had Marion managed to get word through before Kennedy realized what she was doing?

That wasn't likely. Sloan might be following almost any trail; the Copse Cottage murder—Kyle—yes, probably Kyle. That rang the bell. Kyle had been mixed up in big crime, too, and the Yard had known that although he had been caught, his accomplices had kept free. The visit from Sloan, then, had been routine—the Yard thought Kyle would get in touch with his sponsors. But why think Rayner was using an *alias* and was really Kennedy?

Another cloud blew up, tiny, dark; that he was being built up as a stooge. That if plans went awry, he would take the rap for Kennedy. He was the man at whom the police looked askance, now. The pitfalls were many, the path treacherous. He had a dual battle on his hands; fooling Kennedy, and while he was doing that, stalling the police. There wasn't a short cut to either.

It was desperately necessary to find out the whole truth, to smash this man who killed without compunction.

Nothing could ever wholly justify him; but he must keep news, even a hint of the truth, away from Janet and the boys; he must fight the waves of emotionalism which kept sweeping over him.

But Janet was in terrible distress.

Forget it.

.   .   .   .   .

Rose Morgan was forty-ish; plump, shapeless, dressed in a kind of black sack. She had a little beak of a nose, small pale lips which opened very little, a high-pitched, decisive voice. She was efficiency to the last syllable. Her hair was mousy colour and fastened in a bun at the back. She had good hands and perfectly kept nails. She seemed willing to teach Roger everything there was to know about the business.

He saw her for the first time the day after Sloan's visit—a Friday. The office staff was coming here on Monday, she said.

He asked for a list of the staff of nine; she assured him

that all of them were thoroughly reliable and had worked for Wiseman, the previous owner, for several years. He examined the salary list; it was high—he paid his staff well! Rose Morgan received a thousand pounds a year, and the annual wages bill came to a little over five thousand. Rent, rates, other general expenses, were as much again. Before the business paid a penny profit, it had to show income over expenditure of ten thousand pounds. According to the figures it did that without much trouble; the profit for the past two years had been nearly five thousand. The profit was to be his share.

His.

As Charles Rayner, he had a private bank account with a credit of over two thousand pounds, and Government securities which made him worth ten times as much as Roger West.

This opened a completely new vista; he could call himself rich. He felt the lure of wealth; began, as the days passed, to expect the little luxuries he had never had before. He could stand outside himself, in an odd fashion, and watch the effect of this on him. He took to luxury and plenty of money as a duck took to water.

Harry, who " did " for him, was a quiet, vague individual, with a doleful face and big, brown eyes, a perfect servant who never intruded; that was part of the luxury attack on him, every physical want was anticipated. There was tea first thing in the morning, a drink ready before luncheon and dinner, perfectly cooked food, pressed clothes—everything.

He had accounts at three exclusive restaurants and two big stores. He bought clothes of good quality and cut. He could have whatever he wanted, and had only to sign the bill and, later, the cheque. He had stepped into this new identity almost overnight.

Kennedy didn't come again during the next ten days. He heard nothing from Kyle or from Sloan. He was withdrawn more completely from his old life than he had ever dreamed possible. The past had begun as a nightmare and became a distant dream; frighteningly distant. He had to remind himself of it and also to remind himself of his chief objective—to find out the truth about Kennedy and all Kennedy stood for.

He found the business, as such, absorbing; there were many callers. He bought from this man and sold to that; he found that the business had many old and valuable contacts. It could get foods which were in short supply with little difficulty, and therefore could command its own price. There was nothing in short supply in which the firm didn't deal, but he checked carefully and found that everything was above board and legal. He worried at the problem, day in and day out; how was it possible for the firm to get first call on these goods in short supply? Answer that and he might be able to answer a lot of other questions.

There was one thick barrier to all investigations; everywhere he went, he was watched. Waking and sleeping, he knew that he was watched. Sometimes he knew by whom; at others time it was simply awareness, and he couldn't place the man.

Day by day, he grew into life as Charles Rayner.

Day by day, Roger West receded.

By the end of three weeks, he knew that the greatest danger to success would be himself; the new conditions, the constant surveillance and the desire to be free from it— and real freedom would come only when Kennedy was sure of him—worked together to soften his mind. Soften —or harden it?

Exactly a month after Kyle's visit, he sent a registered letter to Mr. John Pearson at the Strand G.P.O. Kyle didn't telephone; Roger was at once pleased and sorry about that. It had been a mistake to tell the man to call him here, but he wanted to see Kyle again and to learn about the man's past, more about Kennedy. He seized on to the possibility of learning more from Kyle until it became an obsession.

It was on the morning after he had posted the money to Kyle that he received a letter marked: " *Personal* ". It was the first he had received since coming to the flat, and Harry brought it to him with his morning tea. He waited until the man had gone, and then opened it with unsteady fingers. Inside was a single slip of paper on which were two words: *Kyle's dead.*

The morning papers confirmed it; Kyle had " fallen " in front of a train at Edgware Road Tube Station.

.   .   .   .   .

It was like living in a fog and never knowing what might loom out of the fog, and hit him.

.   .   .   .   .

Kennedy came on the telephone later in the day.   " Did you get my message? "

" Yes."

" Take it to heart.   I've a job for you."

" Where? "

" You'll be brought to me—remember the male nurse? You can call him Percy.   He'll meet you at the corner of Putney Bridge, near the old theatre.   Know it? "

" Yes."

" Get there without being followed by the police," said Kennedy.

" Are they trailing me? "

" You ought to know. Just make sure you're not followed. Leave at once—Percy will expect you in an hour's time."

Kennedy rang off.   Roger leaned back in his chair and faced up to the new situation.   For the first time he was to be used for a job—that was what the summons meant. For the first time he might get a clear indication of why all this had been planned so carefully.   He hadn't been given much time to think about that; he was to go into action at once, but wasn't trusted.   " Percy " would know where he was to be taken, and he himself would have no knowledge until he got there.   Probably Percy would make sure he didn't even discover then.

He rang for Rose Morgan.

" Yes, Mr. Rayner? "

" I'm going out, and I don't know what time I'll be back."

" Yes, Mr. Rayner."

" Tell Harry he needn't get luncheon, but I expect to be in for dinner."

" Yes, Mr. Rayner."

" See Renfrew when he comes, and apologize—say I'm ill. Handle everything else yourself."

" Yes, Mr. Rayner."

Rose was like a machine.

He put on his hat and went downstairs. The narrow staircase and passage had become familiar now—his haunts. So had the narrow street. It was a blustery day, and there were heavy rain clouds but no rain. He walked towards the Strand, and wasn't followed. He had a curious feeling of freedom; this was the first time he had felt it since becoming Rayner. Kennedy's man wasn't watching, or else Kennedy was using one who was extremely clever.

Was Kennedy beginning to trust him?

He reached the Strand and beckoned a taxi from a rank. " Harrods," he said, and sat back, looking out of the tiny rear window. No one followed him except the usual stream of traffic. He looked for a Yard man; Sloan, anyone; there was no indication that he was followed. He reached the big store, paid the driver off, and walked through the provision and greengrocery departments, then through the tobacco department near the front entrance, and went out into Brompton Road again. He looked up and down; no one took the slightest interest in him. He went back into the store, walked briskly towards a back entrance and stepped into almost deserted streets. A commissionaire saluted. An empty taxi came round the corner, and the driver jammed on his brakes at his signal.

Three quarters of an hour after getting the message, he was at Putney Bridge.

Percy sat at the wheel of a big, roomy black Daimler—an old model, but it had an air. Percy was in chauffeur's uniform and wore a peak cap. He nodded, but didn't smile when he got out and opened the door for Roger, behaving in the same way as Rose Morgan—like a machine. Roger sat back on the luxurious seat, and a feeling of well-being came upon him like a cloud or a shroud. He watched the traffic coming over the bridge and along Putney High Street, with its steep hill. At the top, the driver turned right towards Richmond. Not far along, he heard a whirring sound which reminded him vividly of the cine-camera at the nursing home.

The blinds were dropping at the windows; they were worked from a control button at the front. Gloom drove good spirits away; it was like being driven in a luxury hearse.

The Daimler gathered speed, took corners easily, hummed along a main road where, judging from the sounds, there was little traffic. Roger made no attempt to raise a blind, just sat back and accepted the situation, knowing that Percy's ferrety eyes were on him in the mirror all the time; the feeling of freedom had gone completely.

They went on for more than half an hour, and were well out of London when the car turned a corner sharply and went along a bumpy road. Soon it turned again, at the foot of a hill so steep that Percy had to change gear. They crawled to the top of the hill, and stopped.

The blinds shot up; sunlight streamed into the Daimler, dazzling Roger. When he was accustomed to the glare, he saw that they were outside a small country house. Trees were packed densely behind the house. In front there was a long drive; lawns and flower-gardens, with tulips and wallflowers in brightly coloured beds, misty forget-me-nots adding a background of blue. It was delightful; and it overlooked sweeping country-side. The road along which they had come was hidden by a fringe of oak and beech; this place was as lonely and out of the way as the nursing-home and Copse Cottage.

" Out," said Percy, opening the door.

Roger said: " One day you're going to change your tone, Percy." The little man glared at him, but made no comment. Roger went up three stone steps and stood beneath a brick porch, warm, browny-red. The door was of natural oak, oiled, not painted, and was studded

with iron nail-heads.   As he reached it, a man opened
the door—a stranger and obsequious.

" Mr. Rayner? "

" Yes."

" This way, sir, please."   The door closed behind them,
and Roger was led up a wide staircase : wider than the
outside of the house had led him to expect.   He went
across the square landing.   A passage led to a window
through which the bright sunlight glowed.   Several doors
led off it, and he was taken to the first door on the right.
The man tapped, and opened it.

" Mr. Rayner, madame," he said, and stood aside for
Roger to pass.

Madame?

14

" MADAME "

SHE was lovely.

She wasn't like Marion, Lucille, or even Janet, simply
an attractive woman ;   she was beautiful—and young.
She sat in a chair at a small bow-shaped mahogany desk,
with the sun streaming through the window behind her,
so that her features were in shadow ;   that was perhaps
one of the reasons why she looked so breathtakingly
beautiful.   She smiled faintly, and indicated a chair ;
she didn't get up and didn't offer her hand.

The chair was placed opposite the window, so that she
could see every feature and every line on his face, while
hers remained in shadow.   She pushed a silver cigarette-
box across the desk, and waited for him to light up ;   she
didn't take a cigarette herself.

Her hair was a dark mass of loose curls ;   her eyes, deep
blue ;   her complexion smooth and lovely as a rose ;
her lips the colour of cherries, glistening ripe.   The faint
smile reminded him of Kennedy ;   there was no reason why

it should. She wore a white blouse; that was all of her clothes that he could see. It was simple, plain, and fastened high at the neck, and had long sleeves. All for purity.

Kennedy wasn't here; Kennedy was never where Roger expected him to be.

She studied him coolly, boldly, with obvious interest; he needed no telling that she knew his history. She was sizing him up, asking herself whether he would suit her purpose. That lasted for a long time; half a cigarette. He didn't resent the scrutiny, and said nothing.

Her voice was pitched low; it was somehow less attractive than he had expected, with a faint accent he couldn't place. It tarnished her beauty slightly—very slightly.

" Mr. Kennedy tells me that you will be able to help me," she said. " I understand that you have a considerable experience of police matters, criminal law, and all the relative factors."

" That's right."

" Mr. Kennedy assures me that your services are at my disposal. Is that true? "

It had better be true. " Yes," he said.

She hesitated, as if she weren't quite sure whether to take the plunge. Kennedy believed in leaving plenty to him; too much to him. It was Kennedy's way of making sure that he was resourceful, whatever the emergency.

She plunged.

" My husband is under remand at Brixton Jail. I think it probable that the prosecution would be able to prove their case against him. If it should be proved, he is likely to serve a long prison sentence. He is a man of great sensibility, refinement, and culture. I have copies of all the statements he has made to his legal advisers, and I want you to study them. There are, also, details of the charge and a summary of the evidence against him, so far as we are aware of it. I want you to study all those papers and form an opinion as to the likely result of the trial. If there is, so far as you can see, a weakness in the case for the prosecution, I want you to elaborate it, so that my husband's counsel can be properly primed. Is that all straightforward?"

" Yes, but——"

" How long will it take you?"

" It depends on the length of the statements and the complexity of the case. What is he alleged to have done?"

She smiled slightly at the " alleged ".

" He is charged with smuggling currency from a number of foreign countries into this country; with smuggling sterling out of Great Britain to the Continent. It is a complex case in some ways, quite simple in others."

" I'm no expert on currency."

" You can assess the case in the light of the evidence that will be given you. You will work here—is that convenient?"

It might take hours; a day; or several days. But Kennedy had pledged his services, and the obvious thing was to say: " Yes." It was hardly a murmur, he nodded to give it emphasis.

" Thank you. You were about to ask a question when I stopped you. Or to make a comment. What was it?"

" Your husband's counsel, if he's good—and those who command big fees are usually good—will be able to assess the case better than I."

" Possibly. I have a great respect for barristers, but I have often noticed how they fail because they see the case only from the side of the defence. I want this examined through the eyes of the prosecution—you've been trained to do that."

" It's up to you," he said.

" Yes." She stopped, and seemed to be waiting for him to speak. He returned her gaze levelly. With anyone else, the pause would have been uncomfortable; it wasn't. He had a feeling that he had seen her before, but that might be because she was so beautiful, and beauty reminded one of beauty. She would have been perfect on the stage or screen; she wasn't quite true to life.

Her lips turned up at the corners, attractively.

" Is there a joke?" he asked.

" I had no idea you were an unworldly man. What is your fee, Mr. Rayner? "

" I'll tell you when I've had a look at the job."

" Very well."

" Unless you would rather deal with Mr. Kennedy," he said.

She shook her head.

" I have paid him a fee for the introduction, and this aspect of the matter is now between you and me, Mr. Rayner. If your work is satisfactory in every way, I shall not be ungenerous. It is essential that my husband should not serve a prison sentence."

There was something else in her mind, but he didn't judge this the moment to probe.

" Where shall I work? "

" I will have you taken to your room, and the papers will be sent to you," she said. " You may ring for anything you require. While you are here, I would prefer you not to leave the grounds—in fact, to go no farther than the garden fence. If it is necessary for you to leave the district for any purpose, we will make arrangements."

He nodded.

She rang a bell, and the interview was over; he didn't even know her name.

.   .   .   .   .   .

In fact he did know it; and he knew where he had seen her face before—in the newspapers.

It had been a bad likeness, but he should have placed her when she had talked of currency smuggling—one of the biggest rackets with which the Yard was dealing, one with widespread ramifications and an incredible number of loopholes. She was Mrs. James Delaney—the Honourable Mrs. James Delaney. Her husband was the son of an impoverished offshoot of the aristocracy, and as far as the Press reports had implied, the charges against him were trivial. So this was a job where the Yard had played canny with the Press, giving no indication of the scope of the offences. When Roger had been at the Yard, at least six different organizations, concerned with smuggling, had been the subject of inquiries, most of them small—but it was the kind of job which was unpredictable; what seemed a trifling offence might, on being probed, prove to be a big one—and Mrs. Delaney hadn't minced her words.

His room was large, and had every comfort; it overlooked the garden at the back, sweeping lawns, rose walks, and glowing beds of tulips softened by forget-me-nots. Off with the old luxury, on with the new. Tea arrived; and half an hour afterwards, two bulky brief-cases were brought in. Then he was left on his own. . . .

He felt a strange nostalgia.

Here was *his* work; the careful study of amassed facts, the scrutiny of detail, the building up of a case. This one had started when a Customs officer had discovered that Delaney was taking a hundred pounds above the allowed maximum, in sterling, out of the country— nothing remarkable. But some correspondence had been found in his cases—the fools always had something like that, they seldom destroyed all the evidence—showing a list of French and Swiss people with whom Delaney was in contact. Currency smugglers, all small, had been in touch with the same people. There was an astonishingly detailed account of what the Yard man had asked Delaney and what information he had given away.

Under pressure, he had admitted having a large account in francs at the Madeleine office of the *Banque de France*, under the name of Dinot. He'd given three separate accounts of how he had obtained the money: one, from gambling; two, from friends; three, from business. Mr. Delaney did not seem to have a very agile or retentive mind. Reading between the lines of the police questions, it was easy to see that they knew much more than he had given away.

Delaney had been questioned about banking accounts in a dozen different countries, all in the name of someone beginning with " D ". He had denied knowledge of them all. If it could be proved that he was, in fact, the " D " in every instance, then it would be proved that he controlled well over a hundred thousand pounds in different foreign currencies. Then the questions switched to his accounts in different parts of Great Britain, and other accounts, also in the name of D—this or D—that. The interrogator's questioning had all been aimed at one thing; eliciting an admission that Delaney paid substantial sums to English visitors on the Continent, and was reimbursed, in England, with English currency. The build-up showed it to be one of the biggest organizations that the Yard had discovered.

Roger couldn't be sure what other evidence the Yard had found; he judged that it was plenty.

It was nearly eight o'clock when he had finished, rubbed his eyes after the concentrated reading, and rang the bell. The footman answered him promptly.

" I would like to see Madame," he said.

" Madame would like you to dine with her, sir, and dinner will be at eight-thirty. It is not usual to change."

That was as well; he'd nothing to change into. He packed up the papers and felt oddly dissatisfied. Kennedy hadn't created this new personality so that he could handle bread-and-butter things like this. Unless he was fooling her, the defending counsel could tell Mrs. Delaney at once that there wasn't a hope. It was on far too big a scale for the defence to protest that Delaney hadn't realized the gravity of the offence.

.   .   .   .   .

She had changed into a black dress which had touches of white at the cuffs and neck. She waited for him in a small room, off the dining-room; there was an elaborate steel and coloured-glass cocktail bar—more luxury. She was grave when she offered him a drink; grave while they drank; she looked pale but not worried, and she knew what the answer was going to be. But she didn't ask a question until dinner was nearly over and they were at the sweet; it had been a meal to dream about.

She looked at him suddenly, with a penetrating gleam in those lovely eyes.

" Have you reached an opinion? "

" Yes."

" What is it? "

" You're quite right. He has little chance of getting off. I wouldn't like to say he will get seven years. It depends on whether I've seen everything the prosecution has, and that isn't likely. Three is the probable limit on the available evidence."

" Have you found any loop-hole? "

" There isn't one. He wasn't clever when dealing with the police."

" No," she said, and smiled, as a mother might smile over an erring child. " He isn't used to dealing with the police. He is under remand——"

" There was a note about that. He's at Brixton, and the case comes up at the Old Bailey on Monday or Tuesday next week. I'm sorry, but it's a simple fact that he hasn't a chance. You probably think it's harsh, because before the war this wouldn't have been an offence, but——" he shrugged. " At least he hasn't involved you in any way."

" I am not involved. I didn't know what he was doing. I had no idea that I owed so much to that particular kind of activity." She smiled; she was superbly beautiful. " I am vain enough to think he probably sank deeper and deeper into it, because of me; that is why it is essential that I should help him. He mustn't go to prison."

" You can't prevent it."

" He wouldn't go to prison if he were never tried, would he? "

Roger saw it then, in a blinding flash—doubly blinding because of the delayed action. He should have realized what she was getting at before.

" And he won't be tried if he's removed from Brixton before the trial or on the way, will he? You know the daily routine at Brixton thoroughly—I want you to decide what is the best way to get him out. Then I want you to organize it. What is the term used—a jail break, yes. I have everything ready to leave the country; once I am safely away with him there will be nothing to worry about. Mr. Kennedy is extremely able, and he is arranging all that for me. Don't say that it can't be done, Mr. Rayner. It must be done."

15

JAIL BREAK

SHE was as softly lovely and as distant as the moon—
and she wanted the moon. She looked at him over the
top of her glass, smiling faintly; it wasn't going to surprise
or worry her if he said that it was impossible. He could
almost imagine her thinking that Kennedy would persuade
him that all things, and this especially, were possible.

He finished a trifle which melted deliciously in his
mouth, and sipped his wine.

" Has Kennedy told you to what part of the world he's
sending you? There is such a thing as extradition.
Police forces work well together."

She smiled more broadly.

" Yes, he has told me, and I am not at all afraid of
being caught. I have the necessary passports and papers.
Kennedy is an expert on that kind of thing. Isn't he? "

" He's done some good jobs," Roger conceded.
" Why are you begging the issue? "

" Am I? You say the thing has to be done. All right,
it'll be done." He smiled—and pierced that beautiful
façade. Her eyes sparkled, she stretched out a hand across
the gleaming table and touched his; hers was cold.

" You can do it? "

" With the right men who have a strong enough nerve
I can do it, yes. I know Brixton well."

" When will you try? "

He grinned; he felt almost skittish.

" You'll know, in time. I should be all prepared for
the journey at an hour's notice. I shan't send word to
you until just before your husband is free. It's better
not to know too much. The oddest things can happen,
and the thickest walls have ears."

She laughed.

" I can be ready at an hour's notice," she said.
" Are you quite sure? " It was only now that he

realized how young she was—in the middle twenties?
Young and still deeply in love with Delaney—and storing
up for herself pain and suffering and disappointment,
although she didn't know it.

"Yes."

She jumped up and went across the room, then walked
back, as if she couldn't control her emotions. Once or
twice she laughed lightly—the excitement had gone to
her head. He poured her out more wine, and took the
glass to her. She drank eagerly, gaily. She hadn't
really believed that an escape was possible, and his confidence had poured new life into her. She was lovely
enough to hurt.

"Have you any more work to do to-night?" she asked.

"No. You can have the papers back."

"When will you start preparing?"

"In the morning." He would have to see Kennedy;
but he had no doubt that Kennedy would soon get in
touch with him. The next job—or at least an early job—
was to find out where Kennedy lived.

"We'll have coffee in the other room," she said. She
slipped her arm through his, and they went into the
drawing-room, where a radiogram was playing soft music.
The footman—was it the same man?—brought in coffee
and liqueurs and cigars. Roger selected a cigar, but
didn't light it at once. He leaned back on the couch and
hummed the lilting tune, and after a while Mrs. Delaney
got up and went to the radiogram, putting on several
records—dance tunes. He didn't speak, but he knew
what she wanted.

She was as light as a feather, although not at all like
Marion; but he kept remembering the afternoon tea
dance with Marion. It didn't spoil his enjoyment. He
tried to stand outside himself and judge his reaction dispassionately, and had to admit that he *was* enjoying this.
The soft pressure of her body against his, the delicate
perfume, the radiance in her eyes, all contributed. For
half an hour they danced almost without stopping. Then
suddenly she laughed, broke away from him, and turned
the radiogram off.

" You dance as well as Jim."

" I hope he's good."

" He's wonderful," she said, and came close and took his hands, clenching them tightly. " You won't fail us? "

" I won't fail you."

Her lips brushed his cheek lightly; then she hurried away, and from the door whispered: " Good night."

.   .   .   .   .

Kennedy was determined not to reveal where he lived. Percy drove Roger from the Delaney house to London, and they picked Kennedy up at Putney Bridge. It was high time Roger knew where to find Kennedy; high time he went over to the attack, but—patience was vital, Kennedy was still dangerously wary.

Kennedy sank down in his corner and spoke almost as soon as the door closed.

" She says you're very sure of yourself."

" I am."

" When are you going to do it? "

" Sunday night. There's always less discipline on Sunday night at Brixton—as at any jail. You might not notice it, but it is so."

" I'll believe you. How are you going to do the job? "

" I want two powerful men, one waiter's rig-out, one police-constable's uniform, and a girl, to give me an alibi. The uniform must be a good one, with genuine fixings—numbers and badges. Dinner will be taken into his room that night by my waiter. My constable will follow and deal with the duty warder. I shall want to drill that constable and waiter myself, and they need to be good. You'll have to make arrangements with the restaurant from which Delaney gets his special food to allow my waiter to work for them that night."

" What risks are you going to take yourself ? "

Roger laughed. " I'm not—except that I'll drive the car we get away in, if you call that a risk. If it works, there won't be any."

" I can't see the scheme yet," Kennedy said.

" I'll work that out with the two men and the girl—you're not interested in the scheme, only in the results."

Kennedy laughed; his eyes were half-closed, just silvery slits.

"In some ways you're better than I expected, Rayner! What else do you want from me?"

"Two cars. An ordinary, shabby little thing outside the prison, and a fast one stationed half a mile away. How are you going to get them out of the country?"

"By air."

"Where from?"

"I've a private airfield near Watford."

"I don't want to know where it is, yet," said Roger, "but when I'm in that fast car, I want someone with me who knows the road and can guide me there without losing a minute. Then I want a different car ready at the airfield, to take me away. All right?"

"It sounds reasonable. I'll send the trio to your office, and——"

"You won't! You'll tell me where to meet them. They aren't to come near my office, and they aren't to know who I am. If you want me to keep at this job, you'd better be careful of details like that."

"I'll see you," said Kennedy. He laughed again. "I want you to keep going, don't make any mistake about that."

.   .   .   .   .

It was dark outside Brixton Jail. Only a few lights glowed at the street lamps, beyond the high grey walls, dim yellow squares shone against blackness. Two policemen stood on duty outside the iron gates. A little Morris car, grey, dirty, and with adjustable registration plates which could be changed by pressing a button in the dashboard, was found the corner from the gates. Roger sat at the wheel, with a girl by his side—a pretty little blonde showing no intelligence and no nerves; if she had any, she didn't betray them that night. She would swear, if need be, that he had been with her all the evening, at her rooms.

He knew what was happening inside, could follow every move of the policeman and the waiter.

.   .   .   .   .

The waiter had arrived first.

There was a trail of them, most nights, to the prisoners under remand, who had privileged treatment if they had plenty of money. The waiter came from the nearby restaurant, which specialized in superbly cooked food for prisoners with discerning palates. He carried his tray, with a huge metal cover over it, expertly. The gate guards let him through. He walked to the main doors of the remand building, and there a warder lifted the lid off the tray.

" Don't let it get cold," said the waiter.

" Smells all right." The policeman lifted the lids off the three dishes. The light was good enough to let him make sure that nothing was being taken in which the prisoner might use—to help himself escape or to do violence ; suicide was the most likely form of escape. " You're new, aren't you? "

" Days, mostly. I'm doing a special turn to-night."

The warder laughed.

" Okay."

The waiter went inside. The building was badly lighted, bare, but not like a prison ; the remand " cells " were plainly furnished rooms with low ceilings. Another warder, a tall, gangling man with drooping eyelids, approached the waiter.

" Who for? "

" Mr. Delaney."

" Okay." The warder led the way, jangling his keys. A prisoner had a midget radio on, playing softly ; it wasn't allowed, but there were ways and means, according to the station in life of the prisoner ; you just didn't hear that music if you were on the staff. The warder unlocked the door of Delaney's room, and as he did so, a constable appeared at the end of the passage. He walked smartly along, as the waiter went inside followed by the warder.

The warder would watch every movement, make sure that nothing but the food passed from waiter to prisoner.

Delaney sat in an easy-chair. He was a young Adonis : fair, blue eyed, slim, dressed well—almost an exquisite. His expression spoiled his good looks ; he was frowning, and looked as if he were suffering physical pain. He didn't look up as the waiter approached the small table and began to lay the cloth. A cigarette drooped from his lips, and his eyes were closed; he had long, curling lashes, as fair as his hair.

The constable turned into the room.

" Now what? " asked the warder.

" Mr. Carnody sent me from the Yard," said the constable easily. Carnody was a Yard Superintendent who dealt most frequently with Brixton. " Just seen old Do-Do. He said you could tell me what I want. About him." He nodded casually towards the drooping prisoner.

" Just you wait a minute," said the warder.

" Okay, okay." The policeman unbuttoned the breast pocket of his tunic, and with a surprisingly swift, comprehensive glance looked up and down the passage. No one else was in sight. He drew out what looked like a white pencil, and the warder watched the waiter. Not that there seemed anything to worry about; Delaney was as dejected as usual, he seemed to know that he hadn't a chance.

" Now," said the policeman.

" Shut up," said the warder, and turned his head.

The policeman broke the white " pencil " across the other's chin and drove a terrific punch into his stomach. The warder gasped and doubled up; and tear gas, billowing up in a whitish cloud, stung his mouth, nose, and eyes. As he staggered back, the waiter snatched a gas-mask from his pocket and tossed it to Delaney.

" Put that on—quick! "

Delaney gaped.

" *Put it on.*" The waiter slipped a mask over his own face, the constable did the same with swift, practised movements. The waiter helped Delaney with his. The policeman bent over the warder and struck him on the nape of the neck with a length of rubber; the man stopped spluttering and struggling, but wheezed badly.

The waiter said in a muffled voice: " *Get your top clothes off*," and tugged at Delaney's coat sleeve.

Delaney jumped to it then; behind the mica of the goggles, his eyes blazed. The constable pulled off the warder's tunic and trousers, tossed them to the waiter, who helped Delaney into them.

The transformation took four minutes.

The waiter hissed: "Just follow me. If you see any one, grunt good night. Don't look 'em in the face. As soon as you're outside, pull on a cigarette. Get it?"

"Yes."

"Ready then."

There wasn't time for Delaney to get scared. The policeman took off his mask, opened the door and stepped outside; there was no one in the passage. The others followed, tucking their masks inside their coats. The waiter went ahead, carrying his tray and whistling cheerfully. Delaney followed. The uniform was loose, but didn't look too bad a fit. The policeman walked ponderously in their rear. At the corner, they met a man in civilian clothes, who nodded. "Good night," grunted Delaney. "'Night, sir!" said the waiter. The policeman saluted. But he stayed by the corner, to see where the man in civilian clothes was going. If to Delaney's room, the alarm would soon be raised.

The man passed Delaney's room.

The pseudo-constable hurried on.

The warders on duty at the remand-quarters door had this open by the time the waiter appeared, still whistling. The constable called: "Have you seen Do-Do?" Do-Do was the nickname for the Chief Warder, anyone who knew that had a kind of a password. The warders turned their attention to the constable, and Delaney passed; he was trembling violently.

The cold night air struck at him. The waiter hissed: "*Cigarette*." The pseudo-constable stayed behind, still talking to the warders. The men on duty at the gates unlocked them. "*Nighty-night!*" called the waiter briskly. He slowed down, and Delaney caught up with him, cupping his hands about his cigarette. "'*Night*."

He passed through the gates and turned in the wake of

the waiter. The gates didn't clang; the warders looked
out along the street.

"*Don't look back. Don't run.*" The waiter's voice
floated back over his shoulder, and Delaney tried to stop
himself from trembling, and walked normally. They
reached the corner and the gates clanged.

.   .   .   .   .

Roger felt Delaney's hands and body shaking.

"Take it easy," he said.

They were in the fast car, half a mile from Brixton
and no alarm had been raised. The waiter and the girl
were now in the muddy grey Morris, which was still parked
along the road. This car, a Buick, leapt along.

"You'll be all right. Your wife has fixed this. There's
an aeroplane waiting to take you out of the country.
Everything's fixed—just sit back and don't stare out of the
window."

There was little traffic on a Sunday night, and no need
to go through the West End. Roger kept strictly down to
the speed limit of thirty miles an hour while he was in the
built-up area. Policeman, people, cars, and buses passed
them, cinema lights glowed; but soon they were in the
suburbs and on the main arterial road. Roger opened
out. Delaney, who hadn't uttered a word, said: "Who
—who are you?"

"Never mind."

"Where are we going?"

"Airfield, near Watford."

"Are you sure——"

"There's a whisky flask in the dashboard pocket.
Have a good nip. Yes, I'm sure. You'll be out of the
country in two hours, and your wife will be with you."

Delaney kept the bottle to his lips long enough to drain
the flask. He didn't speak again. Roger watched the
telegraph wires and poles flashing by. He'd altered his
original plans in only one way; he'd driven along this
road the previous night, so as to become familiar with
it, and didn't need a passenger for a guide. They turned
off the main road and drove up a hill. The lights of

Watford stretched out in front of them, tiny glims in the darkness. They reached the airfield, where two aeroplanes, both small, were warming up. A flare glowed like a torch of liberty.

Beneath a tiny hangar, Mrs. Delaney waited. The pilot of their aircraft called: " You ready? " Two or three other people watched from the surrounding darkness, Roger felt their gaze, but didn't look round. Was Kennedy here? Or Percy? He felt the keen wind as he opened the door. Delaney got out the other side, and his wife rushed towards him.

" Save it! " snapped Roger. " Get in."

She turned towards him, and there was just enough light to show her beauty and the glow in her eyes. She thrust a thick packet into his hands.

" Thank you."

" Hurry! "

He watched them climb in; saw the mechanic take the chocks away from the wheels, and stood by the side of the car as the aircraft taxied along the even grassland and then took off. Roger didn't wait any longer, but got back into the car and drove as far as the gates. There, a smaller car was parked with the headlights on.

A man stood by it: Percy.

" Not bad," Percy said. It was the nearest thing to a friendly word that he had uttered.

" Change the number plates of that Buick before you go anywhere," Roger said. " And don't go back along the main road. Risk a late night."

" Think you were followed? "

" I know I wasn't followed. I also know the fantastic coincidences that can catch crooks."

" Okay, okay," said Percy. " Your night out."

.   .   .   .   .   .

No one was in Lyme Street, no one watched from the shadowy doorways. Roger walked briskly from the Strand, and turned into his doorway. As he unlocked the front door he glanced right and left. Now that he was back and it was over, his heart beat like a trip-hammer.

He stepped inside and closed the door, then wiped off the perspiration on his forehead. So often he had waited, at just such a place as this, to catch a crook who believed that he'd been completely successful. He switched on a landing-light, which had another control switch upstairs. The building was silent. He reached his own door—the flat—unlocked it and went inside. It was Harry's night out, and the flat was in darkness. He went from room to room, switching on the lights. Not until he had looked everywhere was he satisfied that the place was empty. He mixed himself a drink, looked at the dish of sandwiches and the plate of smoked salmon laid out for him by Harry, and laughed. He lit a cigarette. Then he caught a glimpse of himself in the mirror. He showed signs of strain ; it had been a bigger ordeal than he had realized, and it wasn't only the risk, it was the *volte face* he had made. Set a cop to fool a cop! He was beginning to see just how much use he could be to Kennedy, yet he knew that this was still only the beginning.

He took the packet which Mrs. Delaney had given him from beneath his coat. It was of brown paper, heavily sealed. He opened it. There were packs of one-pound notes inside, some new, most of them old, all tightly held together by adhesive paper. He counted one pack— a hundred. There were five packs. There was something else, too—a piece of cotton wool, which dropped from the paper and fell at his feet. He picked it up. Something hard was inside it. He unwrapped it, and a single diamond scintillated dazzlingly, the size of a small peanut, worth—he couldn't guess what it was worth.

There was a fortune in crime!

He laughed again, but without mirth, went and washed, then started on the sandwiches—he was ravenous. Half-way through, the telephone bell rang. He had to get up to answer it. He seldom had calls, and they were always from Kennedy or Percy. He lifted the telephone, and was surprised that his own voice was harsh.

"Hallo?"

"Mr. Rayner?"

" Yes, speaking."

The man at the other end hung up without another word—and left his voice ringing in Roger's ears. The voice had been unmistakable: Bill Sloan had called.

Why to-night?

Why now?

.   .   .   .   .

Roger picked up the Sunday newspapers. His own *Times*, *Observer*, and *Express* were there, together with Harry's *Sunday Cry*. He'd seen his own, glanced through the *Cry*—and suddenly stopped breathing.

His photograph—the real West's—looked up at him.

He scanned the article, saw a mention of Copse Cottage, and sat very still.

16

BULL-DOG

THE front-door bell rang.

Sloan couldn't have reached here as quickly as that, even if he'd called from a kiosk nearby. Roger got up, and the bell rang again. He went to it slowly, not worrying about the caller's impatience, searching for any weakness in his own alibi. The girl, if called on, would swear that he had been with her all the evening; everything had been laid on to cover the remotest risk. But Sloan had unnerved him.

The bell started to ring again as he opened the door.

Kennedy said: " Getting lazy? Like someone to replace Harry on his nights off? " He came forward.

Roger barred his way.

" You choose the damnedest times for coming. When you're wanted, you're not here, when you're not wanted you find your way. Is Percy downstairs with the car? "

" No." Kennedy stood on the threshold, too startled

to protest, and worried for the second time since Roger had
known him.   "What's wrong?"

"My bull-dog's biting."

"Talk straight."

"I've just had a call from Detective Inspector Sloan,
and I fancy he's on his way here.   I don't know why he
chose to-night, and I hope the reason isn't what I
think it might be.   If I were you, I'd go into the office,
wait until he's come into this room, and then leave.'"

"I don't think I like your friend Sloan," said Kennedy
in a soft voice.   He glanced over his shoulder towards
the stairs.   There was no sound.   That didn't mean that
Sloan hadn't opened the street door with a skeleton key.
He might be coming up; Sloan could move with uncanny
stealth, and took a lot of chances.

Roger said: "Forget it, Kennedy.   I'll tell you here
and now there's one thing I won't take.   That's violence
against the police."   In spite of his agitation, the significance of that whispered comment had alarmed him.

"Won't you?"

"No.   Get into the office."

"Did he say he was coming here?"

"No, that's why I think he is.   He telephoned.   The
D's have taken off, I can't think of anything that's gone
wrong, except you calling."   The whispered voices
couldn't travel far, but he wondered if Sloan were here
and near enough to see the shadows on the top landing.
"Have you an office key?"

"You like giving orders, don't you, Rayner?   Watch
yourself."

Roger said: "Hurry."

Kennedy crossed the landing and let himself into the
office, making hardly a sound.   Roger went back to the
living-room, put the money and diamond into a drawer,
locked it and pocketed the key, then went slowly downstairs.   He peered into the dark corners of each landing
and the passage; there was no trace of Sloan, and
nowhere the Yard man could hide.   He opened the door
and went into the street and strolled up and down; two
people turned into the street, but neither took any notice

of him or turned into Number 15. Sloan hadn't arrived yet. He withdrew into the doorway and heard a car turn the corner. Headlights blazed and shone on to Number 15, but he dodged back in time to avoid them, left the door unlocked, and went upstairs.

He put on all the lights and was eating another sand- wich when the flat door-bell rang. He let it ring, as with Kennedy, but Sloan wasn't so impatient and didn't ring again. When Roger opened the door, Sloan stood back from it, head on one side, smiling with taut lips.

" Who——" began Roger.

" Remember me? " asked Sloan.

Roger relaxed. " Well, well, it's the policeman who came to my house-warming! Don't you rest on Sundays? "

" Policemen never have any time off."

" Come in and relax," said Roger. He wished the lights weren't so bright; putting all on had been a mis- take. It was easy to understand mistakes which crooks made, now, the list of possible slips was a mile long. He felt a tug of the tension he had experienced when Sloan had first come here, and when he had seen Janet and Mark.

Sloan looked round and tossed his hat into a chair.

" You do yourself well."

" I'm a successful business man. Have a sandwich."

" Thanks." If Sloan had a weakness, it was for food. " You're very affable to-night."

" I've been enjoying myself," Roger said, and grinned.

" You like these unofficial visits, don't you? "

" I never pay calls when I'm off duty, you can call me the man who's always on the job. Yes, you're doing very nicely for yourself, Rayner. I've been checking carefully on your business, and you're obviously pretty smart. I'm a bit worried in case you're too smart."

" For you? "

Sloan grinned and took another sandwich.

" What will you drink? " asked Roger.

" Beer, if there is any."

" Other people besides policemen drink beer." The conversation was too slick. Roger hadn't any idea whether Sloan had come because of the Brixton job, but as his mind roamed restlessly about the possibility, he didn't see where he could have slipped up. He poured beer into a glass tankard and had a gin for himself; gin, because as Roger West, he had never drunk it. He kept his voice hard and spoke with little movement of his lips; he was more afraid of his voice than of anything else, when with Sloan. " What do you want? " he asked.

" That's a leading question. Been places to-night, do you say? "

" A nice little girl," Roger said dreamily. " Sweet and innocent, no intelligence, no questions, a nice little healthy little pleasant little animal. They still grow like that. Do you want to know more about my love life? "

" I didn't think you had any," said Sloan.

There was a weakness in his story, and Sloan had seen it in a flash; he'd not taken a girl out since he had come here, until this afternoon. He laughed easily.

" We have all to begin, you know."

" You're long in the tooth for beginning," Sloan said.

" Supposing you tell me why you want to see me."

" I hope you're in a more talkative mood than the last time."

" You've discovered all you want to know about me, haven't you? "

" Not enough. I don't know all your friends."

" The Kennedy one? " Roger laughed.

" Wrong name, right initial. Remember Mr. Kyle? "

Roger said, " Kyle, Kyle? " He stood his ground, but wanted to sit down. " Kyle—oh, the little crook who came to see me just before you arrived that day. Yes, I remember."

" You've a good memory. Heard from him lately? "

" No."

" Surprising," said Sloan, and grinned. " He carried a slip of paper round in his pocket, with a different name on it, care of the Strand G.P.O. When he was brought in last, that piece of paper turned up. I went and collected a letter addressed to the alias from the Post Office. There was nothing written inside, but there were ten pound notes. Are you a philanthropist? "

"Not yet."

"Did you send that money to him?"

"No. Ask him."

"I didn't have time," Sloan said. He was watching intently, and would notice the slightest change of expression. He gave Roger a half-puzzled, half-impatient look. "Don't you know what happens to your friends?"

"He wasn't a friend of mine. He——"

"Friends of yours are liable to die suddenly, aren't they? By accident?"

"So he's dead!" said Roger, and frowned. "What do you expect me to do? Cry about a man I've only seen once in my life, and didn't want to see again?"

"What about the girl?"

Roger poured himself out another gin, refilled Sloan's tankard, and hoped he was as casual as he ought to be. "I don't follow? The girl I've just left——"

"No, not her. Marion Day."

Sloan wasn't really doing well, and his approach was puzzling. He was giving more away than a good policeman should—and he was a good policeman. He had chosen to come on a Sunday night because it was the least likely time for a detective to call, and that was good tactics—but apart from that, he was being too clever. He did nothing without a reason, so there was a reason for this.

Roger said slowly: "Marion Day? No, it doesn't ring a bell."

Sloan laughed, spontaneously; there was nothing at all sinister about it.

"Ringing a bell is good." He took a photograph from his pocket—of Marion. He thrust it forward under Roger's nose. "Have a good look."

Roger said: "I've seen her before, somewhere, but I don't remember where, just now. I don't know her well."

"You will, if you ever join her," said Sloan cryptically. "Either someone is storing up a lot of trouble for you, or you're storing it up for youself." He came forward and looked hard into Roger's eyes. "There was a telephone number with that alias of Kyle's—*Temple Bar*

89511. Your office number. There was a telephone number in that girl's handbag—*T.B. 89511.* Can you explain either?"

"Kyle, possibly because he'd been here, and might have wanted to try again. The girl——" Roger shook his head, but felt tension rising. The machine of the law, which he had invoked so often and taken so much for granted, was grinding slowly but surely. "No, there's no reason why she should have the number. There's one thing you've probably overlooked."

"What?"

"There are eleven people in my office. One of them might be involved—might be a friend of these people. I wouldn't know."

"I'll find out," said Sloan. "In fact I'm finding out, Rayner. These two people were killed by accident, if you believe the coroner, but I don't always agree with inquest verdicts." He finished his beer and took out cigarettes from a familiar yellow packet. Roger took one. "Remember the Copse Cottage murder?" Sloan asked, and his eyes were close to Roger's above the flame of his lighter.

It wasn't fair; the dice were loaded against Sloan. The slight pause, the nonchalance of manner, were preliminaries to a rapier thrust; strangers wouldn't know, but Sloan had learned the trick from Roger.

"There are so many murders," Roger said. "And I'm not a policeman, I don't like sordid life. Copse Cottage—no. Well, vaguely. How long ago was it?"

Sloan said: "Say a couple of months."

"Murderer still free?"

"Yes. A girl was battered out of recognition. Her killer escaped, and that was quite a sensation, because he was kidnapped from the police. A clever, daring job, which proved that a gang was involved. You wouldn't know anything about criminal gangs, would you?"

"Plenty. I read my newspapers."

Sloan said harshly: "You're just that much too clever. Ever used the name of Kennedy?"

"No."

"Sure? Don't lie to me, it won't do you any good in the long run."

Roger said: "You had this silly notion before. No, I have never used the name Kennedy, and I don't propose to. If I ever need an *alias*, that's the last one I'd choose, I should hate to vindicate you. Relax, tell me what all this is about."

Sloan's eyes were hard; they always were when he wasn't preparing a thrust.

"You'll never use an *alias* in the future, we'll watch you too closely."

"For five minutes." Sloan, with that tell-tale glitter in his eyes, was going farther than he should, making oblique threats to try to throw a scare into him; it was a dangerous mood. "You seem sure that I'm mixed up in some crooked business, and as a policeman, it's your job to make sure. Go ahead and make sure. I've nothing much to hide."

"Nothing *much*?"

Roger laughed. "That's what I said, work it out for yourself."

Sloan said: "I will. Your firm had offices at Leadenhall Street before you came here, didn't you?"

"Yes."

"I can't find anyone who worked near those offices who remembers you."

"I didn't take over in person until we got here."

"Where did you get your money from to buy the business from Kennedy?"

Roger said: "I hypnotized him into letting me have it, and he didn't have a chance. It wasn't from anyone named Kennedy, anyhow, it was from a Samuel Wiseman. I still don't see where all this is getting, Mr. Policeman."

Sloan shrugged and turned to pick up his tankard—danger flared again.

"This is just the preliminary stage, I'm making my man uneasy. What did you do before you bought this business?"

"I made a small fortune in Africa. People still can."

That was in the records Kennedy had provided of his past.

"I'll check that, too," said Sloan. "When you were in Africa, or after you came back, did you ever have a visit from Chief Inspector West?"

17

CAUSE FOR ALARM

ROGER had sensed a thrust coming and had his defences up. They weren't strong enough to withstand that. He jerked his head up. Sloan grinned; Sloan had never seemed so sinister. Roger didn't answer. Sloan moved towards him and put a hand on his shoulder and pressed hard; it was a familiar grip used when a policeman was going to charge a man, and enjoy doing it.

"So you did," said Sloan.

Roger said: "No, I didn't have a call from West." He forced a laugh. "But that name startled me. I was reading an article about him in to-day's *Cry*." That was true enough, but was it a get out? Sloan looked disappointed, and took his hand away, but that didn't mean that it was safe to breathe freely. "He disappeared, after—great Scott! The Copse Cottage murder!"

"Which you didn't remember, although you read about it this afternoon."

Roger said: "The article was about West, the murder was hardly mentioned. Another drink?"

"No, thanks. Sure you've never seen West?"

"He's never called on me, you're the first policeman I've met at close quarters." Roger offered cigarettes, and Sloan took one and examined the tip thoughtfully. "I still don't know what you're getting at."

Sloan said softly: "Roger West was a good friend of mine."

"Was he?"

"That canard in the *Cry* isn't worth the paper its written on. Oh, it doesn't say anything openly, but it makes a pretty broad hint. West was a *very* good friend of mine. I think he was trapped and killed and his name smeared with muck, and I've just one job in my spare time—finding out the truth of that."

" You'd better find the writer of that article."

" I can find him whenever I want him," said Sloan.

" Pity you can't say the same about your friend."

" Yes," said Sloan heavily. " Listen to me, Rayner. I've spent a lot of time checking on your past and what you do. I haven't found anything much against you. I'll tell you something that I wouldn't if I were here officially to-night. I like the cut of your jib. I don't think you're a bad 'un, and I can smell bad 'uns. You might be mixed up in something which you don't know about. The man who owned this business wasn't Wiseman, but a certain Mr. Kennedy. I think Kennedy can tell me something about West."

Was this the moment for a question?

Roger said : " You get odd ideas, but I can't speak for Kennedy. I dealt with Wiseman."

" That isn't an odd idea, it's a sane one. If you come across Kennedy, warn him that I'm after him."

" Unofficially? "

" Please yourself," said Sloan. He half-turned in preparation for another thrust. " Rayner, I've just come from West's wife. She's pathetic. She's afraid that he's dead, but she doesn't know for certain. She's frightened by things she can't understand. She's had a lot of that *Cry* muck poured into her, and it hurts her like hell. She knows what I know about West—there wasn't a straighter man living. I'm going to scrape the mud off West's name somehow. If you're smeared with that mud, look out. If you're not——"

Roger said : " I'm sorry for his wife." He didn't know how he got the words out, but Sloan didn't seem to notice any oddness in the sound of his voice. Sloan might be foxing or, but more likely, had been carried away with his own emotions.

" All right," Sloan said. " Tell your friend Kennedy what I've said."

He went to the door. Roger let him out.

* * * * * *

Roger closed the door and went back to the sitting-room and saw nothing except the image of Janet's face, superimposed on memory of Sloan's. He felt choked with emotion. His eyes stung, his hands were clammy. He sat down and leaned back in his chair and stared at the ceiling and at that image. It wasn't a help to know that Sloan kept faith; nothing was a help. He didn't think of Kennedy or of the questions for a long time.

Then he opened his eyes. The sight of sandwiches nauseated him. He poured himself out a strong whisky and soda.

His mind began to work at last, slowly.

It was a waste of time trying to guess how and why Sloan had so quickly connected Kyle, Marion, and Kennedy with him. He could see the build-up in Sloan's mind; add to that Sloan's tenacity, and in this case his burning desire to get at the truth, and it was all the explanation needed. By far the most important factor was the fact that Sloan had reason to suspect Kennedy.

Again, it was a waste of time to speculate how he'd reached that point.

Roger got up, took the money and the diamond out of the drawer and locked it in the small safe. He knew that Sloan had forced the pace. He himself had played cautiously for as long as he dared. Kennedy was half-way to trusting him. He had never done a thing, since Kyle's visit, to cause distrust. He was no longer followed everywhere, but in spite of that, he hadn't put a foot wrong. He'd have to start soon, and the first task was to find Kennedy's home address.

As he was turning away, the telephone bell rang. It was Kennedy, who said casually:

" Well ? "

" I must see you." That rasping note should shake the other's composure.

" I'll come——"

" You won't, you're to keep away from here. Get that into your head. Where are you ? "

" I'll meet you——"

" Listen," said Roger, " I'm not a stooge any longer,

I'm a partner. We take the same risks, by relying on each other. I'm not going on with hole-in-corner business. Where are you?"

Kennedy said: "Percy will pick you up in half an hour's time, outside the Burlington Arcade. He'll bring you to me."

. . . . .

Roger went into the kitchen, tore some paper into squares, and, with steady hands, shook a little flour out of a tin into each square. Then he screwed the pieces of paper up; he had a dozen little screws when he'd finished. He wiped all trace of the flour away, and put the bags, wrapped in a large handkerchief, into his pocket.

. . . . .

Percy was at the wheel of the Daimler, and didn't get out. Roger climbed in. The car moved off swiftly, and the blinds fell, with the familiar whirring; no, Kennedy wasn't ready to take him on trust. Roger opened the side ventilation window, and waited until the car had turned two corners, then tossed one of the small screws of flour out. He waited for three more turns, and tossed another.

The journey took fifteen minutes, and he didn't think they had gone farther than five minutes away from the Arcade; Percy had been driving over the same ground. As they slowed down, he dropped out another paper-bag.

Percy opened the door without letting up the blinds, Roger glanced up and down the dark street. Except that it was one of London's spacious squares, he couldn't identify it, and they were not near a corner or a name-plate. He glanced down at the pavement; the little white bag had burst ten yards or so away, the flour showed pale blue beneath a lamp. There was no white dusting on the Daimler's wing.

He followed Percy to the house and saw that the number painted on a round pillar was twenty-seven. A sleek manservant opened the door; Kennedy lived in style. Percy came in and, without a word, took him upstairs. It was luxurious: carpets, tapestries on the walls,

good furniture and soft lighting—the home you would
expect of a millionaire. Percy led the way to a room
on the right, tapped and opened it at a call.

It was a study; a beautiful room, book lined, with a
magnificent carved-oak desk; a film set of a room falling
just short of opulence. Kennedy stood by a white Adam
mantelpiece, with a brandy glass in his hand and his eyes
only slightly open. He tipped his head back to look at
Roger.

"All right, Percy," he said.

He was in a dinner-jacket. A cigar, half-smoked, lay
on an ash-tray on the mantelpiece. On another, at the
side of a chair, was a half-smoked cigarette; it was
red-tipped, so a woman had been here to dinner. There
was a faint smell of perfume, noticeable in spite of the
aroma of the cigar.

The door closed with a click.

"What's the cause for alarm, West?"

The slip, West instead of Rayner, betrayed Kennedy's
state of nerves; betrayed the fact that beneath Kennedy's
calmness there was an ordinary jittery man. The smile
didn't hide it, but if Kennedy realized what he had done,
he had the wit not to correct himself.

Roger said: "Why didn't you tell me you were wanted
by the police?"

Kennedy said softly: "But I'm not, and you know I'm
not. You had a previous visit from Sloan, and he slung
the name Kennedy into the conversation. Has he been
at it again?"

"He's after you," Roger said abruptly. "What's
more, he's connected you with Kyle, Marion, and—with
me. Don't ask me how."

Kennedy turned, took the cigar and drew at it, took it
from his mouth and looked at the faint red glow beneath
the pale-grey ash. He was quite steady.

"I should like to hear more about it."

"You can listen to your dictaphone recording in the
morning," Roger said roughly. Kennedy let it pass. "I
thought I was the big risk in this outfit. Now I know that
you are. Have the police got anything on you?"

" They've a name, that's all. You know me as Kennedy. A few other people do. I'm not known here as Kennedy. That isn't my name. I'm careful, Rayner." He slipped back into the use of Rayner easily. " They don't know anything against Kennedy. They might suspect him of a few minor crimes, that's all. There's no need to fly into a panic."

" Call it what you like. This is dangerous."

Kennedy said slowly: " Yes, up to a point. It still isn't dangerous for me. I don't think Sloan has anything but suspicions about this man he knows as Kennedy. I I don't see how he can have. Was it an official call? "

" No. His spare-time job is looking for the man he thinks murdered his friend West."

" And he appealed to you for help."

" He came to warn me that I was playing with bad men when I played with Kennedy."

Kennedy said: " Perhaps he thinks you're honest! " He laughed, but didn't seem to be amused. " I've always been worried by the man Sloan, he got on to Kyle too quickly. He was after the men behind Kyle, of course, that's——"

" How the police get half of their results. They pick up a man on one thing, and find he's connected with another. They're much better than you've ever given them credit for."

Kennedy said: " Maybe. Would Sloan have a dossier on you, this Kennedy, and anything else to do with the case? "

" Not an official one."

" That's no answer."

" He'd keep a record, probably in his desk—more likely there than at his home. Few policemen keep everything in their heads. They never know what they'll forget—and they never know when they might run into trouble, so they leave their testimony behind them. Sloan usually kept his note-book in his desk."

" Would he talk to anyone about this? "

" I doubt it."

" Why? "

" He hasn't any close friends at the Yard. He's young
—young for his rank, too. He and I were usually together
on a job. He'd confide in me. And on this job, he's
more likely than usual to keep it to himself, because I'm at
the bottom of it. He'd feel that the others were laughing
at him for thinking I'd been framed—most of them have
probably assumed the worst by now, that I killed the girl
at Copse Cottage."

Kennedy drew at the cigar again.

" I see. Have a drink, Rayner? I can recommend
the brandy, or——"

" I wouldn't mind a whisky."

" Please yourself." Kennedy poured out. " Do you
know of anyone at the Yard you could bribe, Rayner? "

The question wasn't a surprise, it was no more than
Roger had to expect. He took the glass and didn't answer.

" Do you? " The other's voice was thin and harsh, and
his eyes, wide open now, were like white fire.

He *had* to win Kennedy's confidence; there was no
drawing back, now.

" I wouldn't like to say. There are one or two I didn't
trust, but I doubt if they'd sell anything that mattered.
We had our black sheep, though. There's one——" he
broke off and gulped down his whisky. " No, you're
crazy! The Brixton job was bad enough. Corrupting a
Yard man——"

" You wouldn't have to do it. The man who'd tackle
the job would be prepared for trouble. He'd be safe
enough from our side. But it might take him six months
to find the right prospect. This is just another way you
can help me, Rayner—*and* help yourself."

Roger shrugged. " I can't guarantee anything."

" Who is the man you've got in mind? "

" Well—Detective Sergeant—— "

" Small fry," sneered Kennedy. " Do better."

" He's your best bet. You can't get at the high rankers
—I'll stake my life on any one of them. This man, Sergeant Banister, is an old chap. He's had a raw deal. He
has a damning habit of antagonizing his seniors, especially
Assistant Commissioners, and he's failed at most of his

exams. He's good, but he can't get promotion and the accompanying pay increase, and he has a rough time at home. His wife's on the sick list—a chronic invalid. I don't know how far he would go, but he's your most likely prospect. What do you want?"

"Sloan's desk note-book."

"What else?"

"Anything about the Copse Cottage murder, you, Kyle, Kennedy, and Marion—dossiers on them all. They're easy enough to get for a man inside, aren't they?"

Roger said: "They should be. They might be out— that means with the Assistant Commissioner, the Home Office, or one of the Superintendents. That wouldn't be for long, but if Banister played ball, he might not be able to get everything for a few days. There's a big snag in your notion."

"What is it?"

"Once the dossiers were missed, the Yard would make a grand slam against the people covered by them. It would become the one job that mattered. Sloan's proved that he's guessed plenty, and there must have been indications which others have seen. You'd be surprised what happens when those experts really put their heads together. They know all the tricks, all the answers."

"I wouldn't want the papers for long; just long enough for them to be photolithoed."

Roger said: "Well, try Banister. Don't say I haven't warned you."

"I won't." Kennedy laughed—that curious laugh with his head back, and his whole body shaking. "Beginning to see what a tower of strength you are to me? I've often wondered how much they've got on certain friends of mine. This will help me to find out."

Roger said: "All right. Only remember what I told you."

"You tell me so much."

"No violence—with Sloan or anyone else."

"I know where to stop," said Kennedy. He looked earnest—until Roger glanced round at him from the door, five minutes later. Kennedy was grinning; at the thought of what was going to happen to Bill Sloan. This was like playing with T.N.T. The footman closed the door. Roger crossed the landing, and another door opened. A woman, small, chic, beautiful, looked straight at him. She wore a dinner-gown of black with lace half-revealing her shoulders and the gentle swell of her breast; she wore a tulle scarf, which wisped up at the back of her head. Her hair was corn-coloured; lovely. She didn't smile, but withdrew and closed the door.

Percy was waiting outside in the street.

" Where do you want dropping? " he asked.

" The same place will do."

" Not going home? "

" No."

Percy shrugged; Roger got in. A small car parked farther along the road moved after them. He didn't see it, once he was inside, because the blinds were down, but it was still behind them when he was dropped in Picca-dilly. He walked slowly towards the Circus. It was a fine, starry night, with no wind. The lights of London were on again, and the Circus looked gay with the moving fantasy of the advertisements and the garish display out-side the cinemas.

A man followed him.

He made no attempt to avoid the man, but walked to his flat. He went upstairs and switched on the light, then went cautiously down again. The man was loung-ing in a doorway, opposite. So Kennedy—who *wasn't* really Kennedy—had told Percy that the red light was on; Kennedy was making quite sure that Roger didn't try any tricks. The telephone was tapped, of course. If he'd made a mistake it was in telling Kennedy that he knew of the dictaphones; but Kennedy had probably already realized that he knew. The risk, the great, almost unforgivable risk, was with Sloan.

Sloan was marked down for murder as surely as Lucille had been.

When?

To-night? Possibly to-night, but not if he stayed in-doors; this would be another accident, not open murder.

Roger stood in front of the telephone, undecided. He could switch off the dictaphone, but a different contraption might be fitted to the telephone itself. He suspected that the other offices in the building were owned by Kennedy, but wasn't sure. He mustn't take a risk with that telephone.

How long would the guard remain outside?

He went back upstairs, sorted through a small tool-box in the kitchen, selected several, including a key that would serve as a pick-lock, and then remembered Harry; Harry was usually in by eleven o'clock on his nights off; it was now nearly ten, and an hour wasn't enough for what Roger wanted to do. He would take a chance by waiting until Harry came back; probably Harry would take over from the man on guard outside. Roger picked up a book and began to read, but couldn't concentrate; yet he was past constructive thinking, anxiety was nagging too painfully. He switched on the radio; there was hymn singing. He listened for five minutes, and switched off. He read the *Cry* article again. He didn't like it; he didn't like seeing the names of Janet, Scoopy, and Richard in print.

Then he heard Harry's key in the lock.

Harry walked in, smiling sombrely, asked if there were anything Roger wanted, and went to bed; he had a small room which wasn't included in the main rooms of the flat. Roger waited until the man had had time to undress and get into bed, then went into his own room, adjacent. He hummed to himself as he ran water from the tap, did everything as if he were going to retire. He switched on a small radio; there was dance music. He took fifty pound notes from the safe, then put on a pair of shoes with rubber soles and heels, wrapped up the tools and dropped them into his pocket, switched off the radio, and crept out.

At the front door he paused, to look towards Harry's door. A line of light showed underneath, but he heard no sound of movement. As an afterthought, he went into the living-room, tore a piece of gummed paper off the wrapping of Mrs. Delaney's package, and marked it with a pencil. He stuck this at the foot of his door, sealing door to frame. If Harry looked in to see if he were there, the paper would be broken and he would be warned.

He crept downstairs.

Harry hadn't replaced the guard; the man was still huddled in the doorway.

Roger turned to the ground-floor office of the building and worked on the door with his tools. The lock wasn't difficult, a policeman could crack a crib with any man if the need were great enough. He fiddled for five minutes before the lock clicked back. There were tell-tale signs at the door, marks of the tools, but they probably wouldn't be noticed if nothing were stolen. He crept across a large office to the window which overlooked the yard— as did his office upstairs. The window was latched. He unfastened it and pushed the window up, climbed out into the concrete yard and then closed the window. He did everything with great deliberation. He went to a narrow service alley which led to the next street. He walked past the end of Lyme Street and saw the guard, and then averted his eyes quickly, for Percy swung round the corner in the Daimler.

Was he checking up?

Why not telephone, if that were all?

The Daimler pulled up in front of the watcher, who hurried to it and climbed in. The Daimler moved off and was lost in the streets near Covent Garden. That was conclusive proof that Kennedy relied on Harry to keep a watch on Roger at the flat; and with luck, Harry thought he was in bed. He needed luck. But he had never done anything to arouse Harry's suspicions and had made no attempt at independent action until to-night. He had to do a lot to-night.

The tools were heavy in his pocket as he went along the Strand, then into a side street where he knew there were telephone booths.

He dialled Sloan's private number.

He felt shivery as he did that, and as the *brrr-brrr* sounded. Was Sloan out? The ringing tone seemed unending. If Sloan were out, then he might run into trouble. *Brrr-brrr.* Sloan mustn't be out, and it was too early for him to be in bed. *Brrr-kk.*

"Hallo?"

Roger schooled his voice. Sloan might guess it was Rayner, but he couldn't be sure.

"Mr. Sloan?"

"Yes."

"I'm warning you, Mr. Sloan. They're after you."

"Who——"

"Use your wits. There'll be an attack. Maybe a rundown. It'll come quick. I'm warning you, Mr. Sloan."

"Listen! Who——"

"I've warned you, just look out. And there's another thing, Mr. Sloan."

"Well?" Sloan had stopped expecting to be told the name of his caller.

"Remember the Copse Cottage job. Girl you never traced. Have a try in Paris. 23 Rue de Croix, District 8. Got that?"

"23 Rue de Croix, 8. Yes. Will you——"

"It's the same job, and they mean to get you."

Roger rang off and slipped out of the box. That was as far as he dare go; farther than was safe. He laughed to himself as a little ragged bundle of a woman, passing him towards one of the nearby doss-houses, stared at him in surprise and then whined: "Spare a bob, mister." He laughed again and dropped half a crown into her hand. He knew her; she had been at Bow Street on "under the influence" charges fifty times while he had been at the Yard. He walked to the Strand and beckoned a taxi from the rank near the Savoy.

"Do you know Ealing?"

"Palm of me 'and, brother!"

"Try and find Merrivale Avenue, will you?"

"Orf the Common, 'seasy. There an' back?"

"With a wait in between."

"Okay. It'll cost yer the world." The cabby laughed his joke off. Roger sat back, legs crossed, watching the

passing lights, letting his thoughts roam. A great deal
depended on whether he got back without being missed.
He smoked two cigarettes, and was half-way through a
third when the cabby slowed down near Ealing Common
Station.

" What number, Merrivale? "

" Thirty-five."

" Okay."

Number 35 Merrivale Avenue was a small house, standing in a tiny patch of garden, which even under the light
of the stars, looked neat and tidy. No lights were on;
it was now nearly half-past eleven, and there were few
lighted windows in the long street. Roger rang the bell,
and waited; rang again and knocked immediately
afterwards. ·

A light went on, footsteps sounded on the stairs.

The man coming was Pep Morgan, who knew Roger
West well; once, had known him very well indeed. He
ran a private inquiry agency, was shrewd and cautious
as well as clever, and seldom risked a clash with the
police. He opened the door, a ball of a man wrapped in
a thick dressing-gown. His sparse hair was awry, and
his nose and mouth were screwed up in annoyance. He
squeaked:

" What the hell do you want? "

" Your services," said Roger. " Fifty pounds for a job
that's not worth ten."

" Who are you? "

" I'll tell you when we're inside, maybe," said Roger.
He squeezed past the round ball as a woman called out
from upstairs: " Pep. Who is it, Pep? "

" Just a client, m'dear, just a client." Pep closed the
door and put on the light of a front room. He had
bright-brown eyes, from which all traces of sleepiness had
vanished. He eyed Roger closely. " I don't know you,"
he said.

" I hope you never will." Roger took the fifty pounds
from his pocket and put it on top of a small upright piano.
Pep hardly glanced towards it. " This is a simple job,
there's no risk, and there's nothing illegal, but it's urgent.

First thing in the morning—if you can't do it earlier!—
I want you to arrange for a man on a bicycle to start from
the Burlington Arcade, take the first right and then the
second left—got it? "

" I'll write it down." There was a pad and pencil
near the telephone. Pep's stubby fingers moved swiftly.
" Yes? "

" And around there he'll find traces of flour, which
was dropped from a passing car. There are more traces,
in different streets, usually at corners—always at corners,
except one place. That's a few doors from a house
numbered twenty-seven. The number of the house is
painted in black on a cream, fluted column."

Pep wrote swiftly. " Yes? "

" I want to know the name of the street and the name
of the owner of the house—just that and no more. As
soon as you've got it, leave word at your office. A Mr.
Brown will call you, probably about lunch-time—all he
wants is that name and full address. All clear? "

" What's worth fifty pounds? "

" Being hauled out of bed."

Pep rubbed his button of a nose. " Okay," he said.

.   .   .   .   .   .

Roger went back the way he had come—through the
window of the downstairs office, so that he could latch the
window and lessen the risk that signs of intrusion would be
noticed. He locked the passage door with the skeleton
key and went quietly upstairs.

The piece of gummed paper at the foot of his door was
still in one piece; so Harry hadn't realized that he had
been out. He ripped it off, went in, closed the door
gently, and then sat down in an easy-chair. He felt
shivery hot, but that didn't last for long. When he
started to get ready for bed, he felt more light-hearted
than he had for weeks.

Sloan could look after himself now.

Couldn't he?

18

SLOAN

BILL SLOAN tapped his silver pencil against his strong white teeth as he skimmed through the notes he had made on what he called *The West Disappearance*. These notes were kept jealously, for his eyes alone. They contained a précis of everything he had done in the past two months in his quest for Roger. They showed that he had spent every spare minute of his time on the hunt; it had become an obsession. They showed that he had worked with Mark Lessing, but not consulted any official at the Yard. He had taken the extreme precaution of buying a diary with a lock on it, so that no prodnose could glance through and see where he had probed, what lines he worked on. There were references to Kennedy—a name only—Kyle, Marion Day, and several others, all cryptic; nothing was evidence in a legal sense.

He locked the book, put it away, and pressed a bell on his desk. He shared the big office with five other D.I.'s, but none of them was in. None had seen the book.

A middle-aged man with florid face, straggly grey moustache, barrel-shaped figure, and sullen, disappointed eyes came in. He let the door slam behind him.

"Want me?" he asked gruffly as he approached the desk. He was slovenly dressed. His brown suit needed not only pressing but also cleaning. His hair needed cutting. He looked as if he thought the world were against him, and had an almost furtive expression in his cloudy blue eyes.

Sloan said: "Yes, Banister. Do you know if the Assistant Commissioner is in?"

"Yes, I know the old—yes, he's in." Banister bit on his comment, and evaded Sloan's eyes.

"Been after you again?" asked Sloan.

"He's always after me. Everyone's—oh, forget it."

"All right, that's all," said Sloan. He watched the

sergeant go out; the door slammed again, indicating that
Banister was in a foul temper. Sloan leaned back in his
chair for a few minutes, forgetting West and the A.C.—
that was, forgetting West as nearly as he could. He was
recalling a conversation he'd had with Roger, at Roger's
Bell Street house, a week or two before the disappearance.
Roger had started it.

" Happy about Banister, Bill? "

" Can anyone be? The scales are pretty heavily
weighted against him."

" I didn't mean that."

" What did you mean? " Sloan knew, but wanted it
put into words.

" Would you trust him with much? "

" Well—I've no reason not to, but if I wanted anything
kept right under my hat, I wouldn't chose him to hold my
hat for me."

" That's what I mean," Roger had said.

Roger——

The Yard was full of Roger; his face, his brisk walk,
his crisp confidence, his unorthodoxy, his daring, his
friendliness. There hadn't been a man at the Yard so
often in the middle of trouble, and caring nothing for
personalities or position; only results mattered. If he
liked a man, he shared everything. Sloan owed his quick
promotion to Roger; he felt lost and out on a limb ever
since he'd gone. The odd hint here, a suggestion there,
a chat over a difficult case—Sloan had trained himself
largely on Roger West. Admiration and respect had
grown into confidence and friendship. He was probably
the last man at the Yard who still believed that Roger was
alive; and who believed the sun more likely to fail to rise
than Roger to become corrupt.

He jumped up, and hurried along to the Assistant Commissioner's office. Had he telephoned for permission it
would probably never have been granted. Chatworth
seldom had time for D.I.'s except on a specific case.

Chatworth growled:

" Come in."

" Morning, sir! " Sloan was bright and brisk.

" What do you want? " Chatworth glowered; so it was a bad moment to have chosen. But he didn't say: " Go away! "

He was a big, burly man with grizzled grey hair and a shiny bald patch, a brown, tough, weather-beaten face, which in moments of affability became almost cherubic; then one could see the essential simplicity of the man. He was dressed in green homespun tweeds, and his blue collar was two sizes too large for him, his pink tie badly knotted. He looked like a farmer in a beauty *salon*; for the office was all chromium, glass, and tubular steel, spick and span—cold, unfriendly. No one quite knew how Chatworth had managed to get the Office of Works to make him such an office; his intimates knew that the study at his Victoria flat was furnished on identical lines.

" Can you spare me a few minutes, sir? "

Chatworth might growl " no " and leave it at that; or tell him that if he wanted an interview he should apply through the proper channels. Or he might——

" What about? "

" A personal matter, sir. "

" Come in and sit down." Chatworth pointed to a chair. Sloan sat in it stiffly, feeling on edge, knowing that Roger, in his place, would relax and light a cigarette and not care a hoot what the A.C. thought. That was not simply the difference between a C.I. and a D.I., but the difference between two men.

Chatworth read on for two or three minutes. Then he pushed the papers away, made notes with a slim gold pencil, and at last looked up. The cherub in him appeared. He smiled, showing small teeth, and moved a silver cigarette-box across the black glass of his desk.

" Have a cigarette, Sloan. What's it all about? "

" I'm scared, sir." That was the kind of introduction Roger would have advocated as being sure to grip the A.C.'s attention. Chatworth raised a bushy eyebrow.

" Oh? What about? "

" I've had a warning which I think I ought to take seriously—that there is likely to be an attack on my life in the next day or two."

" Whose corns have you been treading on ? "

" It's a long story, sir, and——"

Chatworth's eyes sparkled, and were frosty.

" Anything to do with West ? "

Roger would have expected that. Sloan hadn't. He gulped, smoke got mixed up with his larynx and he coughed and spluttered. Chatworth tapped the gold pencil on the glass top, and it made an irritating sharp sound—evidence of his own irritation and perhaps of something more.

" Well, is it ? "

" In its way, yes. I——"

" Been devoting a lot of time to West, haven't you ? "

" Not official time, sir, it wasn't my job, but——"

" *Spare* time? A good detective shouldn't have any spare time. He should either be working or relaxing in order to equip himself for the next real job that comes along. You don't think West is dead, do you ? "

" No."

" You don't think he's turned bad, do you? Or this nonsense about a split mind."

Nonsense! Sloan's eyes glowed. " No, sir, it's utter rot. There are times when I feel like murder—did you read the *Sunday Cry* yesterday ? "

Chatworth said: " I prefer evidence. You know the evidence that piled up against West. Never mind—you've been ferreting on your own, you think you've unearthed something and as a result, you've been threatened. That it ? "

" Yes."

" Tell me about it."

Sloan said: " I'm not sure how much you want to know, sir." He meant " ought to know ", and thought that Chatworth understood that. " There have been a lot of loose ends. I've worked on the theory that West uncovered something about a big organization of which we know little or nothing, and they had to get him out of the way. I don't pretend to know how they've done it, but I've a feeling that he's still alive *and* still working."

" Working, eh ? "

" Yes. If he is alive, he's working. It's all vague and ____"

" At least you realize that." But there was no bite in Chatworth's voice, he didn't intend to discourage Sloan.

" I haven't any evidence that West *is* alive, but you remember that after the Copse Cottage job, we had a squeal from someone we brought in that a man named Kennedy could explain a lot about it. We never traced the Kennedy. But I went through the records and turned up another whisper about a certain Kennedy. He was supposed to have been behind the big forgery job up north, when a man named Kyle was sentenced to seven years. I thought it would be a good idea to watch Kyle when he came out, and put a man on it—Mr. Abbott authorized that, sir."

" I'll take the authorization for granted. Go on."

" Kyle went to see a man named Rayner, at offices in Lyme Street, Strand. No need to go into details. This Rayner says he made a pile in Africa and came back and bought a general commission agency. He bought it from a man named Wiseman—sorry if I have to be confusing here, sir—and Wiseman had a sleeping partner, named Kennedy. That's a commonplace name, but it was interesting that Kyle should go to someone who had taken over a business from the Kennedy already referred to in his trial. The Kennedy is only a name—I've never set eyes on him, haven't been able to pin anything on to him. I talked to Kyle myself after the visit to Lyme Street, but he said he'd gone to ask for a job, and didn't get one. I talked to Kyle about himself, and discovered that while he was inside, his wife was killed in a street accident."

Chatworth nodded.

" Although he seemed bitter about it, and scared, I couldn't make him talk freely. But I did discover that one thing frightened him—the possibility that his daughter, who lives in France, should discover the truth about him. The daughter's name was Lucille. We always thought that a French girl was killed at Copse Cottage, if you remember."

" There are other French names," Chatworth barked. " And there are plenty of Lucilles in England."

" I know, sir, but—well, remember the whisper that a Kennedy was involved both in the Copse Cottage job and West's kidnapping. We've been looking for a French girl, and among the missing people reported at our request by the Paris *Sûreté* there was a Lucille Dinard. Just following that line, sir, I slipped over to Paris when I had a week-end off not long ago. I discovered that this Lucille was really English, but I couldn't get the English name she had before she went to live with this uncle and aunt in Paris. My French isn't very good, and the *Sûreté* man who was with me wasn't very interested. I just let it seep into my mind, sir, and watched Kyle. Nothing happened, he reported regularly to Bow Street. But a month after he'd visited Rayner—the Kennedy contact— he fell under a train at Edgware Road. Someone told the police that he'd been pushed, but wouldn't swear to it at the inquest. The coroner had a lot to say about vivid imaginations, and the verdict was accidental death. Like that on Kyle's wife, some months ago. I checked, and Kyle had Rayner's telephone number on a slip of paper, as well as a name—John Pearson—and a Strand post-restante address. There was a letter containing ten pounds at the Strand Post Office, waiting for Pearson, so someone was staking him."

Chatworth rubbed his round, red nose and grunted.

" Then another queer thing happened—a girl named Marion Day was killed in a street accident. It all seemed normal enough, but I had an obsession about street accidents on this job, and spent a lot of time checking them. I couldn't cover them all, but I had a bit of luck with Marion Day. She was killed in a stretch of Kensington High Street which is usually free from accidents—I investigated all of those in the accident-free parts, it narrowed the line of inquiry. When found, she had a telephone number in her possession—the number of the Kennedy contact whom Kyle had gone to see. That made *three* accidents, all connected with Kennedy. It was still pretty vague, but I spent some time checking on this girl

Day. She'd worked at a nursing home—a private asylum, really. They dealt in schizophrenic cases. The home was closed down a few days after Marion Day was killed. The doctor and staff vanished, and very little was known about them. There was no list of the staff, no record of the doctor in charge—named Ritter—in medical or surgical lists. But I spent a few odd hours up there—it's near Worcester—and managed to find an old man who'd worked in the garden. He didn't know much, never went inside the house, was paid by a member of the staff whose name he didn't know. But he told me that a Mr. Kennedy often called there until a couple of months ago—he knew, because Marion Day occasionally had a talk with him, and once or twice she'd said she was expecting Mr. Kennedy. Now, he said that Marion Day had a special patient. She took him for a walk round the garden once, and—well, the gardener wouldn't swear to it, but he thought it *might* be West. The gardener remembered being called away from the back garden on the occasion when he saw this patient. I showed him photographs Slipped up, I'm afraid, sir—instead of giving him a selection to chose from, I let him see just West's. Even then, he wasn't sure, but he was sure about the name Kennedy. And this patient was at the nursing-home immediately after the Copse Cottage murder. As I've said, the nursing-home closed down after the death of Marion Day. I can't swear anything is connected, but it doesn't seem impossible."

Chatworth grunted; that might mean anything.

" So I had another go at Rayner, tried to get him to admit that he knew Kennedy and Marion Day and Kyle. I didn't get anything out of him. I don't rate him as a bad man—that doesn't mean he isn't one, some cover it well, but I doubt if he's a professional crook. I saw him yesterday. Late last night I had a mysterious telephone message, warning me that I was likely to meet with an accident—that rang a bell, sir!—and also giving me an interesting piece of information. The man said that if I wanted to find the identity of the Copse Cottage victim, I ought to try 23 Rue de Croix, Paris, 8. That's the address of the Lucille Dinard whose relatives I went to see. As a result——"

Chatworth said heavily: "You're scared because you think this man knows what he was talking about."

"Yes."

"And being scared, you want protection as well as official support for your line of inquiry, men to work with you, and—you'd like to carry a gun, wouldn't you?" Chatworth glared, but there was a faint twinkle in his eyes.

Sloan laughed and waved his hands.

"That's about it, sir. I know that we've often had a lot of vague stuff like this to work on before, and I can't say that until last night I could see any reason for concentrated effort on the job, but now——"

"Who'd you want with you?"

"Detective Sergeant Peel."

"All right. Make an official report of the threat against your life, an official application to carry firearms until further notice, and see if Peel can be freed for a week. Week long enough?"

"We ought to get something by the end of it, if there's anything to get."

"All right, try."

* * * * * *

Peel was eight years younger than Sloan, and in appearance, might have been his brother. He was also a protégé of Roger West. He was free for the job.

* * * * *

At the top of the steps, Sloan said to Peel:

"I'll go by bus to the Ritz, then walk along to Hyde Park Corner and down Grosvenor Place. You take a car and be waiting at the Ritz. Follow me. If I've been followed, I'll tip my hat on to the back of my head. Right?"

"Right." Peel was eager.

Sloan went briskly down the steps of the Yard, along past Cannon Row police-station, thence to Parliament Street. A small car, parked near Parliament Street, moved after him. It was a Morris, shabby and muddy grey, and the registration number was *XA 124*. Sloan boarded a bus and found a seat in a place where he could watch the road behind him. The muddy grey Morris followed. Something about it touched a chord in his memory. He rubbed his chin, and tried to think why. " Muddy " and " grey " were the words which mattered. He glanced at the *Daily Cry* which he carried—there were front-page headlines about the Delaney escape from Brixton. Ah! " *The police are anxious to obtain information about a small muddy grey Austin or Morris four-seater car seen near the entrance to Brixton Jail about the time of the escape. A man was at the wheel, and a young woman passenger beside him. Information should——*"

Sloan said aloud : " I believe in coincidence, but not in miracles ! " He shrugged the suspicion aside.

The car slowed up in front of the bus when he got off. A passenger climbed out, a small, nondescript man, dressed in navy blue, wearing a trilby hat with a wide brim. Sloan walked briskly past the bus stop and along by Green Park. Chairs were dotted about the grass, a few people were strolling about beneath the watery sunlight. Traffic streamed towards Hyde Park corner, but the muddy grey Morris stayed where it was for a few minutes, and the nondescript little man followed Sloan. Sloan tipped his hat on to the back of his head, but didn't look round to see if Peel were following : Peel would be.

Sloan passed the gates of Green Park, hesitated on the kerb and looked at the square mass of St. George's Hospital. He seemed to change his mind about crossing, and stepped out briskly down Grosvenor Place. His man and the little car also followed—the car never more than twenty yards behind him.

Quite suddenly, Sloan stepped into the road.

He had hardly touched the roadway before the engine of the Morris roared and the car leapt forward.

19

JANET

TWENTY yards wasn't far.

Unwarned, Sloan wouldn't have stood a chance. The driver of another car, who was just pulling out to pass the Morris, jammed on his brakes and started to skid. The muddy grey Morris turned towards Sloan, but couldn't touch him without causing a crash. The driver straightened the wheel. The car didn't slow down. It flashed past Sloan, who was in front of the other car, which had stopped inches away from him. The driver, opening his door, was white with fright.

Peel's dark car flashed by.

The man in the navy-blue suit stood on the kerb for a few minutes, then suddenly turned and hurried back towards Hyde Park Corner. All he'd done was walk along the pavement, there was nothing Sloan could do about him. The driver of the car which had nearly touched Sloan, shouted:

"You ruddy fool! Serve you right if you'd caught a packet. How I stopped I don't know. It's idiots like you that cause the trouble. You're lucky to be alive." The words came out in a furious spate, and Sloan straightened his coat and tried to speak, but wasn't given a chance. Passers-by joined in, all on the side of the driver.

". . . ought to be given in charge, walking across the road like that. I've a good mind——"

"Yes, sorry," said Sloan. "It was my fault." He took out his card.

"I should damn well think it was your fault. Only a fool or a drunk would do that! Don't stick your card in front of my nose." The driver waved it away.

"I thought I saw a man I was after," Sloan said. "I'm from the Yard."

"I don't care where you come from, if—*where* did you say?" The scared blue eyes dropped to the card, everyone else stopped talking. "Oh, the *Yard*."

" Yes, I'm after a man and thought he was over here.
I didn't see you coming. Sorry."

" Well——"

It was ten minutes before Sloan, transformed from
villain to hero in the space of seconds, was able to get away.
He took a taxi back to the Yard, and the first job he did
was to write an official report of the incident, a description of the man who had left the car, and of the car itself.
He made a special note: " *Check with Brixton job* ", and
then went on with routine work, on edge for a call from
Peel. He began to imagine things about Peel; the
possibility that he'd been noticed, that the Morris driver
had turned on him, that—Sloan gave it up, but was on
tenterhooks for the next three-quarters of an hour.

The telephone bell rang.

He snatched off the receiver. " Yes? "

" Peel here," said Peel. " I'm glad you're all ..ght, I
thought you'd gone bang into the other car."

" Trail him home? "

" Yes," said Peel. " A boarding-house in Chelsea.
I'm at the Chelsea Station. Better just have him watched,
hadn't we? "

" Your job," said Sloan, " and keep it quiet."

" I hope it isn't," said Peel. " After this morning's
dose, you oughtn't to travel much on your own."

" Don't worry about me," said Sloan. " You just
concentrate on that man. Where's the car? "

" Outside the boarding-house."

" Ask the Chelsea people to find out where it was last
night—trace the garage, everything. Muddy and grey—
does that mean anything."

" Crikey! Brixton! "

Sloan laughed; he felt on top of the world.

He was still feeling on top of the world when the telephone bell rang again. He let it ring, but it wouldn't
stop. He finished a note and lifted the receiver. " Hallo
. . . oh, hallo, Mark."

His voice changed, and he came off the top with a bump.
Mark Lessing made him think immediately of Janet West.

" Anything? " asked Mark briefly.

" I wish there were." It was all right to use Lessing unofficially, impossible to tell him anything on this telephone, unwise to say anything that would raise Janet's hopes. " How is she? "

" Not too good," said Mark Lessing. "She's convinced that the Yard has completely forgotten about it. Anything you can do to cheer her up a bit? "

" I'll try to look in to-day," Sloan promised.

He couldn't settle to work for the next ten minutes. Visiting Janet West always hurt; it had to be done, but it still hurt. He was back at the old question, too—whether to say or hint at anything that might raise her hopes. He couldn't chance it. Chelsea—odd that the driver of the muddy grey Morris lived in Chelsea, not far from the Wests. Be tempting to go and look at the house, but that would be asking for trouble. It was far too early to show too much interest in that man or that car—except the quiet, persistent interest which garnered information but didn't arouse alarm. He didn't want it known or guessed that he'd been tipped off about the attack. Other tips might come.

Who had given him the tip?

Rayner? Was he fooling himelf about Rayner? The attack was probably a direct result of his second Lyme Street visit.

There might be a way of picking up the driver of the car without revealing the tip-off; by proving it had been used in the Delaney job, for instance. He didn't feel certain about his best course. Roger would have known, he'd have acted on Roger's advice.

Laugh that off!

He had lunch in the canteen. Banister sat on his own at a small table: Banister always sat on his own. He looked morose: he always looked morose. Sloan forgot him.

It was just after four o'clock when he turned into Bell Street, Chelsea. He hadn't been followed; he didn't think there was any danger for the rest of that day, they wouldn't try again so quickly; one accident was an accident, two would make coincidence: coincidences made policemen thoughtful.

He saw two small boys, racing along the street towards him, one hefty and plump and red-faced, the other smaller, thinner, with wavy hair; even from this distance the smaller child's huge blue eyes were noticeable. Both were laughing fit to burst. A young woman stood at a gate—West's gate—calling them. They ignored her. They passed the car without looking towards Sloan, the larger boy nearly up to the first and stretching out to grab his grey jersey.

"*Rich-ard!*" He cried breathlessly. "*That's mine!*"

Richard was clutching something that didn't belong to him as he ran. The young woman called out again and began to hurry after them—and then Richard caught his toe in a ridge between paving stones, and crashed down. There was a moment of breathless silence, followed by a piercing howl. Sloan stopped as the woman hurried past him. She was small, big-breasted, with long, dark hair and a pale face; and her skirts were short. Richard howled wildly. Sloan looked out of the car and saw Scoopy, the elder boy, standing and watching in wide-eyed alarm; and he said.

"It wasn't my fault, Richard took it."

The woman said: "You're a bad boy, Scoopy."

Richard howled.

Sloan got out of the car and said: "Let me give him a ride, that'll make him forget it."

"No, he's cut his knee," said the woman, helping Richard up. His face had gone beetroot red, and he opened his mouth wide as he howled. The woman had dark eyes—and a way with children. She picked Richard up, although he was heavy for her, and began to carry him towards the Wests' house. "Scoopy, walk nicely behind me. What your mother will say, I don't know."

Scoopy defended himself. "Richard took it."

Richard still had it; a small musical box, the shape of a drum, clutched in his right hand.

They trooped towards the house.

Normally, Janet's ears were so sharp that she would have heard that outcry and rushed to see what had caused it. She may have heard it, but hadn't rushed. Sloan drove on, and reached the house just in front of the little group. Scoopy took notice of him for the first time, and his big, broad face lit up.

"It's Mr. Sloan!"

"Hallo, Scoop. What's all the trouble about?"

"Richard wouldn't let me have my musical box." Scoopy knew an ally when he saw one. "It *is* mine. Daddy bought it for me before he went away."

"He *didn't*!" Richard had stopped crying, and was aggressively indignant. "He didn't, *did* he, G'ace? Daddy bought it for *us*. It was my turn."

The woman, Grace, put him down. His knee was bleeding freely, and blood gathered at the top of his sock. She bundled both of the boys inside; Sloan followed— and saw Janet coming downstairs. She didn't notice him. He stood and watched her, hating the lifelessness in her eyes and face and the dullness of her voice.

"Now what have you been up to?"

"Scoopy——" began Richard.

"Richard——" began Scoopy.

"I'll look after them, Mrs. West, it only wants a wash and a bandage. Don't worry." Grace smiled; she had a charming smile which lit up the whole of her face with a lightness that was almost radiance, and made her look a different woman. None of the radiance touched Janet. She stood aside, and Sloan studied her more closely.

She had often been through difficult, dangerous times, known heart-ache and desperate anxiety when Roger was on a tough assignment; but Sloan had never seen her despairing. Her expression made her look years older —drawn lines at her eyes and mouth spoiled her looks. The eyes which had so readily glowed with cheerfulness were dull. She hadn't let herself go completely; she was tidily dressed, in a dark-grey frock, and her hair was brushed; she wore it up, Edwardian fashion. It had lost the lustre which had made it beautiful.

She saw Sloan.

"Bill!" Hope blazed in her eyes—hope without foundation, hope just at seeing him. For the moment she completely forgot the boys, Grace, everything—she saw a friend of Roger's, and there was hope in her, that he had news. But it faded swiftly; and she closed her eyes and stood quite still as he went in.

"Hallo, Janet."

"I'm all right," she said. "Come in." She led the way into the front room—the sitting-room. It was full of Roger; why not? It belonged to Roger. His chair, his pipes, his——

Janet sat down and waved to a chair, then got up.

"Will you have a drink?"

"No, thanks, it's a bit early."

"There isn't any news, is there?"

"No," said Sloan. "Not news—not hard news, Jan. But I've something to tell you that I hope will help a bit."

She became rigid, and didn't speak, just stared at him—and the dark shadows under her eyes made them look falsely bright.

"There's a line on the Copse Cottage job which we hadn't found before," he said cheerfully. "It may lead to nothing, but at least it means that Chatworth has agreed that I should spend more time on it. He knows why I'm anxious to do it, of course. I had a chat with him to-day. He's prepared to back me up, and although he didn't say so, he's right with me in believing that the whole business is a grotesque mistake."

"He hasn't told *me* that," said Janet.

"He won't, unless he gets hold of something that looks like real evidence. I don't know that I should tell you this, but at least it's something to hold on to. I can put some official time into it, now."

She smiled faintly. "You've been wonderful, Bill. You and Mark, I don't know what I'd have done without you. But—oh, I've tried to tell myself that it will work out all right, but if Roger were alive, he'd have got in touch with me, somehow."

Sloan didn't speak—but glanced at the door. He heard a slight sound there, and thought he saw the handle turn. Scoopy liked to listen to conversations, but if it had been Scoopy he wouldn't have come to the door so silently. Imagination?

Janet said: " Bill, it's no use, we just have to face the facts. Either Roger is dead or he *has* had something to do with—crime. That's the only choice we have. And you know he hasn't had anything to do with crime, so he *must* be dead."

" I can't believe it."

" Have you any reason at all for *saying* that? "

Sloan stood up and took out his cigarettes, moved casually across the room without making a sound and without looking at the door. He said:

" No real reason, Jan. But we know the identity of the girl who was killed at Copse Cottage now, that's the line that's opened. I've left my matches in my overcoat pocket —won't be a moment."

He opened the door.

Grace was moving away, back towards him, heading for the stairs. She didn't look round. He went to his overcoat and pretended to take matches from it, returned to Janet who was leaning back with her eyes closed. She'd noticed nothing unusual. Sloan sat down again, although it wasn't much use staying; he hadn't really cheered her up. But over a period it might give Janet something to think about, and save her from touching greater depths of depression.

He left, three-quarters of an hour afterwards, hearing the boys shouting merrily in their bath, and Grace talking to them cheerfully. Janet was, if anything, a little brighter. He got into his car, waved and drove towards the other end of Bell Street and then to the Chelsea Embankment. He wanted to go back to the Yard.

That woman, Grace——

A car swung out of a side turning towards him. He wasn't on guard, because he was concentrating on the woman, Grace. But his sixth sense, awareness of danger, worked as he saw the car. He wrenched the wheel. The other was a powerful Buick, big enough to crush his own car like matchwood. He felt the crash, but the Buick only hit the near-side wing. He lost control of the wheel, and his car swerved across the road. The Buick leapt along the Embankment and swung left, over the bridge.

Sloan regained control.   People ran towards him.   He wasn't hurt, beyond a bruise or two.

.   .   .   .   .

Peel was at the Yard when he arrived, and reported that the Chelsea police were looking after the man with the muddy grey Morris, and being ca' canny.   When Sloan told him of the crash, Peel said:

" I told you so."

Sloan shrugged and said:

" Yes, we've got to keep our eyes open all the time.   But it's coming to a head, Peel."

" Think so? "

" Roger West would call it a hunch.   All right, call it a hunch.   And here's another job, to do very carefully. Check on the nurse, Grace Howell, at the Wests' home. No, I'm not sure there's anything to worry about, but there might be."

Peel went off.

Sloan began another report; an official one, for which he didn't need his private note-book.   So he didn't look for it.   But he wanted the Copse Cottage murder file, and sent a constable to get it from *Records*.   The man was gone a long time, and Sloan looked up impatiently when he came in, empty-handed.

" What's the matter—needing a rest? "

" Sorry, sir, but it's not in its place.   The Assistant Commissioner had it earlier to-day—he may still have it. They're still looking."

Sloan said: " All right, thanks."

If Chatworth was going through that file, it meant that he was in earnest about the business.   That also meant he'd been impressed by the story Sloan had told him, the visit had been well worth while.   Sloan managed without the Copse Cottage file, and went home a little after seven o'clock.

Nothing happened to him on the way.   He didn't tell his wife about the two attempts to run him down.

20

KENNEDY DEMANDS

IT wasn't possible for Roger to telephone Pep Morgan that day. He was followed wherever he went, whether by a Yard man or Kennedy's, he didn't know. He preferred not to take a chance.

He spent a quiet evening wrestling with the circumstances and fighting with himself. At the end of it, he felt sure that there wasn't much longer to wait; he'd been wise to start the counter-moves. He would soon have to decide whether to risk telling Sloan more.

He was still worried about Sloan, and found it hard to settle to any one thing.

Next day, he wasn't watched. He didn't waste time wondering why. He had an appointment in the Strand with a manufacturer of nylon stockings, left before noon, and called Morgan from a kiosk.

.   .   .   .   .

Morgan said: " Mr. Raymond Hemmingway, twenty-seven, Mountjoy Square."

" Thanks, Pep," said Roger.

As the " Pep " came out, he realized the mistake. Not many people knew the private agent as " Pep "—only those who knew or had known him well.

Morgan appeared not to notice the nickname.

" It's still dear at fifty pounds, Mr. Brown."

" I may have something else for you to do later. Not now. Thanks very much."

Roger stepped out of the kiosk, in a corner of a tobacconist's shop near Lyme Street, wiped his hot forehead, and went into the street. That had been a bad slip, his worst. By affecting not to notice it, Morgan had shown that it had registered; and Morgan would start thinking about all the people who knew him as " Pep ". They were mostly Yard men or Divisional detectives, who had started to use the name when he had said the police wanted more pep;

that was years ago. The danger was that Morgan might tell Sloan, Mark, or Janet.

The risk was real; he couldn't afford to relax his guard for five seconds on end.

Two or three people were passing; none showed any interest in him. He walked the long way round back to Lyme Street; no one was watching there.

He was paying dearly for the slip, already. Morgan had probably discovered something about Mr. Raymond Hemmingway of 27 Mountjoy Square. Roger should have asked that, and also instructed Morgan to find out all he could about the man.

It wasn't certain, but it was likely, that Kennedy was really Hemmingway.

Rose Morgan was in his office when Roger arrived.

" Hallo," he said. " Anything for me? "

" I was just putting the letters here for signature, sir," she said. " I'll go to luncheon, now, if there's nothing more you require."

" No, thanks. Suppliers remain compliant, don't they? "

" We're very fortunate, sir, we have such good connections."

" Yes. But this corner in goods in short supply won't last for ever."

" I think it will go on for some time yet, sir, and we needn't cross the next bridge until we get to it." She was smug, and infuriatingly right.

Roger smiled and nodded, and was relieved when she went out. He leaned across and took up a telephone directory. Mr. Raymond Hemmingway was shown at 27 Mountjoy Square—telephone, *Mayfair 12131*. So he'd lived at the house for some time, for this was a year-old directory. Roger took up a *Directory of Directors* and *Who's Who*, but before he opened them he began to think about the ease with which " his " firm could obtain short-supply goods. It remained a simple fact that if any kind of goods were wanted, the firm of Rayner could get them. All quite legal, all above board; the firm had priority, that was all.

Why?

It wasn't just with one or two firms; it was with practically everyone with whom they dealt. He had seen fresh evidence of it every day. Steel and steel parts were desperately short; get them from *Steelers*, who still traded under that name although they had come under the wing of the Board of Trade. Expensive china, which you couldn't buy in the shops except under the counter—*Barry's* of Stoke-on-Trent would supply as much as he wanted. Hand-woven serge, unobtainable in all but the most exclusive tailors and dressmakers who obtained their supplies through Rayner & Co.; Rayner's bought from any one of a dozen mills, and had no difficulty. All legal, all above board, but remarkable. There were a hundred other examples. The Scottish whisky distilleries were open-handed. Imported goods from anywhere in the world, even those which had the tiniest import quotas imaginable, came in without any trouble. There was not even great difficulty in getting import licences.

Other facts: the knowing ones in commerce, hotels, exclusive shops, and little-known organizations knew that Rayner's could obtain almost non-existent goods. The connection was extensive, and world-wide; Rayner's dealt only with the exclusive, and their amount of profit was high; but they kept scrupulously within legal margins. Whoever had built up this business, had genius.

These facts had been floating around in his subconscious for some time, but he hadn't concentrated on them; it was past time he did. Odd that the brisk exchange with Miss Morgan had started his mind off on this track. But once he'd shown interest, she'd closed up as a clam; she might almost have said: " None of your business, Mr. Rayner." The firm, or someone connected with it, had compelling influence with a remarkable number of people.

Mystery Number 2.

Mystery Number 1 was Kennedy *alias* Raymond Hemmingway, and he mustn't forget it. He looked up the entry under Hemmingway in *Who's Who*.

Hemmingway, Raymond Manville, Company director. *b.* 1905, *ed.* Eton, Balliol, *m.* 1931, Desirée, daughter of Sir Robert and Lady Mortimer. *Address*: 27 Mountjoy Square. *Clubs*: Atheneum, Carlton, Pendexeter.

That didn't give much away, except that he had had a better education than Roger had thought; you could never be sure. And that he'd married well. Roger turned up the name in the *Directory of Directors*. One Company was quoted—Hemmingway, Mortimer & Company, Ltd., Dealers in Fine Art.

That might help; dealers in fine art had wonderful opportunities for smuggling antiques, pictures, *objets d'art*, and jewellery. There was a lot of smuggling in that line to and from America, and into Great Britain from the Continent. But this company had all the hall-marks of a legitimate business as well as an address in Bond Street. Bond Street dealers seldom fell from grace, they were the high priests of their trade.

His fingers itched for the telephone.

If he were at the Yard, he need only speak for two minutes and, by the evening, would have a complete picture of Mr. Hemmingway's business activities. Forget that, too. Yet his hand kept straying towards the telephone. The afternoon went quickly; orders and more orders flowed in.

Just before six o'clock, the door opened. Percy appeared, in his navy-blue chauffeur's uniform. He closed the door on the several members of the staff still working.

" Boss wants you," he said succinctly.

" Knock before you come in here, and go downstairs and wait," snapped Roger.

" One o' these days   " began Percy, but he didn't finish, and went out.

The door closed gently behind him.

Roger watched the door handle; it didn't turn again, Percy wasn't waiting just outside.

Roger didn't hurry. The dozen thoughts crowding his mind needed sorting out. It was easy to read too much significance into that " Boss wants you ", but would Hemmingway send for him now unless it were urgent?

Careful; keep the man in mind as Kennedy, not Hemmingway; thinking of the new name might bring about another serious slip of the tongue.

The moment Kennedy suspected what was being planned, he would kill.

Roger picked up his hat and went downstairs: one difference between Charles Rayner and Roger West was that Rayner always wore a hat, and West had always gone hatless; trifles, which mattered. He found the Daimler waiting, and got in. The usual trick with the blinds wasn't played; they didn't go to Mountjoy Square but to a block of flats behind Oxford Street—a small, luxury block.

" Number 15," said Percy, showing no sign of grievance. Roger nodded and went inside.

Kennedy himself opened the door. He was dressed in morning coat and striped grey trousers; he looked as if he had been poured into them. Except for his eyes, there wasn't much to remind Roger of the man he had first glimpsed coming away from Copse Cottage. Why had Kennedy appeared *in person* in that job? That was one of the most puzzling questions, and there was no obvious answer.

The flat was small, but the living-room was big and luxurious. It struck him as being a woman's flat. There was a faint smell of perfume, not the perfume which he had noticed at Mountjoy Place. That meant nothing.

Drinks were out, which didn't suggest a fiery interview. Roger said: " Another little *pied à terre.*"

" I hope you like it. What will you drink? "

" Whisky, thanks."

Kennedy poured out, offered cigarettes, and for him was a long time getting to the point. He sipped, and eyed Roger through his lashes, as if he wanted to hide those fiery silver eyes.

"Your friend Sloan is tough," he said.

Roger stiffened. " I told you——"

" That's one of the things I want to talk to you about," said Kennedy mildly. " You've forgotten to forget your past. You've too much of a conscience. Sloan is tough,

and Sloan isn't a fool. He's got to go. Two attempts
were made on him yesterday. Both failed. I don't
know whether he suspects what happened or not, but he
might, and he's not safe."

Roger said: " I won't stand for it."

Kennedy laughed.

" Won't you? " He turned to a table, picked up a
photograph that was lying face downwards, handed it to
Roger. " Recognize them? "

Two smiling faces and one grave, stared up at him.
Scoopy and Richard, dressed in Red Indian finery—and a
girl whom he didn't know, small, big-breasted, wearing a
skirt much too short for her. He didn't spend any time
looking at the girl at first, just stared at the boys. Wearing
those feathers and waistcoats was one of their great joys.
Janet let them have them for a few days every month;
Janet made sure they didn't get weary of any favourite
toys or playthings.

This had been taken in a garden—his garden.

His teeth clamped together.

Kennedy said: " I've told you before that I don't want
to injure the kids, but you've got to understand that they
don't belong to you any more—and that any of your one-
time friends who get in our way, have to go. Sloan's
one. I can lift up the telephone, and give orders to that
girl to walk out of the house taking the kids with her.
How would a certain widow like that? "

Roger felt sick.

Kennedy said: " I hoped you'd got past the worst stage,
Rayner." He turned from the drinks, went to the window
and stood looking out. " I think you have—this is just a
sentimental hangover. Sloan only spells danger to you.
Don't you enjoy your new standard of living? "

Roger said: " It has its points."

" You can become a much richer man. You can do
what you like and go where you like. I haven't wasted
my time when having you watched. This new life fits you
like a glove. You revel in luxury. Money can buy a lot
of other things for you to revel in. All you have to do is
forget, and everything is yours."

Roger said: " I've warned you not to do anything to Sloan. The fact that he was a friend of mine is one thing. There's much more. He's bristling with suspicion. Do anything to him, and you'll have the Yard down on you like a pack of hounds—and I *mean* like a pack of hounds. They'll tear you to pieces, strip you of everything. This place. Your home. Your money. Your future. You're a fool if you go for Sloan."

Kennedy said: " He's got to go, soon." He moved to a writing-desk, a beautiful walnut piece, and picked up a book, a large diary with a lock and key. "Recognize this?"

Roger gulped.

" Sloan's note-book? "

" He's done a lot of ferreting. He's proved you're right—the police are better than I'd realized. If he talks about this, it might be very bad indeed. Yes, Sloan has to go."

" So Banister——"

Kennedy laughed; that hateful laugh.

" Banister was exactly the right man. He's done this kind of thing before, on a smaller scale. I've had *dossiers* and records photolithoed this afternoon, and know everything that the Yard knows. You'll study it, point out the weakness and the strength, and decide how best to counter what they're doing. But there's nothing in those records half as dangerous as Sloan's private note-book. Sloan *must* go."

Roger helped himself to another whisky and soda.

" Have you been working long enough now to know how valuable you are to me? " Kennedy demanded.

" I've an idea."

" We've hardly started." Kennedy grinned. " When we get at the big stuff, you'll wallow in money. Where does Sloan live? "

" You won't get Sloan's address from me." Keep calm. " If you want to get yourself hanged, send one of your thugs to find out where he lives—they can follow him home. Do the job your own way, and don't blame me."

Kennedy looked at the amber liquid in his glass.

" You seem very sure of yourself."

" I am sure."

" You could go too far with this attitude."

" I've told you before, we're on equal terms because we run an equal risk. You want me to assess the dangers and avert them. I'm telling you that the murder of Sloan would be absolute folly. I won't have any part in it."

Kennedy continued to look at the glass.

" I see. Supposing Sloan were to disappear? "

" Well, supposing? " They were just words, while he took in what Kennedy was getting at; and there was something deep, betrayed by that glitter in his eyes, which seemed to take on the colour of the whisky.

" Would that raise the same hue and cry? "

" Pretty well."

" Go on, finish," said Kennedy. " It would have a different effect, wouldn't it? Sloan was such a good friend of yours. Sloan disappearing would seem almost a natural consequence. And if it happened together with the disappearance of confidential documents, your other friends there would add two and two quite nicely. Sloan took the papers. Banister would remain at the Yard, able to serve us again. Do you like the build-up, West? "

Roger knew that " West " wasn't a slip.

" You might get away with it."

" That's condescending of you. I'd have two of the brightest men at the Yard under my wing, and the Home Office would begin to worry. Corruption at Scotland Yard is a bad thing, isn't it? Afterwards, we might get one or two others to join us. I can imagine this doing a lot of damage at the Yard, but never mind that for now— just concentrate on getting hold of Sloan. There's one simple way of doing it: speaking to him in your natural voice. He'd come running, wouldn't he? "

Roger said slowly: " Yes."

" I want him," said Kennedy.

" When? " The word was dragged out of Roger.

" To-night. Well—to-morrow at the latest."

" Where? "

" At your office. That will——"

" He suspects me as Rayner. He'd smell a rat if he
had the office address. What's the matter with bringing
him here? "

" All right, bring him here," said Kennedy. " Number 15 Balling Mansions, Wild Street." He made the
decision quickly. " When you've got him, Percy will
inform me. No tricks, West. And when it's done——"
he paused, looked round. " Nice flat, isn't it? "

" It's all right."

" Yours. With everything that's in it. Everything
you want, anyhow." He laughed: that hateful laugh
which grated on Roger like a saw on a metal bar. " Don't
slip up, West. If we don't get Sloan, I may have to throw
my hand in and decide that you're not worth the trouble.
I shan't want to do that. I can see a big future for us."

Roger poured himself out another drink.

" Don't get drunk," said Kennedy. He went towards
the door. " Stay and think it over. I'll see you later.
Don't put that picture in your pocket by mistake, will
you? "

He had propped the photograph up against a book-
end; the two boys smiled gaily, and the dark-haired
woman looked across at him sombrely.

.   .   .   .   .   .

Kennedy was clever; Kennedy knew that this was a
crisis, and wasn't sure which way the cat would jump.
So he had increased the pressure. He had also increased
Roger's determination to find out what lay behind it all—
to guess at that " big future ". Get one thing straight,
thought Roger; Kennedy was in big crime and mostly
unsuspected crime. It had something to do with those
short-supply goods; with the forgery racket which Kyle
had helped to run; with the currency smuggling. One
could spend a lifetime at Scotland Yard and scoff at stories
of master crooks, but such men existed—and most of
them worked without the police knowing. Kennedy—as
Hemmingway—had kept himself completely free from
suspicion. But in a show like this, you had to have records,
you couldn't keep them all in your mind. So Kennedy

had records, and there was an even chance that they were at 27 Mountjoy Square.

Roger could spend a lot of time thinking of that and beg the most urgent issue—how to handle Sloan, or the situation which Kennedy had created with Sloan. One thing stuck out a mile: if Sloan disappeared, then everyone at the Yard would assume that he had been in a racket with Roger, and had gone to join him. Beyond all this there was the vague hint from Kennedy, that the Yard could be split from top to bottom with corruption. It had happened before; not recently, but not so long ago that it didn't make old Yard men sore whenever it was mentioned. If a man *could* control a large number of officers at the Yard, he would be in a perfect position to handle any crime, any racket that he wanted. The Yard's tentacles spread far and wide—but he was letting his thoughts run away with him. He had to get down to earth; decide what to do about Bill Sloan.

He heard the door open.

A woman came in.

.   .   .   .   .

You could walk along the Strand or mix with any crowd and wonder where the lovely women of England had gone. Often the succession of dull, nondescript faces would depress you. Then in a short period, you could meet nothing but beauty. Marion, so beautiful in her way; the petite woman at Mountjoy Square; Mrs. Delaney; and this woman.

It wasn't surface beauty, either; didn't owe everything to make-up. She came in and closed the door softly, smiling at him as she approached. Her movements were easy and smooth. She was tall, and no one would ever complain about her figure. She wore an afternoon dress, obviously a model; it was perfection of dark green and pale yellow. Her hair was auburn, and she had fine, grey-green eyes. It would have been hard to put a finger on any feature of her face which wasn't near perfection. Her voice, unlike Mrs. Delaney's, was husky and pleasing.

" May I have a drink? "

He took a grip on himself.   " What will it be? "

" Gin and vermouth, please."

He mixed the drinks. Her fingers were long and slender, pale, with pink nails; she wore a single diamond ring on her right hand, but no other jewellery. He hadn't known that she existed until two minutes ago, but she looked at him as if they had known each other for ages— intimately. That touch of intimacy in her manner was the strangest thing.

" You look thoughtful, Charles."

" There's plenty to think about."

" Too much. Here's success! " She sipped. " And everything you want. It *is* a pleasant flat."

" So you've heard about that."

" He told me. It's my flat. It *was* my flat. I go with it."

It came out as cynically as that, but there was nothing cynical about her expression when she added: " Why don't you sit down and relax? "

" I was just studying the bait."

" How crude! You know that you'll have to do what he says, or unpleasant things will happen. If you have to take the pill, why not look pleased about the sugar? I think you've been on your own too much lately. Far too much."

" I'm a bachelor by habit."

" I know all about you," she said. " You're eating your heart out. I can see it in your eyes. I've told him that it was essential for you to have—companionship. There's nothing that helps one to forget so much as someone else to think about. Has that ever struck you? When your wife reaches the same point, she'll get better. You think it's a tragedy. It's happened to millions of people, and they've lived happy, contented lives afterwards. This sentimental illusion about one woman for one man is just nonsense. You ought to realize that."

" So I'm eating my heart out, and you're going to stop me," he said.

" I'm going to try, because I don't want the unpleasant things to happen. After all, you can look after your wife, if you want to."

This was a new angle—different pressure. He stared at her, the question in his eyes.

" With money," she said.

" I just post a package of money to her, do I ? "

" The worst of men when they're in trouble is that they get childish," she said. " Come and sit down." She went to a couch and smoothed her skirts and adjusted a cushion. He stood staring down at her; she had beautiful legs. One of the ideas, of course, was to get his mind off the crisis, to start him seeing new possibilities, to interest him in—this woman, any woman; to convince him that life could be easy and smooth for Janet and for himself.

" All right, I'm childish." How should he deal with the situation? He poured himself out another drink; he was drinking too much.

" I know," she said. " There are several ways in which you could get money to her without letting anyone suspect how it came. You could have a secret insurance policy, for instance, and details of it could be found and——"

" Officially, I'm missing, not dead."

" They have only to find a body that will serve as yours, and then you'll be over the worst hurdle," said the woman in green, quite calmly. " Ways and means could be found, and you know it. You haven't let yourself face the situation frankly. It's time you did."

He moved to the couch and sat on the arm.

" Help me to," he invited.

" I want to help you. You're an attractive man, and you're wealthy, or on the way to being wealthy. You're quite young. You've been taken up by a man who is exceptional, and who will have very great influence before he's finished—a kind of genius."

Did she know much about Kennedy, or was she bluffing?

" What makes you think he's as good as that ? "

" Ray is my brother," she said. " I've never known him make a serious mistake yet. One or two of his friends thought that it was a mistake to try to use you, but—it hasn't been, and if you're sensible, it won't be. He's quite merciless—that is one of the things that makes him so unusual. Once he thought that you weren't prepared to go on, he would kill you as he's killed the others. With you dead, the police would have a little knowledge of a man named Kennedy, none of my brother. You don't know who he is; only three people, his chauffeur, his sister, and his wife, know who he is and know what he's doing. He leads a normal life, moves in good society, has a great many commercial and industrial interests. He will one day be the richest man in England." She spoke without any hint of doubt.

"A remarkable man," Roger said heavily. There was every reason to believe that all this was true—and a familiar question flashed into his mind: why had Kennedy come to Copse Cottage in person? "He has a small army of thugs, hasn't he?"

"Practically none," said the woman in green. "He has a lot of influence with some, and he can always find men to do what he wants. They don't know that their orders come from him. Some of them get caught, like Kyle, but it makes no difference to him. There's no way of tracing those things back to him. They can only be traced back to a certain Mr. Kennedy, who doesn't exist."

Roger slid from the arm to the couch itself, crossed his legs and looked at her levelly. There wasn't anything the matter with her, except her outlook.

She smiled. In anyone else it would have been seductive; she made it natural, friendly, inviting.

"What is more, if you were to see him as he really is, you wouldn't be able to say for sure that you know him. You're a smart man, Charles, and you're good. Haven't you marvelled that he showed himself to you?"

"It had crossed my mind."

She stretched out her hand, so that it lay near his, palm upwards, slim and white and inviting.

"I think he was right," she said dreamily. "He felt that using you was the most important step he had ever taken. It opened a host of new possibilities, and he had to make sure that it was successful. He couldn't trust anyone else to deal with you—not even me." She laughed easily, at herself; and laughter came naturally to her. " He is a fine judge of character. I often think he can read what is passing through your mind. Is it silly fancy? Look at to-night. He judged your reaction to Sloan perfectly, didn't he? "

" Did he? "

" Fencing with words isn't really clever," said the woman in green. " Yes, he did that. He knows that if you can jump this hurdle, everything will be fine in the future. He's naturally very anxious that you should jump it."

" And you're to help me? "

" That's right," she said, and leaned nearer, taking his hand. Her eyes were lovely, invitation glowed in them. Her glistening lips were slightly parted, he could just see the white beauty of her teeth. Her hand was cool, the pressure firm. " I'm to help you. I'm to show you the real future, to make you understand what it can be. Have you ever been poor? "

" Poor enough." It was impossible not to be aware of her beauty and her nearness, or the soft, insistent attraction of her voice.

" Not *really* poor? Poor enough to be hungry, to wonder where the next meal is coming from, to wonder whether your clothes will hold together for another day, to wonder where you can get new ones, something to keep you from shivering? Have you ever been poor, like that? "

" No," he said; the word came out abruptly.

" I wish you had. If you had, you would understand so much more easily. *We* have. Ray thinks he's forgotten those days, but he hasn't. It was because of them that he turned his brilliant mind to this. We've touched the depths, and now we're touching the heights. There is nothing money can't buy, Charles. Beauty, lovely things, travel, comfort, luxury—everything but life itself, and we start with that. Ray hated the old days and loves the new. He's very generous. You know that. Hasn't he been generous with you? Is there anything you lack? "

Roger said : " No."

" You think you lack the past, but the past is a thing best forgotten—or put into the back of the mind, to take out again occasionally and think about sentimentally. You're out of the old life, and the new is already closing about you—you can feel it, can't you? Sweet and inviting, better than you've ever known. It can be the same for your friend Sloan. And it can be so much worse. Ugly—black. Not for you—you haven't really a choice."

Her hand was tight on his now, and she was closer to him, still looking at him with those glowing green eyes and the sweeping lashes. She raised his hand, held it close to her, pressed gently—so gently. " You either have to go on, doing what he wants—and what you will want eventually —or you will be killed. But the others will suffer so much, if you die. He might take your children away from their mother; that would really be cruel. She would have no idea where they were and wouldn't have a moment's rest. Think of it. And somehow he would make sure that she would spend the rest of her life in poverty. He *can*. Your friends, too—this man Lessing, Sloan—they would all be on his list, marked down, treated so cruelly. Yes, he can be cruel, and has to be in order to obtain what he wants. What happens to them is in your hands, Charles. Wouldn't it be foolish to take risks? "

Then softly, she added:

" You have so much."

She closed her eyes; and her lips were very close to his.

He kissed her gently, feeling the pressure of her lips, the closeness of her body.

.   .   .   .   .

" You'll send for Sloan? " she said quietly.

He was standing by the cocktail cabinet, smoothing down his ruffled hair.

" Yes."

" To-night? "

" If two attacks have been made on him, he isn't likely to come at a mysterious sum. ions after dark. He'd take the risk in daylight."

" He must come by himself."

" I can't guarantee what he'll do." Roger poured drinks; champagne, which fizzed and bubbled and sparkled. His hands weren't as steady as he would have liked. " I think it would be crazy to stipulate that he must come alone, it would sharpen his suspicions. Much better to be ready to look after anyone he brings with him. Better not come here, either." He took her a glass. " I thought that would be a good idea, but he might tell the Yard where he's going." He didn't want Hemmingway under suspicion at the Yard yet. " Better to take him to some place which can't be traced afterwards."

She took the glass. " Yes. I'll speak to Ray." She clinked glasses with him. " Happy future, Charles!"

" Happy days." He sipped, hating her. " When will you see—your brother?"

" I am joining him later to-night. We have some business to discuss—no, not you and Sloan, one of the other projects." Her eyes glowed. " If you really work well, Charles, the day won't be far off when you'll be in our full confidence."

He frowned.

" What's wrong?" she asked.

" Do you have to go out to-night?"

" Yes, Charles, and I shan't be back until the morning, we're going——" she paused, and added quickly: " To have a long session. But that doesn't often happen at night. Will you stay here, or go back to your flat?"

" If you're not here, I may as well leave." Was he pretending well enough to fool her?

" When we have Sloan, you'll be able to tell me when to go and when to stay." She laughed and drank deeply. " It's glorious, Charles, you'll never regret it, never."

The door opened, and Kennedy came in. His eyes were narrowed, there was the merest sliver of silver light in them. He grinned.

" What did I hear?"

Roger saw the flashing glance which she sent him, and read the triumph in it, as he sipped his champagne.

" Charles is going to send for Sloan," she said, " and he's made several suggestions . . ."

. . . . .

" Good night," Kennedy said, at the door.

Percy stood by the Daimler, outside.

" Good night."

" I'll see that you have the address for Sloan, early in the morning."

" Thanks." Roger hurried out to the car, Percy opened the door and looked at him without favour. Percy was never likely to become a good friend of Charles Rayner, there was instinctive animosity in him.

" I'll walk," said Roger.

" You won't! " Percy snapped.

Roger turned away from the car and walked towards the end of the street. He couldn't see Percy; guessed that Percy was sending an SOS to Kennedy, who was probably still at the door. At the corner, Roger turned. A man came out of the block of flats, walking swiftly, and turned in his wake. Roger affected not to notice him, and strolled on. It was a warm, friendly London night. In the distance was the hum of traffic and a glow of lights against the starlit sky. There was hardly any wind, and he didn't need his overcoat. He dawdled. The man who had come from the Mansions also dawdled, a little way behind him. He was still being followed when he reached Lyme Street, twenty minutes later. He stood at the doorway, lit a cigarette, and looked up and down; his shadower stayed in the doorway of a shop at the corner, appearing to take no notice of him.

Roger went upstairs, leaving the street door unlatched.

When he pulled aside the curtains and looked out of a front window the man was opposite, in the doorway from which he was always watched in times of tension and suspense.

Harry, quiet and unobtrusive as ever, asked if he wanted dinner.

" Please. A snack will do."

" Very good, sir." Harry went into the kitchen.
Roger put on some records; Wagner—Wagner suited his
mood, the melancholy made a background to his thoughts.
They were fragmentary. The clever cunning of it! The
sugar coating over crudeness. The continued attempts to
break down his resistance and corrupt his mind. Whether
he got Sloan or not was to be a vital test; Kennedy might
regard it as final. Succeed, and he would be close to the
black heart of this affair; fail, and the woman in green—
he did not even know her Christian name!—would be
able to say: " I told you so." No use arguing with himself about that. Succeed, and Kennedy would lower
most of the barriers. Fail—and die.

Fail—and take terrible risks with Janet and the boys.

He stirred in his chair, smoking, restless.

The woman in green was now with Kennedy, sure of
herself, yet human and prone to mistakes. She had
started to tell him what they were going to do that night
and had broken off; that was the mistake. Turn " long
session ", which she'd substituted for the truth, into " long
journey ", add the fact that the journey couldn't start
until after he'd left, and it became obvious that they were
going out of town. Kennedy's wife would probably be
with them; Percy would almost certainly drive them.
They probably wouldn't be back that night. Kennedy
was away from Mountjoy Square, then; and Percy, too.
Kennedy's wife? He couldn't guess.

Kennedy was sure that he didn't know the address at
Mountjoy Square.

Kennedy and his sister were now sure that he would
" play "; the shadow and this caution was routine. It
was too big a thing on which to take a chance. He would
be watched, everything he did until Sloan was caught
would be noted, he had no real freedom of action, unless
he took a desperate chance.

It would be the only chance, leading either to complete success or abject failure. It meant breaking into
27 Mountjoy Square. He'd need a skilled cracksman;
he could find one, if necessary. He laughed——

If he held on, sent for Sloan and trapped him, then afterwards success would be much easier. On balance, he ought to wait; he'd gone so far, and Sloan would be the last man in the world to blame him for going on. Sloan was one of the few who would really understand what he had been doing, but—there was one incalculable factor.

If he caught Sloan, what would Kennedy do?

Use the other Yard man? Or kill him?

Could Kennedy use Sloan successfully? Hadn't he all that he wanted, already?

Roger stood up suddenly. "He'll kill——" he began.

The door from the kitchen opened silently, and Harry came in with a tray.

"Did you speak, sir?" His sallow face was expressionless.

"Talking to myself." Wagner was at a rare, low and mournful ebb, but the music had probably been enough to keep the words away from Harry. He smiled. "I'm too much on my own, Harry!"

"That has been my opinion for some time, if I may say so, sir." Harry put down the tray, took a silver-plated lid off a dish of mixed grill. "That is the best I can do at such short notice, Mr. West."

He drew back; his doleful brown eyes had an unusual glow. He seemed to come alive. And by saying "West" he had flung a verbal hand grenade.

Roger said slowly: "I don't think I heard you."

"I think you did, sir."

Keep *calm*.

"How much do you know about this, Harry?"

"A little, sir. I have my ears." He was solemn again, the glow had gone, but there was something in him which hadn't been there before. "Also, I have had my instructions to report on your movements and your telephone calls while at the flat, sir. I have duly carried out my duties. Except——" he paused.

This was a form of torment. It was impossible to know what was in his mind; Roger felt as if he were in the midst of a furious explosion, but Harry's voice went so quiet. He'd known the man for nearly two months, and studied him. All he'd seen was a well-trained automaton, obeying orders with smooth precision, never obtruding, always at hand.

Now, he was a man; a human being primed with dangerous knowledge.

"Except what?" Roger held the arms of his chair tightly.

Harry gulped; he had screwed himself up for this— yes, he was frightened. Tension, springing out of nowhere, was brittle and dangerous.

"When you went out the other night, sir."

Roger didn't speak, but thought of the dictaphone he knew was hidden in this room. He'd never located it; it had been wiser to leave it untouched, and guide all conversation into channels which Kennedy could safely hear. He couldn't control this conversation.

"I saw the brown paper at the door, and that told me you had gone—I thought I heard you," said Harry. "But I didn't report to Mr. Briggs."

"To whom?"

"Mr. Briggs—Percy, sir. Percy is the man to whom I have had to make all my reports."

"I see. And why didn't you inform him of my excursion?"

"I weighed everything up and decided that it wouldn't be in the best interests," said Harry. He formed every word carefully, had to force it out, because of his fears. Of what? Of Roger's reaction, when he knew the truth? Was this—blackmail? The word seemed to scream at Roger.

Harry was a crook, and must be a professional, or he wouldn't have this job; Harry had a stranglehold over his "boss". Roger stood quite still, watching his composure break now. The grill stood on the table, getting cold. Harry seemed to shrink, yet there was a form of courage in him. He licked his lips before he spoke again.

"You see, sir——"

No, he couldn't get it out.

Roger said slowly, forcing down his rage. "All right, Harry. Let's have it. How much do you want?"

Harry raised his hands, a swift, startled gesture.
"*Want?* It's not blackmail, I wouldn't put on the black,
it's——"

The front-door bell rang.

21

INTO THE PARLOUR

HARRY jumped, as if someone had kicked him, and darted
a glance over his shoulder.

Roger said: "Never mind that. If it's not blackmail,
what is it?"

"I—I think I had better see who that is," said Harry.
The ringing had made him turn pale, his hands weren't
steady. "It might be Mr. Briggs." Fear of Percy was
uppermost.

Roger grabbed his arm.

"Forget it. What——"

Harry pulled himself free and hurried to the door.
Short of grappling with him, which would probably be
heard outside, there was nothing Roger could do. He
watched the man's thin back and sloping shoulders as he
opened the door of the tiny hall. He heard the outer door
opening. He looked round the room, in a despairing
effort to locate the dictaphone; he was reduced to despairing efforts. He heard a man's deep voice:

"All right, I know he's in."

It was Sloan.

"Really, sir." Harry's voice rose in a protesting
squeak. "Mr. Rayner is just having——"

Sloan filled the doorway.

Roger said evenly: "Getting tough?"

"I'm always tough when I'm in a hurry, and I'm in a
hurry now. Is there a place where your man can go without hearing us?"

Harry's eyes became cloudy again.

"Kitchen, Harry," said Roger. He might have said:

" Kennel, Fido," and meant the same thing and had the same effect.

Harry went off, hurriedly, and closed the door leading to the kitchen. Sloan went across to it and turned the key in the lock. He looked very big, powerful, and aggressive; but he was alone, and he hadn't come with any real or trumped-up charge. This was another personal interview—off the record.

Roger said: " I don't know that I like you in this mood, Inspector."

" Forget I'm a policeman. Did you telephone me on Sunday night? " Sloan was in an angrily aggressive mood.

There was a dictaphone, taking all this down.

" I did not."

" I want the truth, Rayner."

" I can't imagine any reason why I should telephone you. Why don't you ask your friend Kennedy? "

" Don't be smart. After I came to see you, I was twice run down. Nearly run down. They were murder attempts. They came immediately after I'd called to see you. I'm giving you a chance to save yourself from trouble. Did you telephone me? "

" No."

Sloan said: " So you fixed those attacks."

" You're crazy."

" We'll see." Sloan moved across the room. He had his right hand in his pocket, holding something which made a considerable bulge; the kind of bulge that a gun would make. If a Yard man had reason to suspect that his life was in danger, he could get authority to carry a gun. There was something new in Sloan's expression, as if he felt sure he could force a showdown, and meant to.

Roger said: " Calm down. Have a drink."

" I've finished drinking with killers."

" All right, please yourself. Mind if I get on with my supper? " Roger sat down and picked up a knife and fork.

" Where have you been to-night? "

" Out."

" Don't evade my questions. Where have you been? "

" Continuing my experiments in romance. Auburn, this time, and very sophisticated. I don't think she would be quite your type."

" Don't you? Not the type you had with you on Sunday night? "

An alarm bell seemed to ring in Roger's head. He cut into a kidney and put it to his mouth; it wasn't the easiest thing in the world to keep steady.

" No, not the same type at all. The first was a sweet little innocent animal, didn't I tell you? There was nothing innocent about this one, and I don't know that you could call her sweet. Sure you won't have a drink? "

" What was the name of the girl you were out with on Sunday? "

" Doris."

" Doris what? "

" That's as far as I went, and as far as was necessary. She was quite satisfied to know me as Charlie."

" Where did you take her? "

" I didn't. She took me. A pleasant little two-roomed flat. She was *very* sweet." He ate some bacon and toast; it nearly choked him. " I wish I knew why you were getting so worked up."

" You're lying. You took her out in a car."

" Have it your own way."

" The car was a Morris. Colour, grey. It was muddy because it had done a lot of country running and hadn't been washed down. It's still muddy. You took her out in it—let's have the truth, Rayner."

" I haven't a car."

" This one was lent to you."

Roger finished his mouthful, and leaned back.

" No, take it easy, Sloan. I didn't go out in any car on Sunday night. I spent the evening with Doris, and came back here in time to have a talk with you. Remember? If I wanted to hire a car, it wouldn't be a poky Morris."

Sloan took a step forward and grinned into his face.

" A *poky* Morris, is it? How did you know the size of that car, *Mister* Rayner."

Roger would never feel contemptuous about a crook who made a simple slip again. But he laughed.

"When I think of Morris's, I also think of size eights. I still wish that I knew what's under your skin."

Sloan said: "You will. We've picked up your Doris."

"Really? What's she done? I didn't know that she was a crook in her spare time. I—oh, she's a pro, is she? Pity." He laughed, and again he nearly choked himself, but helped it to seem more natural. "Sweet and innocent! What mistakes a man can make, can't he?"

"So you're learning that. She isn't a pro. She's a girl who lives on the fringe of a small East London gang. You know the gang—Myers runs it. She was in that muddy Morris outside Brixton Jail on Sunday night. You were with her."

Roger said: "Well, well! Did she say so?"

"You were with her."

"At her flat. If she's said anything different, she was out with another man after I left her. That was quite early, remember. She——"

Sloan took out his gun—an automatic. He held it pointing towards Roger. He was a Scotland Yard Officer, and a Yard Officer never used a gun to threaten, or hardly ever. He used a gun in self-defence only, and there was no reason for self-defence here. Sloan was going too far, and the glitter in Sloan's eyes suggested that he wasn't himself. There was a dictaphone too, and it was at least possible that the watcher across the road had telephoned to report Sloan's arrival. If so, others might come to collect the fly that had walked into Roger's parlour.

"Let's have the truth," growled Sloan. "Go back a bit, Rayner. You killed West. All the rest is unimportant. You killed West. I may not be able to pin it on to you, but I've promised myself that I shall kill the man who killed West. I can shoot you in self-defence and get away with it." His voice was low-pitched, he wasn't so far beside himself that he risked Harry hearing the conversation. *Could* he mean this? Was it just bluff? All the experience of years told Roger that it was bluff, but he had never before seen Sloan in a savage, unreasoning mood like this. There was something more than the suspicion about the little grey car burning in Sloan.

Roger said: " I did not kill West. I have not killed anyone. I was not out in a grey Morris on Sunday night."

" I don't believe you."

" All right, get on with your romancing. I'm hungry." Roger turned to the mixed grill. It was cold, the fat had congealed on the plate. A piece of sausage had no taste at all, and that wasn't the fault of the sausage. Sloan towered over him; nothing was beyond Sloan at that moment.

He said slowly, deliberately: " West's body was found this morning. Until then, I wasn't sure that he was dead. Now I know. Now I know that you killed him.. But there are others, higher up than you. Kennedy—others. Let's have the truth, Rayner. Give me the story, and the other names, and I'll let you take your rap for the Brixton job and forget the rest. Keep it to yourself, and——"

He wasn't even consistent.

Take it one at a time, and quickly. Kennedy's sister had said that Janet could be " looked after " with a big insurance about which she had known nothing; that had been a strong hint that plans were in the making to produce his " body ". Sloan had jumped to the conclusions, when a policeman should have taken much more trouble to make sure that the body was really the one suspected— but Sloan wasn't in a normal mood.

He heard a car pull up, outside. Percy? Or men summoned by the man across the road?

" You can't make me take a rap for a job I didn't do," he said. " You've got the wrong end of the stick, Sloan. Put that gun away and be sensible. How do you know your friend West is dead? "

" His body was found. He'd been drowned. Face battered, fingers amputated, all the usual tricks to prevent identification, but they made a mistake. *You* made a mistake. You fools always make one. West had a scar or two which served as identification. I saw the body myself. I've seen those scars myself. I've seen them before—I was with West when he was wounded, and got one of them."

Brilliantly clever; they had even scarred a man, so that the identification would be to the satisfaction of the police. And Janet—did *Janet* know? He felt a des-perate surge of anxiety, he had never been nearer telling Sloan the truth. But he daren't, yet. He heard a sound, metal on metal; a key was being inserted in the lock of the outer door.

Sloan didn't seem to hear it.

" I'm sorry about West," Roger said. He felt sick— *did* Janet know? " If this girl Doris told you that I was with her in the car on Sunday night, she lied."

Doris hadn't said anything of the kind. Possibly she'd been held; probably she had been recognized by someone who had passed the car. You couldn't cope with the fantastic improbabilities of life, which so often helped the police to catch a man or woman who thought they were absolutely safe. Someone passing Brixton Jail knew Doris, had seen her in the car, and told the police—that was how it happened, time and time again.

Sloan thrust the gun forward.

" I'll give you half a minute," he said. His eyes glared, all *finesse* had gone, but even now it must be bluff; he hadn't been driven to such heights of madness even by the discovery of the body. Or—had he?

The door of the hall opened softly. Sloan had his back to it.

" I mean it, Rayner."

" Oh, no, you don't."

A man slid into the room, gun in hand, and spoke. Sloan spun round. The man at the door fired. The bullet smacked into Sloan's gun and wrenched it out of his hand. It dropped to the floor, between him and the gunman, who moved forward swiftly and kicked it away. Two other men came in swiftly. Both had guns.

Sloan drew back. " Get out. Get——"

They approached, remorselessly.

Roger screwed himself up. If the order had gone out, " Kill Sloan ", then they'd shoot again, whether Sloan took this lying down, or put up a fight. But if they had orders to kill, would the man have shot the gun out of

Sloan's grasp? Wouldn't he have killed him with that first shot?

Sloan said: "Get away."

"Don't try any rough stuff, Sloan," said the man with the gun. He was small, thin, evil-faced: evil because of his grin. Roger knew him slightly, as one of the most corrupt and vicious East End gangsters, a race-gang type, and one of Oily Joe's mob. His name was Myers. He took another step forward, the gun still raised.

A third man came in.

Sloan said: "Get—away."

And then he jumped——

Roger shot out his foot. Sloan kicked against it and went sprawling as the gunman squeezed the trigger. The bullet spat out, the sharp crack echoed. The bullet buried itself in the wall, and Sloan sprawled forward, unhurt. The two men from behind the gunman pounced; wolves couldn't have moved quicker. Before Sloan could save himself, he was manacled with regulation handcuffs. He fought and struggled until the thin-faced crook cracked him high on the nape of the neck with the butt of his gun.

Sloan suddenly became still.

Myers grinned at Roger. "Saved a lot o' trouble, ain't it? Okay, get him out." He nodded to the others, who dragged Sloan towards the door, and at the doorway hoisted him between them so that they could carry him downstairs. He disappeared, and he was alive: they'd gone to a lot of trouble to keep him alive. That was on instruction, so the kill order hadn't gone out. Kennedy wanted to use Sloan, or else hold him as an added pressure on Roger.

The thin-faced man said: "All okay?"

"That made a lot of noise."

"Nice and quiet up here. You don't have to worry. If anyfink was 'eard, we'll fix it. So long." Myers swaggered out of the room and closed the door behind him. The footsteps on the stairs sounded loud as the other men carried Sloan.

.   .   .   .   .   .

He'd let it happen.

Could he have done anything to prevent it? Even if he'd thrown everything else to the winds, caution, hopes, plans, could he have prevented that from happening? He might have shaken the little gangsters, but he had no gun, and the others had been armed. There hadn't been any way of preventing it from happening, but if Sloan died, he would for ever blame himself.

He sat over the cold mixed grill.

He didn't know how long he sat there before he heard the tapping. At first, he hardly noticed it, but it continued so persistently that he raised his head and looked about him. It came from the kitchen door—Harry, of course. He had forgotten Harry, forgotten his urgency when Harry had gone to open the door to let Sloan in.

He went across the room and turned the key.

" Thank you, sir," said Harry. He didn't look any less frightened. " I was afraid that you might get hurt."

" What else are you afraid of? "

" I—I don't think I'm afraid of anything, sir. I spoke out of turn. I'm sorry your supper was spoiled. Shall I prepare something else? I will gladly——"

" Do you know where the dictaphone is in the flat? "

Harry gulped. " I've disconnected it, sir. I did that before I spoke in the first place."

Roger said abruptly: " Do you drink? "

" I don't mind a beer." Harry looked startled.

" Get me a whisky. Help yourself to what you want. Then come and sit down." He wasn't sure that these were good tactics; one man would be more at ease with drink and in a chair; another would feel acute embarrassment. Harry poured out with steady hands and came and sat down. He didn't perch on the edge of his chair, but settled back—they were the right tactics for Harry. He had poured himself out a beer, in a glass tankard. Roger gave him a cigarette.

" Thank you, sir."

They lit up.

" If it's not blackmail, what is it? "

The fear was there, hovering in Harry's eyes, but the

new situation had given him confidence, and his voice was
steady as he answered :

"I've noticed a lot while I've been here, Mr. West.
One day before you arrived a lady came asking for you.
I was here, fixing the place up. A Miss Day she was,
Miss Marion Day. I noticed in the papers what hap-
ened to her afterwards. It was from her I got an idea who
you *really* were, sir. And I—I was a friend of Ginger Kyle's.
Very good friends we were in our young days. We got
mixed up with the same bunch. I'm not pleading inno-
cence, sir. We went into it with our eyes open, and we knew
the risk we was taking. I was lucky—I've never bin inside. Made a little packet, and if it wasn't for—for pressure, Mr. West, I would be retired now. Ginger ought to
have had a nice little pile waiting for him when he came
out. Instead o' that, they didn't look after him. They
killed his wife, or he thought they did. Saw him while he
was in London, he told me all about it. And when they
killed *him*—I can't help it, Mr. West. If I've judged you
wrong, I'm for it. I'll take my chance, same as Ginger did.
And others. But it seemed to me you slipped out the
other night so's they shouldn't know, and you wasn't
working with them whole-hearted. *Are* you, sir? If you
are, then okay, I'm for it. If you're not, if you're *against*
them—I'll help if I can. My word on it, Mr. West."

He sat back. His forehead and long upper lip were
beaded with sweat, and that cloudy fear hovered in his
eyes.

But—was that put on?

Was this another of Kennedy's trick tests?

22

27 MOUNTJOY SQUARE

Roger could tell him the truth; and Harry might send
word to Percy, and so bring about the end of it all.

He could be non-committal; but if Harry were still
spying on him, that would be as damning.

He could reject the offer, report to Percy—and if it were genuine, damn Harry, send Harry to his death. You slid into accepting that as a fact. You didn't tell yourself that no one would kill as freely and as ruthlessly as Kennedy; you knew that it was true. The man was completely amoral, he didn't regard killing as most men did. It was necessary, it was done—an obstacle removed, like a chalk mark wiped off a blackboard and leaving only a smear as trace.

Harry sipped his beer; his hand was unsteady.

Look at the other facts.

They'd got Sloan; they'd kept him alive for a while, anyhow. But Roger could no longer lift the telephone, in emergency, and call for help from Sloan. He could do the obvious, and try to persuade the police to raid 27 Mountjoy Square. Sloan might have been persuaded to do that, no one else at the Yard would take a chance with a man as highly placed in Society as Raymond Glanville Hemmingway. The anonymous report would be noted, and filed, but no action would be taken on a simple telephone call. He could—in the absolute last resort, he would—visit the Yard himself, and make a full statement. They'd act then; but there was no guarantee that incriminating evidence would be found at Mountjoy Square; and there was Kennedy's sister's statement, made so easily and confidently, that he himself would find it difficult to identify Kennedy as the man really was. This wasn't the time to wonder whether that was true; he must assume that it was true and worry about how the trick of disguise was worked afterwards. Kennedy was full of tricks.

Harry stirred in his chair and stubbed out his cigarette.

Roger said: "Where do you report, Harry?"

"To Percy, sir."

"Yes. Where?"

"I have a telephone number. There is another way of communicating, also—through the men who sometimes are on duty outside. No doubt you've noticed them—I saw you looking out of the window to-night. There was one there. I always assume that when there is a special job on, they take extra care because they aren't sure of you

yet. I hope they never will be, sir. It's a dirty business—
it stinks. I've done a lot of things in my life, but murder—
I stop at murder. I'm scared. I don't mind admitting
I'm scared. But I've taken a chance, and I hope it's
justified."

" Don't you know where Percy lives? "

" No, sir."

" Kennedy? "

" I've heard the name, that's all, and I think he's called
here once or twice, but when he's been coming, I've had
ordees to keep out of the way."

" How do you get your instructions? "

" From Percy, sir."

" And he blackmails you into obeying? "

" That's right."

" What jobs have you done? " Roger asked, and his
voice sharpened. Harry put down the empty tankard and
half-closed his eyes. It was very quiet in the room.

" Safes, mostly, sir. And breaking and entering, more
lately. One of the places I went to, an old man was killed.
I didn't do it, but Percy says he can pin it on me. I don't
doubt he can. I get well paid for this, I didn't see any
reason why I shouldn't do what I was told. You were just
another dope. But after that Miss Day and Ginger was
bumped off—I couldn't settle. There's some things you
can take, and there's others that you just can't swallow,
and cold-blooded murder's a thing *I* can't swallow. I
weighed it all up carefully, and decided to take a chance
on you, sir."

Roger wanted a cracksman. He said: " Have you
got any burglar's tools here? "

Harry's eyes opened wide.

" Well——"

" Good, up-to-date stuff, not just a jemmy and a screw-
driver."

" I haven't got any *here*, but I know where I could lay
me hands on some."

" Will you take a big risk?"

" Nothing much to lose, now," said Harry, and his face
became more animated, a little colour glowed in his

cheeks. " So I was right, you've been putting one across Percy and his boss."

" That's right, Harry."

Harry leaned back in his chair and gave a little, satisfied smile. There was no gloating in it, but much relief. There remained a risk that Roger was wrong in trusting him; he didn't think it was a grave one.

" How long will it take you to get the kit? "

" In a cab, about an hour, Mr. West."

" Then get it, and——"

" Isn't there something you've forgot? " asked Harry. He looked at the window. " That fellow will report if I go out and if you go out. No doubt about that, is there? "

" He won't report until he's relieved or they come to relieve him. He won't be able to. They'll find that he's missing," Roger said. He stood up abruptly. " The one thing he won't expect is a direct attack from you or me, Harry. I'll fix him, first. You slip out after me. When we leave here, we've burned our boats."

" Might as well make a good bonfire when you're at it," said Harry. " May I ask what job we're going to do? "

" No."

The gentle smile came again.

" You're wise not to tell me too much, Mr. West, but you needn't be afraid, you can trust me. I was a long time making up my mind about this, but when my mind's made up, I don't shift easy. I'm like that. Have you got a gun, Mr. West? "

" No."

" Perhaps it's a good thing," said Harry.

*   *   *   *   *

Roger stood in the doorway and looked across Lyme Street. The guard was still there. He himself was in the shadows, and the man couldn't see him. He saw the other put his hands to his pocket and take out a packet of cigarettes; a moment later, a match flared. The man moved out of his doorway and strolled along the street—and Roger moved forward, but drew back suddenly. A policeman had turned the corner and was

walking along, that was why the guard had moved. The
guard crossed the road and stood outside a small café
which was still open; a man looking into a café and
studying the menu card in the window wasn't going to
attract much attention. He peered along the street.
The policeman passed him. The guard waited until the
policeman had turned the next corner, and then went
back to his usual stand. The cigarette glowed pink,
showing the tip of his nose, his eyes, the curly brim of his
hat. Roger moved again, quickly. He saw the man
stiffen. He crossed the road, but didn't look at the man—
whose job it was to report, and perhaps to follow. He
walked towards the dark dinginess of the market lanes
and alleys, and the man followed him. He slipped round
a corner; it was very dark here. He heard the man
hurrying after him, and knew when he was at the corner.
   The man turned.
   Roger grabbed him by the neck, stifling a cry, drove a
fierce punch into his stomach, let him go, then struck at his
chin. Two blows knocked the man out. No one was
here, the policeman was out of sight. Roger dragged the
unconscious man across the bumpy, cobbled road, into a
narrow alley leading towards the main, covered market.
He took out a length of cord, bound the man's ankles and
wrists, dragged him farther—into a little alcove—and
stuffed a handkerchief into his mouth. Then Roger
straightened his back, and considered the chances. The
man couldn't escape, but might be found by a patrolling
policeman; this wasn't quite concealing enough. He
dragged him, by his coat collar, farther along—and saw a
dark pile of empty wooden crates. He shifted some of the
crates, dumped the man behind them, and put them back
into position. He wouldn't be found until those crates
were moved, and that wouldn't be for several hours, at
least. Hours were all he wanted.
   He went back to Lyme Street.
   Harry came out of the doorway. "All okay, sir?"
   "Yes. Get a move on."
   "I had to see this through," said Harry. "See you at
the Burlington Gardens end of Burlington Arcade in about

an hour, then.   It's just on eleven—I ought to be there by
midnight."
    " Fine."
    Harry turned and hurried towards the Strand and a
taxi.
    Roger had an hour to kill.

·   ·   ·   ·   ·

    There had never been a longer sixty minutes.   He
walked to Burlington Arcade, and his mind wouldn't stop
working, weighing up the chances; especially those against
him.   Kennedy would have his home well protected.
Kennedy, as Hemmingway, wouldn't be likely to keep the
records at the home where he was so safe.   Harry might
fail him.   Harry might get cold feet.   Harry might have
fooled him.   At least Harry didn't know where he was
going, but Harry would be able to report that he would be
in Burlington Gardens at midnight.   Death didn't take
long.   A man might come towards him, walking, or in a
car—and shoot just once.   It only needed one bullet.
Kennedy was ruthless, and he wouldn't dare to take
chances.   Roger tried not to think of Janet or of Sloan,
but now and again he felt a cold shiver of excitement.   If
he succeeded, it would all be over by the morning.   If he
failed——
    He walked along to Bond Street and towards Oxford
Street.   There were few people about, and most of those
who were came from the Æolian Hall, where they took
the overflow from Broadcasting House.   Taxis passed.   A
sleek car came from Oxford Street and slowed down as it
drew near him.   It was ten minutes to twelve.   He turned
his face towards the car, prepared to spring to one side if
the driver or the passenger moved.
    The car stopped.
    A man in evening dress and a woman with beautiful
furs round her shoulders, sat there.
    Roger felt as cold as ice.
    " Can you direct me to Shepherd's Market? "   The
man sounded anxious.
    Roger said stiffly: " Turn right along Piccadilly and

take the little narrow road after Half Moon Street, that'll
take you into the market—it's about the eighth turning
along . . . " he spoke so quietly that the other had to strain
his ears to catch the words. There was no need to worry,
for the car moved off. Roger walked back towards the
end of the Arcade. It was a warm night, but he didn't
feel warm. A clock struck sonorously—midnight. Each
boom seemed louder and more threatening than the last.
No one approached the Arcade. Harry might have
taken fright; Harry might have fooled him. Harry
might——

He walked away again; it was a dangerous spot to
stand. Another car passed, slowed down at the corner,
and then turned without the driver taking the slightest
notice of him. Another—this wasn't a car, but a taxi!
It came along at good speed, it wasn't going to stop here.

It slowed down.

Harry might——

Harry, carrying a big suitcase, climbed out of the cab
and paid the driver off. It wasn't imagination that the
driver looked at him curiously; but cab drivers were
often curious about mysterious night passengers, it would
have been better to have met outside a hotel; there were
dozens nearby. Forget it. The taxi moved off, and
Harry came forward briskly.

" I've got everything I could lay my hands on, sir.
Had a bit of luck." He was chirpy.

" Yes? "

" One of the new kind of burners, better than the old
oxy-acetylene jobs, not so heavy. Heavy enough, but I
can manage to carry it, need two and a car for the other
kind. Are we within walking distance, sir? "

" Yes. Let me have the case for a bit."

" I can manage, sir, thank you."

Roger felt like laughing. Or screaming. " I can
manage, sir." He let the man have his way, and they
walked briskly up Bond Street as far as Brook Street, then
turned left. He took the case; it was heavier than Harry
had let it appear. They changed it over three times
before they reached the corner of Mountjoy Square.

Roger said : " Have you had a go at one of these houses in the past ? "

" Not this kind, sir—done country jobs, mostly. I never liked working on the big places in London. Too many flatfoots." The street light showed his pawky smile. " Is there a back way ? "

" May be."

" It's safer at the back, sir."

" Yes." They turned a corner, and a few yards along came upon a service alley which led to the backs of the houses in the Square. Mountjoy wasn't typical of London squares. On small iron gates, to the tiny courtyards, there were house numbers. Roger didn't light his torch. He peered closely at the numbers, found 23—it was white paint on a black gate, and there was some light from a house opposite. No one stirred, and there was little sound of traffic until a car turned a corner and snorted past the alley.

Next door—25.

And here was 27. He had to make sure and couldn't see the number on the gate. There was no light from the house beyond. He took out his torch, covered it with his fingers and showed only the merest glimmer of light—27.

" All right," he said.

" I'll see to the gate," said Harry.

He didn't add " sir " ; he had dropped the handle. It wasn't the only change in him—the other was so great that it was almost metamorphosis. Harry seemed to grow in stature and sureness and confidence. This was his real job, and he was a craftsman. The gate was simple, but it was locked. He opened it with a picklock, making no sound at all on the metal. The gate didn't squeak when it swung back.

Roger had to say something : " First hurdle."

Harry grunted.

The courtyard was flagged. Their rubber-shod feet made hardly a sound. As they drew nearer the dark shape of the house, Roger saw a light ; it hadn't been noticeable from the gate. It was at the top of a window, where light crept past the curtains ; and it was at the top floor—the servants' floor. Harry glanced up, and then looked at the door. He didn't use a torch, and there seemed to be hardly any light. He ran his fingers over the door gently, gingerly; he wasn't worrying about leaving finger-prints.

"No can do," he said. "Good job, that, it's got a burglar-proof fastening on the inside. Think they're wired up for an alarm?"

"Probably."

Harry sniffed. "Alarms," he said; but for the need for silence, Roger could have sworn that he would have scoffed at alarms. He pushed past Roger and went to the long, narrow window near the door. Here, for the first time, he used a torch—one with a hood which could be opened or closed at a touch, and which regulated the beam of light and prevented too much from showing. He stood with his back to the alley and the other houses, and peered into the window. Blinds were drawn, but he was looking at the sides, for the alarm wire. He switched off the light suddenly. Roger just stopped himself from saying: "Found it?" Harry obviously had. Harry backed away.

"Lot o' trouble there. Might be a first-floor window open. May be a ladder. Stay here."

He vanished, leaving the tool-kit by Roger's side. He was gone for what seemed a long time, and came back silently as a wraith.

"Found one?"

"No. Careful, aren't they?" Harry's words came in a faint whisper. "Quiet."

Roger stood aside.

Harry took what looked like a folded rag from the tool-kit, then a small can. He poured water over the rag, and then spread it over the window; gummed rag, or paper, deadened sound; but Harry might have forgotten one possibility, that the glass here was toughened. Harry took out a hammer and gave the covered glass a sharp tap.

It gave out a curiously dull sound.

He sniffed. "Triplex." He pulled the rag away, wrapped it up in newspaper and dropped it into the box. Then he took out a drill and, working swiftly and with very little sound, drilled four holes, close to each other in the wooden frame. Next, he used a narrow saw, which was just thin enough to go through one of the holes. The saw made hardly a sound, so it was loaded with grease. The line of the cut seemed to leap into the green-painted wood. In less than five minutes, he took a piece of wood out, making a hole big enough for him to reach inside. He did so, using the torch with one hand, groped for the catch and found it.

That made the first real sound—a sharp clang. He sniffed, and stood absolutely still. Roger could hear him breathing. There was no other sound, no alarm. Harry poked his arm inside again; he was pushing the alarm wire up, away from its wall-fastening. It took a long time, and another car passed in Mountjoy Square, head-lights glowing against the houses opposite. Harry didn't stop working. A faint sound came from the window, and he withdrew his hand.

" Okay," he said.

He pushed the window up. It made little noise, and there was no clangour of an alarm.

" Kit," he ordered as he climbed through, pushing the curtains to one side. Roger handed him the suitcase, open; it was as much as he could do to lift it. Then he climbed through.

" Going to switch off the current at the main? " he asked.

" Not me! Light on upstairs, ain't there? If it goes out, they'll come and investigate. We can manage."

How many cracksmen were as good as he?

He adjusted the curtains and then switched on the light. They were in a long, narrow kitchen. White tiles glistened, a chromium sink fitting showed; it was somehow remini-scent of Chatworth's office. The door faced them.

" Know where we want to go? " asked Harry.

" For a start, the first floor—I know the room."

" Any vaults here? "

" We'll have to look and may have to get inside."

" Okay. Try upstairs first. Know what, don't you? "

Harry looked at him, with a hand on the switch.

" What ? "

" There's one certain way of getting the dicks to have a look round. Ring 999 and report a burglary."

" That will come later."

" Why later ? " Harry kept his finger on the light. " I don't mind taking what's coming to me."

" It's no use bringing the police if there's nothing here to find. And they won't break into vaults or force a safe—they'll just look at the damage done."

Harry sniffed and switched off the light.

There were two more rooms before they reached the passage leading to the hall. All was in darkness, and only the faintest glow shone from the torch, but it was enough to show the staircase. The thick pile of the carpet became their ally. Harry took the case, shut now, and they went upstairs, Roger in the lead. He passed the doorway in which the small, lovely woman had stood when he had first come here. Kennedy's wife ? There was no reason to doubt it. Was she out with him and his sister ? There was really no reason to believe that the woman in green was his sister.

Harry whispered : " Who's at home ? "

" I'm not sure."

" They haven't any guards." The words suggested that Harry was beginning to feel nervous ; but that was probably due to the fact that the first, worst job was finished and he was suffering from reaction. Give him a safe to open and he would forget his nerves. They reached the door of the study. Harry lost no time, put the case down softly and tried the handle ; the door was locked. He examined it, partly in the dim light from his torch, partly by sense of touch. He nodded, and set to work at once with a pick-lock. Roger thought he could use a pick-lock himself ; Harry's speed made him seem slow. It was as good as using the ordinary key.

Harry pushed the door open, gently ; there was no light inside. He nodded and stepped in, shining his torch brightly now, but careful to make sure that it didn't shine on the window. Roger closed the door. It closed too sharply, and he heard Harry's soft intake of breath.

Nothing happened.   Harry moved away from him, his
cat's eyes getting him past the furniture without difficulty.
He reached the window, and his curiously soft and penetrating voice even when lowered, came clearly:
   " Curtains are drawn—okay."
   " Door," said Roger.
   " Not a chance."
Roger groped for and switched on the light.
   Only two wall-lamps came on; they spread a quiet,
subdued light.   The room was familiar.   He looked at
the door, and remembered that he had noticed, on his
first visit, that it was specially protected at top, sides, and
bottom, to make sure that it was sound-proof; that also
made it light-proof when closed, and Harry had realized
that.   He now had a lot of respect for Harry.   The curtains were heavy green velvet with a large, deep pelmet,
and they were wide and dropped well below the window.
There was little chance of light showing.
   Harry said: " Where? "
   " You're the boss."
   Harry grinned, his confidence fully restored.   He
roamed about the room, moving this picture, that piece
of furniture, scanning the walls with expert eye.   Roger
took one end of the room, Harry the other.   Roger wasn't
surprised when he heard Harry whisper: " Okay."   He
turned.   Harry stood by a bookcase which he had eased
away from the wall.   Roger crossed the room and saw the
wall-safe behind it.   There were wall-safes and wall-safes,
and it was impossible to judge the really good ones from
the outside.   All there was to see were round pieces of
metal and a bright steel knob.   Harry pushed the bookcase farther away;   it moved at a touch.   He pointed,
and showed where it was fastened to a spring hook in the
wall;   at the first tug, it would seem too heavy for one man
to shift, but Harry hadn't been fooled.   He behaved, now,
as if he were a man setting about an everyday task.   He
pulled a lamp standard nearer and switched it on.   Then
he took a pair of thin asbestos gloves from the case, drew
them on, and picked out a tiny piece of needle-fine wire.
He held the point against the steel of the knob;   nothing

happened.   He held it at one of the ridged circles.   There was a tiny blue flash.   He drew back and grinned.

" Difficult? " Roger asked.

He knew that the orthodox move was to switch off the current at the main.   But Harry was teaching him much about the practice of cracking cribs.

" Could be.   But if it's electric it isn't so bad.   Could be infra-red."   Harry sniffed.   " That means an alarm, too—wired up like this, they always ring the alarm."

" Main switch? "

" You and your main switch."   Harry grinned.   " Stop the alarm where it rings, that's the idea.   Most likely place is somewhere outside this room.   Maybe there are two, but if we find the control alarm and put it out of action, that will stop the other one.   Staying inside? "

" I'll come with you."

They went out again.   Harry looked sharply at him when he opened the door, but didn't speak.   They stood in darkness on the landing.   Then Harry put down a light switch; subdued light came on.   Nothing stirred, there was no sound.   Harry began to roam about the landing, looking towards the ceiling.   He didn't have to look far.   A box was fastened to the wall, near the ceiling, just beyond the doorway from which the woman had stared at Roger.   He sniffed, and brought up a chair; it wasn't high enough.   He pointed to an oak chest, and they carried it to the wall and then placed the chair on top of it.   Harry still wasn't satisfied, took the chair away and brought a cloth from a large table.   He spread the cloth over the chest; that wasn't to prevent scratching; he took infinite pains to be silent.

He could reach the box comfortably, now.   He opened it gently, and inside a large brass bell gleamed dully. He worked on it for fully five minutes; they were nerve-racking minutes.   Then he turned and whispered:

" Hand me down."

Roger gave him a hand.

" Okay now," said Harry.   " Let's get back.   Never did like working in the open."   They reached the door of the study.

They went across to the wall-safe, and Harry put a cold chisel between the wainscotting and the wall, and levered part of the wainscoting away. Wood groaned and splintered, but he went on until he had room to work behind it. He had laid bare the electric cable leading to the safe. He put on the asbestos gloves again and took a pair of wire cutters with insulated handles. He cut the cable quickly; the powerful jaws snapped through at one nip. There was a fierce blue flash and a hissing sound; that was all. Harry nodded with satisfaction, straightened up, and turned his attention to the wall-safe. He could have spent time trying to find the right combination; he didn't, but took out a compact-looking instrument like a blow-lamp. It was fastened to a small iron cylinder by a long rubber cable. He fiddled with the blow-lamp for a few minutes, and then pressed a lever; a tongue of white-hot flame spat out towards the circular handle.

" Glasses," he said, and then growled : " Only one pair. Look away." He put on a pair of goggles, and then turned his attention earnestly to the safe. Roger turned his back on him. Bluish white light filled the room with a garish brightness. He smelt something; molten metal? He was tempted to turn and watch, but knew that it would be crazy, he wouldn't be able to see for an hour or more if he looked at the flame with his eyes unprotected, so he stared at the door.

He saw the handle turn.

23

KENNEDY'S WIFE

THE flame hissed and glowed as Harry knelt by the safe, intent, unaware of that movement at the door.

The handle turned slowly.

Roger moved towards it. The door was locked, was light-proof and sound-proof. Why had anyone come? Why was the handle being turned so cautiously? Had

Kennedy returned, with suspicions at fever-pitch? Roger waited, watching the handle in that garish light. It didn't fall back, and instead the door began to open.

It opened slowly and slightly, not wide enough for anyone to look into the room, but wide enough for them to see the light and know that burglars were here. It stayed open; the handle didn't move again. He wanted to warn Harry, but a call, even a whisper, would warn whoever was outside. He stepped a pace nearer and glanced over his shoulder. Harry bent low over the safe. The flame dazzled Roger, and he averted his gaze quickly; that glance had been folly.

He closed his eyes to shut out the image of that fierce flame, opened them again cautiously. Door and handle were blurred, but he could see that the door was still open, and the handle hadn't dropped back into position.

It began to move——

The door began to close.

He waited for ten pulsating seconds, then stepped towards it swiftly. Harry said something he didn't catch. The hissing stopped, and only the subdued light of the lamps was on.

"What——" began Harry.

Roger waved a hand to silence him, reached the door and turned the handle as stealthily as it had just been turned. He heard Harry grunt as he straightened up, glanced over his shoulder and saw the man approaching. He waved him back again. He opened the door an inch. A light was on in the passage, but no one stood outside the door.

"What is it?" hissed Harry.

"Someone outside. *Quiet.*" The whisper was agonizing, because it might be heard. He opened the door a little wider and looked round. He saw a bright light coming from a door which was closing—Kennedy's wife's door. He saw her shadow on the landing; then it was shut out.

Harry was close behind him.

"Who——"

"Hold it. Watch." Roger went across the landing,

heart thumping, touched the handle of the other door and pushed—she hadn't locked it yet. He heard a *ting*!; a telephone being lifted. He thrust the door open. Kennedy's wife, so small and exquisite, stood by the side of a bed in a luxury room. The telephone was at her ear, her great eyes were staring towards the door. At sight of Roger, she drew herself up and terror flared in those eyes. But she didn't take the telephone from her ear. Instead, she grabbed at something on the silken pillow—an automatic.

She didn't speak.

She hadn't had time to finish dialling.

Harry said: " *Strewth* ! " His heart was in the word. He stood behind Roger, who moved slowly towards the woman. This was a room of silver and gold, the right setting for beauty. She wore a flimsy, filmy dressing-gown which trailed on the floor, a pale-gold creation. She looked like something out of another, lovelier world— and the automatic was steady in her right hand. She put the receiver down slowly, and it clattered on the table; a faint burring sound came from it, she was connected with the exchange. She stretched out her hand and put a finger in one of the dialling holes, but she couldn't judge which to turn while watching him, and she had to watch him.

He took a step nearer.

Harry followed, and closed the door.

" Open it, " she said.

It was the first time he had heard her speak. Her voice was taut with fear, but she was full of courage. Harry didn't respond. Roger took another step towards her. This was a long room, she seemed a vast distance away from him—ten or twelve yards.

" Don't come nearer. Open the door. " Her voice was icy cold, now.

Roger said: " Put the gun down if you don't want to get hurt, and come away from the telephone. " He whispered, although there was no danger of being heard outside the room. He went another step forward, and the gun was trained on his stomach, held so steadily that he knew she wouldn't miss. He couldn't watch both her eyes and her hand, and he had to watch her hand. He would see the sudden spasmodic movement if she were going to squeeze the trigger. So he watched her hand, not her eyes, and took another step forward. He felt prickly sweat over his face and neck, and he shivered; he knew that he was looking death in the face. The hand holding the gun was small and beautiful, everything about her was beautiful.

He said: " I don't want to hurt you. I——"

Her forearm rippled.

He jumped to one side as she fired. The bullet spat out, with a bright flash. He felt it tear through his coat—and he heard Harry cry out. The bark of the report seemed like a thunderclap.

Roger leapt at her.

She was staring at Harry with horror in her eyes. That was for a split second. She jerked the gun up again as Roger sprang forward, but she had lost her composure; she fired again, but the bullet smacked into the floor. He reached her, hand thrust out, swung it and pushed her to one side. She struck the side of the bed and toppled on to it, still holding the gun. He grabbed at her wrist, and twisted; the gun fell. He snatched it from the bed and backed away. He breathed harshly, and wanted to look behind, at Harry and the door, but he watched her. She straightened up, slowly, her eyes blazing; there was a touch of evil in her beauty. Her tongue darted out, a red tip against pale lips.

Harry gasped: " She—she got me." His voice had a strained, wondering note in it.

Roger glanced at him. He was kneeling, with his right hand pressed into his side, and blood already seeped slowly through his fingers. He tried to get up, but couldn't. He stared at the woman, without hate, rather in disbelief. He had his mouth open, and he gulped as if he were in pain.

Kennedy's wife stood tiny and erect by the side of the bed, as if trying to defy Roger by her strength of will. The humming sound still came from the telephone, but he wasn't worried about that, only about the door. Had the servants heard those shots? Only seconds had passed, but it seemed an age before he moved. She shrank back. He grabbed her shoulder and spun her round, then reversed the gun in his hand. Her hair was short, a cluster of curls. He struck her at the back of the neck, and it was like striking a Dresden figure; or a child. She groaned and pitched forward.

She lay still, against the bed.

Roger put the telephone back on its cradle.

Harry said: "I'm—done for."

There was no sound outside on the landing, but whoever came would come stealthily.

"Nonsense." Roger stepped past him. "You'll be all right." Gun in hand, he opened the door cautiously, then drew back and switched off the lights. The landing light glowed faintly. He peered towards the stairs, saw no one and heard nothing except the thunderous beating of his heart. He waited; there was no creaking of approach, no visible shadowy shape.

Nothing.

The study door was ajar.

He turned, passed Harry again and said: "You'll be all right, Harry." Harry still pressed his hand to his side, and the blood smeared the back of his hand, his face was ghastly. He reached the woman, lifted her and carried her across the landing to the study. She was as light as a child. He dropped her into an easy-chair, and turned and went back for Harry, who knelt in the same awkward position, and licked his lips.

"I'm going to take you into the other room. Take it easy. Just hold your side."

Harry didn't speak.

How did a lean man come to weigh so heavy?

Roger grunted with the strain as he lifted him and took him across the landing. He laid him on the floor, stretched out. He went back into the bedroom, dragged a sheet and two pillows off the bed, and hurried out, closing the door. He closed the study door firmly.

Neither Harry nor the woman had moved. He pushed

her chair away from a table, so that there was nothing she could pick up, stealthily, while he was looking away from her; she would soon come round and might try to fox him. Then he put a pillow under Harry's head.

" Let me have a look."

" I'm—done for," gasped Harry.

" Not yet—not by a long way. A doctor——"

" Don't you—send for one." There was pain instead of fear in Harry's eyes. " You finish the job." He licked his lips again.

Roger said: " Let me have a look at you." He forced Harry's hand away, and the blood dripped on to the carpet. The wound seemed to be on the left side, not dead centre. He unfastened Harry's waistcoat and trousers and pulled up the sodden shirt. Blood oozed sickeningly out of a wound. He folded a handkerchief into a wad and pressed it gently on to the wound to staunch the flow. " Hold it there, Harry." He put Harry's hand on the pad, and then turned to the sheet. He started a tear with his knife, then ripped off strips. With one, he made a second pad, with another he began to bind Harry's waist. It wasn't easy to pass the bandage beneath the man.

Harry clenched his teeth now, fighting against the pain. The bandage was in position at last, with a thick wedge over the wound.

Get Harry into hospital now, and he'd have a chance; leave him for an hour, and he'd probably die. Roger glanced at the woman. She seemed to be as he had left her, unconscious.

The safe gaped open, the tools and case stood on the floor near it. Roger went across. The edge of the metal was still warm to the touch. The safe was much larger than the opening seemed to suggest. There were rolls of paper—thick rolls. Jewel-cases, money, a dozen oddments. He pulled out several of the rolls, which were fastened with thick rubber bands. One lot of paper was stiffer than most—like photographs. He slipped the band off, and saw that these were lithographed prints of the *dossiers* taken from the Yard.

He felt sick with hope and anxiety.

He unfastened another roll, and found sheet after sheet of paper with names and addresses and a few remarks against each. Dozens of the names were familiar; they were people with whom Rayner & Co. dealt, who supplied the short-supply goods—and the type of goods supplied was noted in the remarks column.

Another roll unfurled; more names and addresses, none of them in England—there were several sheets of paper for each country on the Continent. He'd seen some of these names before, too—when he had studied the case against Delaney. So Kennedy had been behind that. Another list of names followed, with a familiar look about them; peers of the realm and—*Members of Parliament*; peers and members of all the political parties. Yet another list showed stockbrokers of irreproachable reputation.

There were many more, but Roger didn't look at them. Kennedy kept his records here, that alone mattered. The Delancy contact would give the Yard sufficient to hold him on, and there were other things that would give them the excuse he wanted. He wiped the sweat off his forehead, and turned away.

Kennedy's wife sat in her chair, eyes wide open, staring at him. Harry's eyes were closed.

He said: "You've had your run. It's all over."

She didn't speak.

He went to Kennedy's desk, glancing at the papers which littered the floor, picked up the telephone and began to dial WHI——.

"Don't do that!" Kennedy's wife called. "Don't do it. You're throwing everything away."

"Some will go as far as the gallows." He dialled two numbers—1–2. The last time he had called Scotland Yard was to make that silly inquiry about Sloan, to give Sloan plenty to think about. Where was Sloan now?

"You can be so wealthy——"

"I'm sick of riches." He finished dialling with another 1–2. He heard the ringing sound. He hardly knew what he felt or thought, except that he was tired—not exhilar-

ated or excited, but tired. He could see Harry's pale face
and closed eyes and didn't think he could see any sign of
breathing. *Brrrr-brrrr*; *brrrr-brrrr*. Why didn't they
answer? *Brrrr-ck*!

" This is Scotland Yard. Can I help you? "

Roger drew in his breath.

" Can I help you? "

" I am speaking for Detective Inspector Sloan. He
wants Squad cars at twenty-seven Mountjoy Square, at
once. Also, an ambulance—a man has been shot and
badly injured."

" Is Mr. Sloan there? "

" He's busy. Hurry."

" Very good, sir." The operator didn't go away.
" What is your name, sir? "

West!

" My name is Rayner, Charles Rayner. Will you get a
move on! "

" Yes, sir, I'm calling the Squad Room on another line.
Let me make sure I have it right, sir. Twenty-seven
Mountjoy Square and you are Mr. Charles Rayner."

" That's it."

Roger put down the telephone. The woman hadn't
moved; nor had Harry. It was deathly quiet in the
room. He brushed his hand over his forehead, and it
came away filmed with sweat. He didn't smile or feel
like smiling—and he didn't know why. The Squad Room
always moved fast, cars and ambulance would be here in
ten minutes. In ten minutes it would all be over, except
the proving. He'd taken the chance, and it had come off.
There were risks still; to Janet, the boys, and Sloan.
How could he persuade the Squad cars to move off as
soon as the police were here, so that no one would warn
Kennedy, when he arrived. How——

The door opened.

Kennedy came in, with the woman in green behind him.

24

HEMMINGWAY

KENNEDY had a gun in his hand.

He stepped into the study quietly, and looked round—and although it was Kennedy, there was something different about him. What? The woman's automatic was in Roger's pocket. He put his hand to his pocket, and Kennedy said: "Don't." The gun covered Roger, and there would be no warning when this man fired.

Kennedy's wife said: "He's just telephoned Scotland Yard, Ray." She was breathless. "Hurry!"

The woman in green walked across the study, stood in front of Roger for a moment, and then struck him across the face. It was a savage blow, as savage as the blaze in her eyes. But she didn't speak. She put her hand into his pocket and drew out the automatic, then backed away.

What was the difference in Kennedy? He was the same man, yet not the same man?

His *eyes*: they weren't orbs of silver fire, they were ordinary eyes, with nothing remarkable about them. It made a great difference to his appearance.

"What did he tell them?" he asked.

"He just asked them to come here."

"Were there any other men with him?"

"Only that one." Mrs. Kennedy pointed, and stood up. By her husband's side, she looked ridiculously small.

There was a movement at the door, and Percy came in. He started, quickly recovered himself, and said: "I warned you." Kennedy nodded. Not two minutes had passed since his arrival, but they were two precious minutes. He was badly shocked, and hadn't really recovered yet.

"What——" began Percy.

Kennedy said: "Collect all the papers, Percy, and take them away. Don't go to Miss Kennedy's flat—take them to one of the other places. First thing in the morning, tell Grace Howell to take the kids away from West's house.

I'll deal with his wife afterwards. Tell Myers to put Sloan away, we won't need him now—he wouldn't be safe. They can do that whenever they like, the quicker the better."

Percy was already picking up the curled papers, and stuffing them inside his coat.

" Hurry," said Kennedy dispassionately.

" Okay, okay," said Percy. " No need to panic, we've looked after emergencies like this before." He stuffed the last rolls of papers away, straightened up—and struck at Roger as he passed. That was the second blow—vengeful, hate-ridden.

" Don't waste time," said Kennedy.

The Squad cars might be on the way already, but they might not be here in time to prevent Percy from leaving. There was no way of stopping him, except going for him now. That wouldn't stop but only delay him. The woman in green slapped Roger's cheek again, as if she read the thoughts passing through his mind. Percy passed Harry—paused again, and drove his foot into Harry's side. Harry whimpered. Roger felt the blood rushing to his head in rage. No one spoke, and Percy went out. Kennedy backed after him, and closed the door. His wife went across the room and opened a cocktail cabinet and poured out three drinks. The seconds dragged. Kennedy looked at Roger with those dull eyes—the eyes that weren't really his, and the eyes which had made Kennedy so noticeable among a crowd. The woman in green had said it would be impossible to swear that Kennedy *was* Kennedy. Impossible?

Kennedy came slowly. " Your mistake was in thinking we didn't check up on your guard, West. We sent a man to see him, every couple of hours. When he wasn't there, we guessed what had happened. I wish I knew why you did it."

" Change a face, yet you don't change a mind."

" I offered you everything——"

Roger said: " Why talk about it? You wouldn't understand." He spoke stiffly. His cheeks and chin were smarting. He didn't see how it would end, now, but

Kennedy would get away with it for the time being, because that damning evidence had gone. He wondered what was in the man's mind, what thoughts were passing behind those odd eyes. Kennedy didn't look himself; looked a different man; he had become Raymond Hemmingway.

Kennedy shrugged.

" I still don't understand it, West, but I won't be able to trust you again, it's all over."

Of course it was all over—for him, Janet, the boys.

" No, you wouldn't get it. Small minds get filled up so quickly."

" Small minds? " Kennedy smiled, but didn't like that. " Now what's in that thick head of yours?"

Roger said: " You can judge a man by his actions, but not by his grandiose plans. You tried with me and failed. You used every pressure you could think of—threats to my wife and the boys. You failed. I'm no further use to you. My wife and family can't be. They'll have enough to worry about, but just to get your petty revenge, you'll make it worse for them. Small minds do that."

Kennedy laughed. " That's right, West. I shall use someone else at the Yard and hold up what happened to your wife and the kids as an awful example. I've others marked down. Before I'm through, I shall have several contact men at the Yard. Banister is a good start, but a small one. I shall be able to get away with a lot of crimes with help from the Yard. But there isn't time to go into detail." He laughed again. " Just one more detail will interest you. I'm going to shoot you." He raised the gun. " When the police arrive, I shall tell them the simple truth: my wife heard someone about, came to investigate, found you two in the house, shot one of you, and was overpowered by the other. Then I returned, and caught you red-handed. There's the open safe, all the evidence. I am not Kennedy here, I am a respected society and businessman, named Hemmingway. I suppose you knew that. I shall pretend to know nothing at all, except that there were burglars and both were shot while trying to get away. That's justifiable homicide.

To make it more realistic, I may wait until the police are at the door—the sound of a shot would be most impressive, and would prove that I'd waited as long as I dared, and that you made a final desperate attempt to escape." He laughed again. "It was a good throw, West, you almost deserved to succeed. Harry was the weakness, of course. I suppose it was a mistake to use a friend of Ginger Kyle's. Never mind."

The gun covered Roger's stomach.

There was a thing he'd forgotten, and his wife might forget; that Roger had used Sloan's name. How would he explain that away? Somehow—yes, he'd find an explanation, and his first was foolproof.

It was very quiet in the room.

"I'm disappointed," said Kennedy. "Really disappointed." He drew nearer and stood by Harry, without looking down at the injured man. "This evening, I thought we really had won you over."

The woman in green said: "I shouldn't lose any more time, Ray. I shouldn't wait for the police." She was nervous.

"Perhaps you're right," said Kennedy, and raised the gun a fraction.

Here it came.

Roger braced himself. Better fling himself forward, make a pretence at fighting. Death had an ugly face, and he was looking right into it, it mattered little which way it came.

Then Harry kicked Kennedy.

．　　．　　．　　　．　　．

Kennedy, caught unawares, staggered and turned on Harry, who kicked again. Roger swung round on the woman in green. Gun in hand, she was staring at Harry. Roger snatched at the gun. She pulled it free. They grappled, and she fell backwards.

Kennedy fired at him. He felt nothing.

He grabbed the woman's gun and flung himself towards the bookcase which stood at right angles to the wall. He felt a bullet tear at his coat and heard the second bark.

He thumped against the wall, on the turn. Kennedy was out of sight. Roger waited tensely. All he could see was the desk and the woman, picking herself up. Kennedy was creeping towards him, his only chance now was to shoot on sight. Never had seconds seemed so long.

Then the door opened; he heard it bang back against the wall.

" What's all this? " a man asked.

Roger knew that voice: this was Peel of the Yard.

.   .   .   .   .

Roger kept behind the bookcase. Other men came into the room. The woman in green said in a choking voice: " Be careful, he's armed! "

" Who's armed? " demanded Peel.

" The thief, behind here."

Peel came forward slowly and steadily. " Don't try any funny stuff," he said. He appeared and didn't flinch, didn't look at the gun.

" We caught them red handed," said Kennedy, and there was a catch in his voice. " Two of them—he's dangerous, be careful."

" He won't do any harm," said Peel. He held out his hand. " Let me have that gun, please." He was crisp and authoritative, and didn't seem to have a nervous qualm at all. " You're Charles Rayner, aren't you? "

Kennedy said: " Yes, he is. And——"

" We'll talk later," said Peel. " Your gun, Rayner, and don't try any funny stuff."

Roger said: " Get after Myers, the Bilk Street mobsman. He's got Sloan. He's going after West's wife. The maid at the Wests' home is going to kidnap the children."

He held out the gun.

Peel said to a sergeant: " You heard that. Better put in a call. Have Myers picked up and the Wests' maid questioned."

He swung round on Roger. " Where'd you get all this? "

There was a chance for Janet.

" Never mind."

" Inspector——" began Kennedy.

Peel relaxed: " All safe now, Mr. Hemmingway."

Roger moved forward. The woman in green joined
Kennedy's wife. Their tension reached screaming pitch.
Kennedy, with those pale, dull eyes, was rigid, frowning.
He was envisaging the accusations and counter-charges;
his mind was working already on a way to discredit
" Rayner ". It would have been impossible, had those
papers been in the room. Now——

There were three men with Peel—familiar Yard men,
big, comforting, confident. Two of them came forward
and looked at the safe and began to talk in undertones.

" Now I'll hear what you have to tell me, Mr. Hemmingway." Peel was formal, and not particularly friendly.
" You say that Mrs. Hemmingway surprised the two
thieves and shot one. You arrived and were about to
shoot the other——"

" After he had drawn a gun on *me*."

" Yes, I see. Are there any servants here? "

" On the top floor."

" Weren't they disturbed? "

" No. The burglar alarm had been put out of action."

" You returned with your wife——"

" No, with my sister." Kennedy spoke quietly, and his
eyes narrowed in that familiar trick. " My wife was
alone on this floor. Do you mind if I get her a drink,
Inspector, she has had a nasty shock." He moved towards
the cocktail cabinet. " And may I warn you not to pay
any attention to this man, Rayner? He has a remarkable
repertoire of lies." He reached the cocktail cabinet, and
picked up a bottle.

" No drinks just now, please," Peel said. He was
brusque. Kennedy looked at him, as if in surprise. The
tiny china doll who was his wife sat down heavily, and
buried her face in her hands. The woman in green stared
at Roger—only at Roger. The tension in the three of
them was at its height.

" Why not? " Kennedy snapped.

" I'd rather you didn't, sir."

Kennedy submitted, evidence of nerves.

" Very well. As I say, Rayner will doubtless——"

" What a man says isn't evidence, sir, at this stage—he would have to offer proof of any charge which he might prefer against you." Why was Peel so brisk and formal?
" Has Detective Inspector Sloan been gone long? "

Mrs. Kennedy caught her breath.

Kennedy said calmly: " Sloan? I don't recall the name. Oh—Rayner mentioned it just now."

" The man who called us said that he was speaking for Sloan. Didn't you call us? "

" It must have been a mistake, Inspector. I didn't——"

Mistake! That was Kennedy's biggest! Roger felt warmth pouring through him.

Peel said: " The name of Detective Inspector Sloan was undoubtedly mentioned, sir. Did you call the Yard? "

" No, my chauffeur——"

" I understood that the servants weren't disturbed."

Good work, Peel! Keep at it!

" My chauffeur drove me back here. He tele phoned——"

" Would he know Mr. Sloan? "

" How the devil do I know? " Kennedy rasped. " He may—he may have mentioned Sloan in order to get you here quickly."

" We always come quickly, sir. Where is your chauffeur? "

" He's not here." Kennedy licked his lips. The woman in green sat on the arm of the china doll's chair. Both of them stared at Peel, now, ignoring Roger.

" So I observe, sir," said Peel. " That is what puzzles me—why isn't he here? Why did you send him out? "

" I didn't send——"

" Then why did he go out? " asked Peel.

Peel had grown into a giant. Roger moved away and sat on the edge of the desk. The two sergeants talked in whispers, but he hardly noticed them, only heard Peel and Kennedy.

Kennedy said: " I have no idea. I didn't know that he had gone out."

" You didn't know that we caught him, either, did you, sir? A patrol car came here immediately on receipt of the alarm, and your chauffeur was met on the doorstep. He had a number of papers with him—papers apparently taken from the safe here. He said that you had instructed him to leave with those papers. He was quite surprised by his detention, and had no time to think up a lie for us—*sir*. Why did you send your chauffeur out with papers taken from the safe? "

Kennedy didn't speak; his face worked.

His wife leaned forward and hid her face in her hands.

"We'll have to know sooner or later, sir," said Peel, whose voice kept on the same monotonous level all the time. " Is there something you wish to hide from us? "

Kennedy said: " I think you're exceeding your duty, Inspector." He glanced at Roger; and he still held the gun. He raised it slightly. " I have charged these two men with——"

A sergeant, behind Kennedy, came up quietly. Before Kennedy knew what was happening, the sergeant took the gun. He swung round, fist clenched to strike, stopped himself, and glowered at Peel.

" I insist——"

"Just a moment, sir, if you please." Peel raised his hand—and footsteps sounded outside on the landing; one or two men were coming in. Roger watched, with increasing tension, not yet sure that it was over and that he could live again. Percy came in—thrust by someone whom Roger couldn't see at first. Percy's face was as pale as Harry's, and his eyes glittered with fright. He felt Kennedy's gaze on him, but couldn't meet his employer's eyes. He came forward, pushed again—and then *Sloan* came into the room.

Roger cried: " Bill! "

Sloan, one eye closed, coat dirty and torn, grinned across at him. Peel jumped in astonishment. A sergeant stood impassively by the door, holding the gun he'd taken from Kennedy.

" Hallo, Roger," said Sloan easily. " I felt pretty sure who you were, earlier to-night."

Peel choked: "Roger *West*——"

Kennedy took a step forward. "Yes, the renegade policeman! The man who forced me to——"

"All statements will be taken down in due course, sir," said Peel. But his voice was unsteady, he gaped at Roger. "A superintendent is on his way, he will take charge." He gulped. "It can't be," he whispered.

"It is," said Sloan. "What a present for Janet!"

Kennedy's face had turned a dirty grey.

25

PRESENT FOR JANET

IT was nearly three hours later before Roger talked.

Chatworth, who had arrived soon after Sloan, sat with Sloan and Peel in the drawing-room of 27 Mountjoy Square, and listened. A sergeant took the statement down in shorthand. It began unsteadily, almost incoherently, grew steadier as the minutes passed. The picture of those two sombre months gradually filled in, both for Roger and for the others.

Upstairs, men were going through the papers.

Kennedy and his wife and sister were held in separate rooms. Percy was on his way to Scotland Yard, Harry was already at the nearest hospital.

Roger knew a little more: that Peel and two other men had followed Sloan that night, and had seen him taken away from Lyme Street by Myers and his men. They'd followed, and rescued him; Myers and the men who had come to Lyme Street were already in custody, so was Grace Howell.

Roger talked on. . . .

He was dry, but forgot the whisky and soda by his side; tired, but talking vividly, with words welling out of him. He didn't smile, didn't alter the pitch of his voice, just talked—as he might have talked to a doctor, about nightmares—a two-month nightmare. Detail after detail built itself into the picture, giving it light and shadow.

He stopped, and sipped his drink.

Chatworth said after a long pause: " But *why*, Roger? Why? "

" You mean, why did I allow myself to be established as Rayner? Why didn't I come to you?' '

" No, no, you've made that obvious. You'd a chance to find who this Kennedy was, what he was doing. I think I see what drove you to that." Chatworth was gruff. " Only way you could make sure of the proper finish was to trap him—Kennedy. Can't imagine any other man standing up to the strain. Never mind that now. What I mean is, why did Kennedy do all this? *Why?* "

" We'll know better when we have finished an examination of the papers upstairs," Roger said.

" Inspector Chubb is going through them, he ought to have some ideas now." Peel stood up. " Shall I go and see, sir? "

Chatworth grunted: it might have been " Yoo."

Peel went out. Chatworth drummed his fingers on the arm of the chair. Sloan sat back, with a fatuous grin on his bruised face. Peel was gone for a long time, but none of them moved. Chatworth couldn't keep his eyes off Roger. He was looking at the new man, trying to see some semblance of the old. He shook his head, slowly, three or four times.

Peel came in, with glowing eyes and a sheaf of papers.

" Well? " barked Chatworth.

" Got it pretty well sewn up, sir! These lists and some other documents tell a tale! Kennedy has been at this for years, gradually building up a system of *blackmail*. He can put pressure on hundreds of people. Hundreds! " Peel was so excited that he rapped a table with a roll of paper. " It's so big, it's frightening. The key is blackmail, everywhere. He got something on these people and put the black on them—people who supplied those goods to Rayner & Co. did so because Kennedy squeezed— they had to. That was the smallest angle. He's had his claws in Members of Parliament, peers of the realm, people of influence everywhere. He's deep in the currency racket and other forms of smuggling. There's a list here of his contact men—all crooks we've got on our records. He told them what to do, gave them a rake-off. Myers has admitted that—he got his orders from the chauffeur, Percy Briggs. There's an elaborate organization, and we only know the beginning of it yet. Kennedy lived here as Hemmingway, and trusted only his wife, sister, and Briggs.

" He was planning wholesale blackmail and corruption. At the Board of Trade, the Treasury—any Government Departments that would be profitable. He wanted a good cover, and didn't want to show himself much. A man named Rayner, who worked with him for some years, backed out and went to Africa, where he made a packet in diamonds. He——"

"Who's told you this? It isn't in those documents, is it?" Chatworth was abrupt.

Peel grinned. "No, sir, but Myers and Briggs have let a lot come out. I've just had a word with the Yard, sir. This man Rayner died some years ago. When Kennedy planned to corrupt West and turn him into a big cover for the whole job, he gave West Rayner's name, passport, background—everything. I've got some other details, too. Kennedy himself—that's his real name—first thought of getting at men at the Yard, and incidentally he *did* get at one, sir, more of that later." Chatworth opened his mouth, closed it again. Peel went on eagerly: "Then Kennedy had his big notion, having a prominent Yard man to work for him. He plumped for West. He probed a bit, and discovered that Mrs. West had a cousin who lived in Surrey, and worked out the whole frame-up from there."

" That French girl——" began Sloan.

Peel said: " Yes, Briggs has talked about her, too. She was in love with Kennedy. He went to see her, in Paris, calling himself Arthur King, to find out whether she knew anything about her father, Kyle. He fascinated her, and he was always after beautiful women. Ginger Kyle knew more about Kennedy than anyone else alive, and Kennedy was just checking up and fell for her. But he didn't bargain on her following him to England. Kennedy thought that she was really probing into his plans, and she fell in nicely with the plot to frame Mr. West. Kennedy took over Copse Cottage, and arranged for her to meet him there. It was he who actually killed her and attacked West." Peel was hoarse from talking and from excitement now. " Of course, there are a lot more details to come, but the general scheme's pretty obvious. Percy Briggs can't talk fast enough, he knows it's the only way to save his neck. When Kennedy wanted a job done—murder or any job—he knew exactly whom to use. He was born in the East End, according to Briggs. The real Hemmingway—the man he's supposed to be here—lived and died abroad. Kennedy took his place. As Hemmingway had no close friends in England, Kennedy got away with it.

" We've enough to charge Kennedy and the women with now—shall I take them to the Yard? "

" Do that," said Chatworth.

.   .   .   .   .

Chatworth said slowly: " I can't take it all in, Roger. It's too much for me." He pulled his lips. " Never heard me say that before, and you never will again. How any man kept the truth away from his wife for that time— and knowing you and your wife——"

" And knowing what Kennedy had fixed against me," Roger said.

"" Yes, yes. Well—it's nearly five o'clock. Er— what *about* your wife? You can't spring yourself on her. She—damn it, she won't recognize you! The boys won't——"

" I'll ask Mark Lessing to go and see her," said Roger at once. " I'll see Lessing right away, if that's all right with you."

Chatworth said: " Do what you like." He shook his head, wonderingly. " When this breaks—oh, never mind. Never mind. Go and see Lessing."

.   .   .   .   .

Sloan drew up in his car and waved as Roger stepped out of Hemmingway's house.

" They're under lock and key, Roger. Briggs is still talking. Man of ideas, this Kennedy. He had a trick of putting drops in his eyes—not bella donna, but something like it. It gave them an unnatural look, and changed his whole appearance. Very few people would have thought them the same man, when with Kennedy, you would be so fascinated by his eyes you wouldn't take much notice of his features."

" You're telling me ! " Roger said.

Sloan grinned ; he was a happy man.

" He thought you were safe when he fixed that body. Remember I told you ? "

Roger said : " Yes, Bill. You've been——"

" Forget it ! "

" Never."

.   .   .   .   .

Later, Roger sat in Mark Lessing's car, outside the Bell Street house.

It was a little after six o'clock. Some traffic was on the road, and two or three people walked past the end of it. In Bell Street, there was sleepy quiet—even the boys were still asleep.

Mark was gone a long time. Cigarette after cigarette stub joined others on the kerb by the car.

Then Mark appeared, and beckoned.

He didn't speak when Roger passed him at the gate.

Janet stood in the doorway.

The early morning light fell on Roger's face. He approached her slowly, his heart beating furiously and breath bated.

It was more than two months since they had met, and Roger saw all the evidence of strain ; and he also saw the light in her eyes. She watched him, studying every feature. Slowly, she stretched out her hands, and they were trembling. He took them ; they were hot. He drew her gently towards him, and then suddenly she began to cry.

.   .   .   .   .

Janet sat on a pouf in front of him, head back, radiance
in her eyes again. She held his hand tightly, as if she
were afraid that if she let it go, she would never touch it
again.

Upstairs, Scoopy called: " Richard. *Richard*! "

There was no answer.

" *Richard*! " Scoopy's voice grew louder. " I'm awake.
Wake up, I'm awake."

Roger felt as if the fierceness of his thumping heart
would suffocate him.

He said: " What will they say? I've thought about it
a million times. They won't know me, they——"

" They'll know you. Just talk to them." Janet's voice
broke. " I'll tell them—you've—oh, I'll tell them anything, it doesn't matter, they've got you back, I've got
you back! Roger, it was terrible, I just hadn't any hope.
I——"

" I daren't——"

" Of course you daren't. Don't blame yourself, don't
worry." Tears welled up in her eyes, but she didn't
really cry as she went on chokily: " It's not a bad
face. Roger, I think I like it better, in some ways
it——"

She couldn't keep the tears back; but a moment later
she was laughing loudly.

There was sudden silence upstairs, and then Richard
said in his clear voice: " Mummy's downstairs."

" Grace isn't in her room," said Scoopy.

" Mummy! "

" *Mummy*! "

" I'll be up soon, boys. You can go into—Richard's
room, Scoopy. Don't make too much noise."

They laughed, delighted.

Roger said hoarsely: " He was in Richard's room
already. Nothing's changed. God! I've got to see
them, Jan. I must see them. I——"

" I'll go and talk to them," said Janet. " I won't be
long." She stood up, then leaned over him and kissed
him, and he felt her damp cheek on his. She swung
round and hurried out of the room.

Mark was in the garden, hands in pocket, back towards the window, shoulders squared; cheerful again.

Janet said clearly: " Now listen, boys, I've a surprise for you."

" You've been *crying*," accused Scoopy.

" I didn't do anything," said Richard, defensively.

" No. No." She could hardly get the words out. " Now—listen, boys. I've a big surprise. I'm not really crying, I—I'm laughing. Something wonderful—wonderful has——"

Scoopy cried: " Daddy's back! Daddy's come back! "

" Daddy! " shrieked Richard.

" *Boys*! Just a moment, it is Daddy, but——"

They were tumbling about on the landing as she tried to tell them what to expect.

.   .   .   .   .

It would be all right; everything would be all right. He was alive again.

THE END